Critical Acclaim for
American Mystery Award Winner
Joan Hess and her *Maggody* Mysteries

"To create living, breathing characters takes talent. To create a whole town inhabited by such characters borders on genius—and this is what Joan Hess has done with Maggody, Arkansas. I love the place and everybody (well, almost everybody) in it."
—Barbara Michaels

"At last! A hilariously funny mystery that touches all the bases and leaves you yelling for more. Joan Hess has found real gold in the tawdry little town of

—Charlotte MacLeod

MADNESS
IN
MAGGODY

JOAN HESS

AN ONYX BOOK

ONYX
Published by the Penguin Group
Penguin Books USA Inc., 375 Hudson Street,
New York, New York 10014, U.S.A.
Penguin Books Ltd, 27 Wrights Lane,
London W8 5TZ, England
Penguin Books Australia Ltd, Ringwood,
Victoria, Australia
Penguin Books Canada Ltd, 10 Alcorn Avenue,
Toronto, Ontario, Canada M4V 3B2
Penguin Books (N.Z.) Ltd, 182–190 Wairau Road,
Auckland 10, New Zealand

Penguin Books Ltd, Registered Offices:
Harmondsworth, Middlesex, England

Published by Onyx, an imprint of New American Library,
a division of Penguin Books USA Inc.
This is an authorized reprint of a hardcover edition
published by St. Martin's Press.

First Onyx Printing, April, 1992
10 9 8 7 6 5 4 3 2

For Ellen Nehr,
a wise and funny lady
and a very dear friend

1

"The picnic pavilion," Ruby Bee read aloud with enough sarcasm to choke the cud right out of a cow, "has comfortable seating for twenty-four diners, who will be only a few steps away from the most incredible display of hot and cold entrées in the county. Don't miss our grand opening." She whacked down the newspaper and folded her arms across her chest. "Well?"

The customer at the counter hunkered over his blue plate special and wished mightily he was elsewhere, because he knew damn well he was in for it, no matter what he said.

"Well?" Ruby Bee repeated, her eyes flashing like the one traffic light in Maggody. "Aren't you impressed with shiny plastic tabletops and an international deli only a few steps away? Everything from tamales and ribs to fresh peach cobbler and that mush they call mousse?"

"Nothing's as good as your chicken-fried steak and turnip greens, Ruby Bee. Why, when I'm hauling a load cross country, I don't think of anything else except getting back to Ruby Bee's Bar & Grill for the best home cookin' in the whole damn county."

"Are you telling me that you're not going to try their Frenchbread sandwiches and chocolate mousse?"

The trucker shoveled in the last bite of mashed potatoes, drained the iced-tea glass, and put an appropriate number of dollar bills on the counter. "I got to run," he said over his shoulder, not actually running but nevertheless making pretty good time. "See you next time, Ruby Bee."

She snatched up the newspaper and squinted at the description of meats and cheeses available for sandwiches

7

and party platters. "Italian baby Swiss! Pro-choot-o!
Kosher Polish pickles! What in tarnation's wrong with a
nice bologna and cheese sandwich, with a dill pickle and
potato chips on the side? I wish you'd tell me that, Gilly
Jacana. I wish you'd tell me that."

Gilly was already revving the engine at the stoplight,
praying it'd turn green. He swore later he could feel the
hairs on the back of his neck rising like there was a spook
in the back of the cab.

"Genuine homemade Mexican tamales," Geraldo Mandozes read, struggling with the longer words. He rolled
up the newspaper and began to slap it against his leg.
"How in the name of sweet Jesus can a bunch of Arkansas grocery clerks make genuine Mexican tamales? I
make genuine Mexican tamales because I am a genuine
Mexican who came from Mexico, not from some little
redneck town. You think my tamales are the best, don't
you?"

Kevin Buchanon bent down so he could look through
the Dairee Dee-Lishus counter window. He was nervous
because Geraldo Mandozes looked like one of those ban-
ditos—what with his shiny dark hair, mustache, and
stocky body—and everybody knew they could be dangerous if they got riled up. Nobody knew much about this
Mexican fellow who'd bought the Dee-Lishus a couple
of months back; Maggody's version of the Welcome
Wagon (the contingency of church ladies who dropped
by in a neighborly fashion to appraise the furniture)
tended to roll right past foreigners and other suspicious
types.

Kevin cleared his throat. "Sure, Geraldo, your tamales
are real good."

"And genuine?"

"Sure, Geraldo. Like you said, you're a genuine spic."

A tamale hit the countertop in an explosion of greasy
white paper and greasy orange chili sauce. "I did not say
spic, you skinny little turd. I said Mexican, as in a person
from Mexico."

"Yeah, I remember now, Geraldo . . . and this tamale
looks real good." Kevin fumbled with the paper until he

had secured it around what would be his lunch, then scattered change on the counter and pedaled away before the genuine spic started throwing chili straight from the pot.

"A total-service supermarket with fully trained employ-ees who are dedicated to your needs," Elsie McMay read, her head tilted back so she could see through her bifocals and also keep the perm solution from dribbling into her ears and shorting out her hearing aid (she'd read about such a fatal tragedy in a tabloid and was always careful). She stopped to dab her forehead with a tissue, then met Estelle's gaze in the mirror. "Now just where is Jim Bob finding these fully trained employees? At the Maggody Academy of Supermarket Studies?"

"I couldn't say," Estelle said, more concerned with a pesky wisp of gray hair that seemed to have a mind of its own. "Rumor has it Dahlia's going back to work for him, and as the head cook in the deli, if you can imagine that."

"Dahlia O'Neill couldn't heat up a can of corn. Remember when she worked at the Kwik-Screw? All she ever did was stuff candy bars in her face and guzzle orange soda pop. It wasn't any mystery to me why she topped three hundred pounds a few years back. I once asked her real nicely where to find the kitchen matches, but I might as well've asked her in some foreign language like French."

"Or German," Estelle mumbled through a bobby pin between her lips.

"Or Swedish."

"Or American." Estelle started chuckling, and then so did Elsie, and the bobby pin fell on the floor and the little pink curler unwound of its own accord, but neither one of them cared at that moment because of Estelle's undeniable wit.

"Open from seven in the morning till nine at night," Buzz Milvin read aloud, his frown getting deeper by the word. He aimed it in the direction of his mother-in-law, who was on the settee reading the directions on a bottle of medicine guaranteed to make her regular. "But that don't make no sense, Lillith. When Jim Bob hired me on as night manager, I could've sworn he said the store was going to be open later than that."

"Doesn't change your salary, does it?" Lillith said, more interested in the promises she'd just read.

"No, but . . ." Buzz took a long swallow of beer as he scratched his head. "Well, it's just that I thought I'd be overseeing the cash-register lines and okaying checks and making sure the employees stayed busy. Jim Bob said he was real impressed with how I'd been line foreman at the plant for more than four years now. The money's still good, but I'm wondering if I'm gonna be a manager or a custodian."

"Excuse me, Buzz, but I've got business to attend to." Lillith headed for the kitchen.

"Jim Bob's in for a surprise if he thinks I'm mopping any floors," he said to himself, since he was the only one in the room except for his daughter, Lissie, who was in the corner whispering to her doll. "I worked my way up to line foreman 'cause I was willing to assume responsibility and keep the line at top productivity. Had to keep the guys happy, the production supervisors happy, the front office happy." He finished the beer, then with slow deliberation crumpled the can in his hand.

Lissie flinched at the sound, but she didn't say anything. She hardly ever did.

Brother Verber, the spiritual leader of the Voice of the Almighty Lord Assembly Hall, was reading, too, but he wasn't exactly reading the full-page ad in the weekly newspaper, nor was he fretting about the impact of Jim Bob's SuperSaver Buy 4 Less on the various citizens of Maggody, not even those in his flock.

He was doing research. He was doing this on his couch, with the fan whirring and a pint jar of iced tea handy on the floor beside the couch. He was doing this in his pastel blue boxer shorts and nothing else, due to the heat in the silver trailer parked beside the Assembly Hall—and the intense nature of his study material.

To be honest—as all God-fearing folks should be—

even during the week, he wasn't reading so much as looking, because the study material leaned heavily in the
direction of photographs rather than print. But the photographs were educational, to say the least, and Brother
Verber made a point of reading the captions that explained why the various participants had selected their
positions and what precisely was going through their
heads.

Because, Brother Verber thought as he stopped to
mop his gleaming forehead and blow his fat red nose,
there was depravity in Maggody and the more he knew
of the origin of such sin, the better equipped he would
be to wrassle with that particular devil. There were things
right there in the pictures that he hadn't known were
possible, much less popular with the younger set.

It was clear to him that God wanted him to study this
variety of depravity, because if God hadn't wanted him
to subscribe to *Kittens and Tomcats*, there wouldn't have
been enough money in the collection plate.

He took a steadying gulp of tea and turned the page.

"Our amazing variety of fresh produce will be the lowest-
priced anywhere," Ivy Sattering read with a scowl. She
turned the scowl on her husband, who was flipping hap-
pily through the latest issue of *Organic Gardening*. "Did
you hear what I said, Alex? This supermarket ad says
they'll have fresh produce. If they buy in bulk, the prices
will be lower than what we can afford to sell for."

"Ladybugs," Alex said wonderingly. He lit a cigarette
and held the page closer to admire the amazingly sym-
metrical pattern of black dots on the little orange crea-
tures. His ponytail swung like a fuzzy brown pendulum
as he shook his head in awe, and behind thick spectacles,
his faded eyes of indeterminate color flickered. The
extent of his hallucinogenic experiences in the late sixties
had left him a pleasantly addled child twenty years later.
He enjoyed talking to himself in the mirror, even though
he had a tendency to forget what he was going to say in
the middle of a sentence.

"Would you please pay attention?" Ivy said with mea-
sured impatience, resigned to his limitations after fifteen

years of marriage but not ready for sainthood just yet. "This supermarket's going to put us out of business. No one's going to come to the produce stand if they can get fruits and vegetables more cheaply elsewhere."

Alex wrenched his gaze from the ladybug ad to smile at his wife, who was attractive in a comfortable way and clearly peeved at him. "But we're organic. Our customers won't buy anything sprayed with pesticides and herbicides."

Ivy looked back at him, her eyes unblinking behind wire-rimmed glasses. "We have customers because we have the only source of fresh produce between here and Starley City. The majority of our customers would drink pesticides if it saved money."

"Whatever you say." He returned to the ladybug ad, which promised the nifty little things could rid a garden of aphids in a matter of days.

Lamont Petrel, the occupant of unit number four at the Flamingo Motel, was reading fine print on various legal documents. His thick silver hair was combed in a sweeping pompadour to draw attention away from his slightly protruding ears, and he was often mistaken for a televangelist. He had twinkly blue eyes ringed with lines, an affable voice with only a tinge of southern refinement, and a firm handshake that'd served him well in many a meeting fraught with peril. His teeth were perfect, but his smile went no deeper than his tan. His wife had told him on more than one occasion that he was a cold-blooded bastard who'd sell his grandmother's soul for a fistful of dollars and his own for a few dollars more. Lamont found that a reasonably accurate description, although he hadn't said so.

He'd already checked the infamous ad for typos, but it looked pretty good and he was pleased with his work. Jim Bob had yelped about the cost, to be sure, but Lamont had convinced his partner that advertising was the only way to go, and he'd finally won the argument.

As for the documents, the fine print was pretty spidery for his sixty-year-old eyes, but he'd instructed his attorneys to go whole hawg in terms of complicated language

and meaningless legal jargon. By the time you stumbled
into the fifth or sixth "wherein the fiduciary obligations
of the party of the first part blah blah the reciprocity of
obligations of the party of the second part, heretofore to
be identified as the blah blah," it made about as much
sense as the federal government's simplified tax form.
Which was what Lamont wanted, because he sure as hell
didn't want to stay partners with the dumbshit mayor of
Maggody.

And unless Jim Bob hired himself a bunch of eagle-
eyed lawyers to plow through the partnership agreements,
Lamont wasn't going to have to put up with him much
longer. This was going to be more of a "Slam-bang,
thank you, ma'am" arrangement.

"This is the smartest thing I've ever done." Jim Bob
Buchanon chortled, studying the ad like a proud papa.
"Lamont wasn't crazy about running a full page, but I
told him how we've got to get everybody's attention
before the grand opening in two weeks. I'll bet you
twenty bucks every single sucker in the county will come
by for a look-see and free samples from the deli."

"Gambling is a sin," Mrs. Jim Bob said automatically.

"You know what I mean." He leaned back and put
his feet on the coffee table, cringed at his wife's sharp
intake of breath, and got them off real fast. "I get all
fired up thinking about being the owner and manager of
a great big supermarket. The whole county's gonna shop
at the Jim Bob's SuperSaver Buy 4 Less. We got ourselves fifteen employees, and most of them's at minimum
wage and glad to get it. I think I'll mosey down there
and see how the roofers are doing."

"The construction supervisor assured you this morning
that everything was on schedule, and more likely to
remain so without your continual interference." Mrs. Jim
Bob said all this without interest, being more concerned
with her study of the Book of Corinthians II, because it
was going to be discussed in her Sunday-school class and
she intended to be prepared. Only three weeks ago, Lottie Estes had won a minor skirmish involving an obscure
verse from the Gospel of Luke, and it had taken all this

time for Mrs. Jim Bob to overcome the humiliation. It would not happen again.

Jim Bob finished his beer and did his level best to hold in a belch, which would make it all the harder to get his ass out of the living room and its suffocating piety. "Maybe you're right," he said magnanimously. "I guess I'll go over to the Flamingo and visit with Lamont about the grand opening. He's apt to be lonely sitting all alone in a shabby motel room with nothing to amuse hisself."

"The motel room to talk business . . . or Ruby Bee's Bar & Grill to guzzle beer?"

"I'm just trying to do the neighborly thing for Lamont. You're all the time saying how it's your Christian duty to visit with those who are lonely and bereft in their time of need." He wasn't sure this made a whole helluva lot of sense, since Lamont was probably drinking bourbon and watching a football game. Jim Bob was doing neither, because the smell of whiskey made his wife nauseous and the noise of the television disturbed her Bible study. He waited for a minute, then stood up. "I'll be back before suppertime."

"Dinnertime. Common folks have supper. In this house, we have dinner."

"Right," Jim Bob muttered on his way out the door. He'd already decided to forgo comforting Lamont in order to find out if sweet Cherri Lucinda might be in the mood for company.

I was reading a travel guide to Europe. I was dressed in my uniform and sitting behind my desk at the police department, however, in deference to my position as chief of police of Maggody, Arkansas, population 755 at last count. Nobody counted very often because there wasn't much need. The outside world was not obsessed with an accurate head count, and the good citizens knew what every last person was doing and therefore could keep a running tally of births, deaths, and escapes.

I was in Maggody because I'd skulked home from a posh Manhattan existence to recuperate from a tasteless divorce (as opposed to an elegant one, in which both parties fall all over themselves to be fair about the property settlement and fondly kiss each other on the cheek on the courthouse steps . . . in Disney World). It wasn't that I was covered with oozing sores; there were only a few scabs to be picked at on a regular basis. I figured it would be only a couple more years before I was ready for the real world, which wasn't ringing all that much anymore.

I was the chief of police because I was the only applicant for the position who'd had any police training. I'd managed to avoid brain petrification only by spending most of my cognizant hours imagining myself elsewhere. And not with a capital *E*, either, since almost anyplace else was preferable to a one-street town noted for its ornery citizens, dusty weeds, boarded-up storefronts, and artful display of litter that ranged from rusted beer cans and disposable diapers to unmentionables.

At this point, I'd just left Florence, after a delightful stay at a quaint pensione that served robust breakfasts and elegant dinners at a reasonable price. Thus far, excluding airfare, I was well within my fabricated budget and I was considering a few days in Rome in a seventeenth-century villa overlooking the city. I could take a bus in every morning to sightsee, and idle away the evenings on the broad balcony, sipping wine and chatting with the resident contessa.

When the telephone rang, I marked my place (just south of Siena) and, in further deference to my position, answered it with, "Police department, Chief Ariel Hanks speaking."

"Ruby Bee's Bar & Grill, your mother speaking," came a most unfriendly voice. "I thought you were coming down here for supper."

"I am, but it's the middle of the afternoon. I still have time to check in at the Villa della Gatteschi and do the Colosseum before it gets dark."

"Don't give me any of that smart talk, young lady. Are you coming down here for supper or not?"

"Can I expect lasagna and osso buco?"

Her voice was so icy that my eardrum tingled. "Are you coming or not?"

"Of course I am," I said, trying not to sound as irritated as I was. It's not wise to mess with Ruby Bee, who looks like a chubby grandmother with her rosy round face and improbable blond hair but has a streak of something hard to define but best to avoid. Every now and then, one of them good ol' boys drinks one pitcher of beer too many at the bar and learns the hard way. One of them limps to this day. Truth.

"Well, then, get your fanny off your chair and get down here," Ruby Bee snapped, then hung up before I could think of anything else, smart or not, to say.

I got my fanny off my chair, vowed to renew my passport, and went out of the relative sanctuary of the PD into the whitewashed August heat of Maggody. A lone pickup truck was heading south, leaving a ghostly swirl of dust in its tracks. A car was parked in front of Roy Stiver's antique store, and I supposed some naîve tourist was in there trying to pull a fast one over on potbellied, slow-talking Roy, who has more CDs in the bank than a cow patty has flies.

My efficiency apartment was above the store. I gave it a wistful look but obediently trudged along the highway to find out what species of bee was buzzing in Ruby Bee's bonnet this time. I winced as I passed the site of the new supermarket, thinking about the poor souls putting on a tar roof in the heat. The building itself was rather peculiar. Jim Bob was too cheap to tear down the old Kwik-Screw, an ordinary convenience store, so some of the facade remained—like a boil.

As I watched, several trucks rolled in loaded with refrigeration equipment and metal shelving units. A beefy man in a hard hat came out to bellow at the drivers, most of whom ignored him and ambled over to the soda machine in front of the Suds of Fun Launderette next door. I didn't blame them. One of the roofers came to the edge and let out his version of a wolf whistle, presumably intended to flatter me into scampering up the ladder for a quick romp in the tar. I'd lived on the Upper East Side in another life, and responded with a minute yet succinct gesture.

Estelle's station wagon was the only car in front of Ruby Bee's, which was odd on a searing Saturday afternoon. There was a black Cadillac parked in front of the motel unit out back, which was odd, too. No one stays at the Flamingo Motel; its sign is a perpetual V CAN Y and every year its neon flamingo looks a little more inclined to molt into oblivion. Ruby Bee lives in number one and swears she prefers the solitude. I've always thought she didn't want to change the linen or mess with registration.

The bar and grill was bright pink on the outside but dim and cool on the inside. And pretty much deserted. Estelle was sitting at the bar with a glass of sherry, listening as Ruby Bee raged and sputtered over the sink.

Estelle, the owner and operator of Estelle's Hair Fantasies, is the antithesis of Ruby Bee. She's as tall as I— five nine—but she towers over me with her six-inch fiery red beehive hairdo. As a child, I'd kept a cautious eye on it, not sure what would happen if it slipped to one side. It never had, to my disappointment. It didn't even sway when she walked.

"It's about time," Ruby Bee said by way of warm welcome. "You want iced tea or milk?"

"Neither, thank you. I'll just sit here like a little mouse until you tell me all about whatever it is that's disturbing you." I climbed onto the stool next to Estelle and propped my elbows on the bar.

"This is hardly the time for jokes," Estelle said with a snort of disapproval. "You might show some concern for your own flesh and blood, Miss High Horse."

Ruby Bee grabbed a dishrag and began to wipe the counter so hard it squeaked. "Now, Estelle, there's no point in giving Arly a lecture on manners. She lived in Noow Yark, you know, where people don't pay any mind to anyone else. They make you turn in your party manners when you drive across the Brooklyn Bridge."

"I forgot," Estelle said, slapping her forehead like a heroine in a melodrama, which wasn't too far off base. "People in Noow Yark just watch out the window when someone gets mugged, and they can't be bothered to learn their neighbors' names or have a nice conversation in the elevator about the weather."

"Hot enough for you?" I inserted quickly.

Ruby Bee shot me a beady look, then attempted to wrest the starring role away from Estelle. "So there's no reason why I should expect Arly to be concerned about me having to live out the last years of my life in the county nursing home. Isn't Adele Wockermann out there?"

"Yes, but last I heard, she was visiting with aliens through her hearing aid," Estelle said, giving me her version of the Beady Look. It's not as effective, since one of hers wanders. "It's a crying shame, Ruby Bee, you not being able to enjoy yourself in your golden years. No grandbabies, no daughter who worries about you, no little cottage with a nice flower garden. A crying shame."

"A crying shame," Ruby Bee echoed. She wiped her eyes with the dishrag, then bravely straightened her shoulders and prepared to crumble into dust in a rocking chair next to Adele.

"A crying shame," I said to complete the symmetry. I had no idea what was up, but I had no doubts I would find out in the next thirty seconds.

It took sixty because we lapsed into a temporary standoff. Ruby Bee and Estelle exchanged looks and waited for me to demand to know the cause of this bleak vision. I contemplated the gold flecks in the mirror and waited for them to spit it out.

"Don't you want to hear about it?" Estelle finally said, pissed because she'd caved in and knew I knew it.

"Sure," I said. "Can I have that iced tea?"

"It's that monstrosity Jim Bob's putting in across the street," Ruby Bee said. "It's going to put plenty of folks out of business, and you got to do something about it."

Realizing I wasn't going to see iced tea anytime soon, I leaned over the bar and got myself a glass of water. "It's ugly, it's been tying up traffic for six months, and it's likely to be staffed by Buchanons from under half the rocks in Stump County. Who's it going to put out of business?"

"Your mother," Estelle said. "The ad says it has this big deli section with tables and plastic silverware so you can eat right there in the store."

"The picnic pavilion," Ruby Bee added in a dull voice.

I shook my head. "It may hurt business for a few days, but it's not going to win anyone's heart for long. That kind of food's never good, and you're the best cook in the county."

Ruby Bee pointed a shaky finger at the empty room. "Just take a look for yourself. Nobody's here."

I tried to figure out how to tiptoe around this one, but nothing all that clever came to mind. "I've heard lately that you've been . . . confrontational with your regular customers," I said carefully. "You've been getting hot under the collar, demanding loyalty oaths and, in general, running everybody off." Valuing my life, I did not add that the hottest topic at the pool hall was whether or not she was too old for PMS (she was).

"I never!" Estelle gasped.

Ruby Bee once again began to wipe the counter, but without her earlier energy. "Maybe I have. I'll be the first to admit I'm not pleased with this pavilion directly across the street. I'm too old to learn how to make croissant sandwiches and mousse. All I know how to make is regular food like meat loaf and scalloped potatoes."

"And all your customers will try the new place and then come right back here like they always did," I said soothingly.

"What about the Satterings?" Estelle demanded. "You think Ivy and Alex can count on folks' loyalty when their produce costs more?"

"I don't know what to tell you. What about you, Ruby Bee? You buy from them because the stand's convenient. Are you going to buy produce at the supermarket because it's cheaper?"

"Of course not," Ruby Bee said, although not with enough conviction to fool a toddler.

Estelle was still into the voice of doom. "And that Mexican fellow that bought the Dairee Dee-Lishus is right upset, I heard. Dahlia said Kevin said he liked to throw a pot of boiling chili at him. The Mexican at Kevin, not the other way around."

"There's not anything any of us can do about it," I said. "Believe it or not, not even Maggody can withstand a spurt of progress every now and then. We used to gripe about the lack of merchandise and the exorbitant prices at the Kwik-Screw. Now we're going to have to face a larger selection and reasonable prices. I'm afraid we're stuck with it, ladies."

"Unless this picnic pavilion at Jim Bob's SuperSaver Buy 4 Less goes belly-up the first day it opens," Estelle said in a casual voice.

"Why would it?" I said in an uncasual voice.

"You just never know."

"That's right," Ruby Bee said, gazing over my head. "You just never know."

The last bit of reading matter of any significance had not yet been read. It was a letter addressed to the Maggody town council, and it lay in a well-polished silver tray in the foyer of Jim Bob's house. He had ignored it on his way out the door, and Mrs. Jim Bob, who opened whatever mail caught her eye, was much too worried about the upcoming Corinthians II face-off in Sunday school to bother with local affairs.

Jim Bob would read it over coffee the next morning, and it would take him all day to figure out how best to use it to his own advantage, which was pretty much how he approached everything.

The letter was from the Starley City Youth Center and was thick with dates, guidelines, rules, regulations, methods of compliance, and boring stuff like that. The gist of it, however, was that Maggody was invited to enter its local championship baseball team in the Starley City Labor Day Weekend Invitational Intermediate League Baseball Tournament (in subsequent paragraphs referred to as the SCLDWIILBT, but don't try to sound it out, 'cause you can't without coming off like you're drunker'n Cooter Brown).

Maggody didn't have a local championship baseball team, but not because there wasn't a competitive spirit. It had a good high-school football team, and a darn tough basketball team. The local 4-H'ers always picked up their fair share of blue and red ribbons at the county fair. The Future Homemakers of America thrived under the enthusiastic guidance of Miss Lottie Estes, and the club's secretary-treasurer had won third place in the state bake-off with her Lemon-Lime Surprise Dinner Rolls.

Maggody didn't have a soccer team, though, because it was a sissy foreign game where you wear shorts and don't get dirty. It didn't have a chess team or an IQ Bowl team, for obvious reasons. And because nobody'd ever given it any thought, it didn't have a championship baseball team. Not yet, anyway.

2

—————▼—————

"Then the high-school band plays, right?" Lamont asked, a small notebook in one hand and a much-gnawed pencil in the other.

Jim Bob poured himself another four fingers of bourbon and sat down on the edge of the lumpy bed while he tried to remember exactly what the band director had said. "The band's going to gather behind the store at one-thirty, get theirselves lined up however they do it, and then come marching around to the front at exactly two o'clock."

"In full uniform?"

"Yeah, full uniform. White bucks, brass buttons, feathers on their heads, all that shit. But some kids are away for the summer, so there'll be holes. Both tubas are gone, along with all but one of the drums and a goodly number of the clarinets. There wasn't any way Wiley could make them come back for the grand opening."

"I suppose not," Lamont muttered, "but if we're down to a fat flutist and a pimply trombone player, I'm not sure it's worth it. We don't want to look foolish in front of the media. The ribbon cutting's at two-fifteen, and then we'll try to keep the camera crew and reporters around as long as we can with free food. I'll have a bottle of booze in the office."

Jim Bob bunched the pillows against the headboard and settled back on the bed, taking a wicked pleasure in putting his dusty shoes on the motel-room bedspread. "Hey, Lamont, I had a helluvan idea over the weekend. You're going to love it."

"Yeah, go ahead," Lamont said, making a note to check that the store uniforms were starched before they

were distributed to the employees. Who were the dumbest people he'd ever met. Three-quarters of them were
named Buchanon, and all of those blessed with simian
foreheads and nasty little yellowish eyes. And therefore
resembling, in varying degrees, Jim Bob Buchanon and
his tight-assed wife, who'd been introduced as Barbara
Anne Buchanon Buchanon. Lamont had been appalled,
but not surprised.

Jim Bob looked as smug as a retriever with a splattered
duck in its mouth. "I got this letter from the Starley City
folks saying Maggody could enter a team in some damn
fool baseball tournament. I started thinking about it, and
I finally called over there and got some information."

"We're opening a supermarket, not a baseball season.
Now I want to meet with the entire staff first thing
tomorrow to review the stock procedures. Tell them to
be in front—"

"Hold it, Lamont," Jim Bob said, his feelings hurt just
a smidgen. "I know we're opening a supermarket, but
there's a way we can get a whole lot of publicity and
community goodwill without it costing us a plug nickel.
I realize you own three supermarkets and know a damn
sight more about it than I do, but I'm a businessman,
too, and I can appreciate the value of gettin' something
for nothing."

Lamont accepted the distasteful fact he was going to
have to hear Jim Bob out before they could get back to
business. He flipped a hand in the general direction of
the bed, made himself a stiff drink, and lit a cigarette,
all the while admiring the overall composition of his
demeanor in the mirror. Jim Bob's brown hair was showing a trace of gray, but it lacked the impact of sterling
silver.

"This baseball team has to be sponsored by a local
business or civic organization, see? The boys wear uniforms saying who's sponsoring them so everybody knows.
Then they go play ball in front of a whole bleacher of
parents, who tell each other how nice it is of the Lions
Club or the beer distributor or whoever the hell it is to
encourage these little boys to play baseball."

"So?" Lamont said real quietly.

"So we round up ten or twelve boys, dress them up in uniforms that say Jim Bob's SuperSaver Buy 4 Less, and send them out to do some free advertising for us." Jim Bob rubbed his palms together and gave his partner a sly grin. "Pretty damn smart, huh?"

Lamont found a certain joy in preparing to prick the prick's balloon. "Yeah, pretty damn smart, Jim Bob. But aren't you forgetting something?"

Jim Bob conscientiously searched his mind, because according to Mrs. Jim Bob, he was all the time forgetting something, even though she was usually referring to hoity-toity table manners or saying amen in church. "Are you worried about finding enough boys? I already asked around and I can get at least ten, most of them pick of the litter. Maybe we'll get some walk-ons once we start practicing."

"Good, Jim Bob, good. I was thinking about something else. As you explained so well a minute ago, we sponsor the team, which means we provide the equipment, the uniforms, and the registration fees. My store in Farberville sponsored a team one year, and it wasn't cheap."

"No problem there. The letter said we should enter our local championship team, so I figure the town ought to foot the bill. All I have to do is call a town-council meeting and run it through before anyone can blink an eye. After all," Jim Bob said, puffing up just a bit, "I am the mayor of Maggody."

"I'm keenly aware of it," Lamont said in all sincerity. No one else could have rezoned the land adjoining the Kwik-Screw with a mere flick of a pencil.

"I was thinking we could have the Jim Bob's Super-Savers at the grand opening, too. All shiny-faced and dressed in clean uniforms, ready to play good ol' American baseball."

"Sounds great, Jim Bob. One other minor . . . very, very minor thing. Who's going to coach the SuperSavers—you?"

Jim Bob choked on a mouthful of bourbon, spewing amber droplets all over himself and the bedspread. Even though he was coughing, he stuck out his glass. Lamont silently refilled it and returned to the chair, where he picked up his notebook and scribbled a memo to buy a whole damn case of bourbon next time he went home.

Jim Bob downed half the whiskey, wiped his eyes with the corner of the pillowcase, and said, "Why, one of the boys' daddies. You know I'm as busy as a stallion in a field of fillies. As much as I'd dearly like to, I don't see how I could make any time to coach the boys." He wiped his eyes again, pretending to be misty about not getting to coach the boys but actually thinking what sweet Cherri Lucinda would say if he started showing up less often at her door. She had the longest dadburned fingernails in the state and wasn't averse to making a point with them if she was in one of those moods.

Lamont, who knew all about Cherri Lucinda, among other interesting tidbits, had no problem reading Jim Bob's mind, which was pretty much printed in crayon. "See if you can talk someone into being the coach. It's not a bad idea, and we might be able to get some free publicity. The media's real fond of little boys with tooth-less grins. Shall we get back to the grand opening?"

Dahlia O'Neill snuggled up to her honey-bunny and said, "Kevin, my honey-bunny, would you be so kind as to read me again that part about employee break time?" She was perfectly capable of reading it herself, but she had a bottle of root beer in one hand and a tantalizingly soft cream-filled sponge cake in the other, and she knew in her heart of hearts that Jim Bob and that other fel-low'd be sore if her employee manual was sticky.

"Oh, yes," Kevin cooed, seizing the opportunity to burrow into her pillowy, billowy (but not willowy) soft-ness until he could swear it was her breast against his elbow. It wasn't that she was a prude, he thought as he opened the manual. It was downright amazing the things she'd taught him when they first started keeping com-pany. Things that brought tears to his eyes just remem-bering. Things that caused him to gulp several times before he could trust his voice. But now that they was officially engaged, Dahlia had insisted they stop doing all those amazing things. Which Kevin didn't rightly follow but went along with his apple dumpling, anyways.

"It says we get fifteen minutes at the end of two hours, twenty minutes for lunch, and one other fifteen-minute break, depending on how busy the store is," he said after some studying. "Doesn't say anything about calls of nature."

"Well, of course not, Kevin Buchanon! They don't talk about that kinda thing in books. It's not nice to write about potties and a person's private business. I don't even want to think about someone who'd write that kinda thing in a book!"

Kevin waited until she'd popped the last of the little cake into her mouth and methodically licked her fingers, then half-closed his eyes and, in his sexiest voice, said, "Do you recall that night we spent in Robin Buchanon's outhouse, and how the moon shone through the knotholes and you were so scared you thought you was going to get sick? Then you realized I was going to protect you no matter what, and we got to kissing and—"

Dahlia's eyes bulged like charred cherries embedded in a piecrust. "I told you not to talk like that anymore. I am the head cook in the deli and you're the assistant night manager. We are engaged to be married and we have to behave like respectable folks. Furthermore, I seem to recall you was the one moaning about throwing up and making me squish against the wall so's you could bend over the hole."

"You held my face amongst your soft breasts and—"

"You stop right this instant!"

"And your nipples was like rosebuds, and I—"

"I'm warning you, Kevin Fitzgerald Buchanon—you stop this filthy talk right now or I'm gonna climb out of this porch swing and march right into the living room to tell your ma what all you're saying to me. She'll tan your hide till you can't sit down at the supper table for a month of Sundays."

Kevin wanted to stop. He didn't want to distress his goddess of love, nor did he want to even think what his ma would do. But he couldn't. He was possessed by the devil. And all of a sudden, he realized the devil was putting pictures in his head and licking on his loins with a fiery serpent's tongue.

Kevin fought as long as he could, but, with a yowl not unlike that of an alley cat, succumbed to Satan. He clambered onto Dahlia's broad, cushiony thighs and put his mouth right on her best blue blouse and tried to gnaw through it like he was a gopher burrowing for grubs.

Dahlia grabbed his shoulders to push him back, but the devil was bracing him from behind. "Kevin! Stop that! You're ruining my best blue blouse! What do you think—stop it, I said! Stop it now! Kevin!"

He could smell the tang of bleach from her brassiere and feel the roughness of lace against his lips and he could almost taste her damp, salty flesh and he knew—

"Stop it . . . !" Dahlia wailed, thinking of her best blue blouse.

"I cain't . . . !" Kevin wailed, although for an altogether different reason.

"Kevin Fitzgerald Buchanon," said a new voice, a voice cold enough to make his forehead seize up like it did when he ate ice cream too fast. "You stop this very minute."

"Yes, Ma," Kevin said, having been flung into reality hard enough to make his adenoids tingle. The devil departed with a chuckle and an uncomfortably wet goodbye kiss.

"I can't imagine what's gotten into you," Eilene continued in the same voice. She waited until he flopped back onto the respectable side of the porch swing. "I do believe I'm going to have to have a word with your pa. Dahlia, honey, are you all right?"

"This is my best blue blouse," she sniveled. "Look where Kevin tore it with his teeth. I can't even sew it back because of where the rip is and everything."

She and Eilene stared at the perpetrator, who had managed to cover an awkward problem by crossing his legs and folding his hands in his lap like he did at church. He couldn't think of a single thing to say, which was probably just as well.

And now, sated with wine and moonlit nights at the Colosseum, it was time for me to say "Arrivederci, Roma" and take a train to Venice. The weather had been glorious thus far, but I was hoping there might be a gray drizzle when I arrived in Venice. It seemed more appropriate for the darkly romantic decadence of the neglected palazzi, the narrow canals, the Bridge of Sighs, the haunting lament of a gondolier guiding his craft in a—

The telephone rang. "Police department," I said in my darkly romantic, decadent voice as the gondolier gazed up at me with a sad, knowing smile.

"You coming down with a summer cold?" Ruby Bee demanded.

With a sad, knowing smile, I put the travel book aside and propped my feet on my desk. "I'm thinking about it."

"Sometimes I just don't know what gets into you. I really don't. If you're so all-fired bored, why don't you go have your hair fancied up or buy yourself some decent clothes. No man's gonna look twice at a girl who wears her hair in a bun like a schoolteacher and walks around in baggy pants and a faded shirt."

"It's official police camouflage," I said, "designed to allow me to blend into a baggy, faded town where nothing happens. Well, that's not true. Raz Buchanon came by to lodge another complaint against Perkins, who's been slandering Raz's prize sow, Marjorie, by casting aspersions on her purported pedigree. Raz says he has the papers to prove—"

"You need to come down here. There's something important I need to talk to you about, and Joyce can't wait around all afternoon while you make smart-alecky remarks."

"I didn't start this," I pointed out in an admirably reasonable voice. "I was exchanging looks with a swarthy gondolier named Riccardo. I was thinking of meeting him at a tiny outdoor café for a glass of chianti. You called *me*, Ruby Bee."

"Because you need to come down here. I already told you that Joyce can't wait all afternoon. She needs to strip the kitchen floor on account of company coming this weekend."

I admitted defeat, promised Riccardo I'd be back, and went down the highway to Ruby Bee's to find out what was important enough to make Joyce Lambertino delay stripping the kitchen floor.

Joyce was sitting at the bar, dressed as usual in worn jeans and a high-school sweatshirt that had seen the tenth reunion but might not make it to the twentieth. Her face had acquired a few more lines and her ponytail quite a few more gray hairs. She gave me a wan smile as I perched on the stool next to her.

"Sorry I got Ruby Bee all stirred up," she said in a low voice.

"Don't worry about it, Joyce. Last season, they named three hurricanes after her. What's the problem?"

A tropical storm slammed out of the kitchen, banged a glass of iced tea in front of Joyce, and turned inland on yours truly. "Did Joyce tell you about this outrageous business?"

I shook my head, Joyce opened her mouth, and Ruby Bee continued. "It seems that Mayor Jim Bob Buchanon, in a fit of civic pride, has decided Maggody is going to enter a baseball team in a tournament in Starley City. What's more, in this same civic fit, he and the town council voted to pay for the team's uniforms and equipment out of the budget. Now isn't that the most generous thing you ever heard?"

"It's not the most outrageous thing I ever heard," I said cautiously.

"Oh, no?" Ruby Bee rolled her eyes around for a minute, no doubt wondering how she could have produced such an obviously dim-witted offspring. "Would you like to hear about these uniforms the town's buying? I'm just a simple widow woman, and I haven't ever been to college or lived in Noow Yark, but I assumed when Joyce started telling me this that the uniforms would have the town's name across the back. But I'm just a simple widow woman, so there isn't any way I should be smart enough to know what to put on the uniforms."

I looked at Joyce. "The simple widow woman's incoherent. What do the uniforms have across the back?"

"Jim Bob's SuperSaver Buy 4 Less, with the address underneath. The only thing missing is a coupon to cut out at the end of the tournament. Larry Joe's going to coach the team. He brought home the uniforms yesterday and told me about the tournament and all." Joyce caught the end of her ponytail and began to twist it around her finger. "I asked Larry Joe if my little niece Saralee could play on the team. She's visiting this summer while her parents get divorced, and she loves all kinds of sports. I said it might help take her mind off things and he said it was okay with him. Then last night he talked to Jim Bob about it and Jim Bob said absolutely not because she was a girl—but she could be a cheerleader. Saralee is not the cheerleader type, Arly. She's been in two wrasslin' matches in Sunday school already, and half the time I can't find her at suppertime because she's climbing trees or fishing in Boone Creek."

"That's outrageous," Ruby Bee cut in. "Even you got to agree it's outrageous."

"It's certainly not fair," I said, "but I don't know what we can do about it."

The door opened behind us, allowing in a flash of sunlight. Estelle marched across the room, a piece of paper in her hand and an excited look on her face. "I got it!" she crowed. "I told you I could get it, and now I got it!"

"Lemme see," Ruby Bee said. She took the paper from Estelle and moved into the muted blue light beneath the neon Pabst sign.

"What it is?" I asked Estelle.

Estelle waited for a minute to savor the triumph. "You know how Perkins's eldest cleans every other day for Mrs. Jim Bob? She used to clean every day when Jim Bob's illegitimate children was there, but now that they've been packed off to some special school, Perkins's eldest comes every other day."

"Fascinating," I said.

"Well, this very morning Mrs. Jim Bob went to Farberville to look at some fabric samples, so Perkins's eldest slipped into Jim Bob's little office off the sun porch and found the letter about the baseball tournament."

I managed not to flinch. "At your request, of course."

"Goodness gracious, Arly, you don't think Perkins's eldest would snoop through Jim Bob's office on her own, do you? Not all the burners on her stove get real hot."

"It's just what we thought!" Ruby Bee said before I felt obliged to mention conspiracy, theft, theft by receiving, and so on. "It says we're supposed to enter our local championship team. It doesn't say anywhere that Jim Bob can just put his supermarket's name on the uniforms and send the team out to advertise for him."

"We don't have a local championship team," Joyce contributed.

"Because we can't have a play-off," Ruby Bee said, giving Estelle a sly look. "If there was another team in Maggody, the two teams could have a play-off like they do in the television leagues. Then we'd know which team was champion of Maggody."

The stage was set, but one of the players didn't have a copy of the script. On the other hand, she had a long history of being manipulated by her mother, and she was beginning to catch the drift of the production. "You thinking of sponsoring a team?" I asked.

"What a novel idea," Ruby Bee said, getting slyer by the second. "And that way, Joyce's little niece Saralee could have an equal opportunity to play instead of being made to be a cheerleader. This letter says the players have to be entering fifth or sixth grade this fall. It doesn't say one word about boys; it says players."

"Saralee's going into fifth," Joyce said.

"Hizzoner's not going to like this," I said, shaking my head.

Ruby Bee slapped down the letter so she could get both fists on her hips. "And that's going to keep me awake nights? How about you, Estelle—is that going to keep you awake nights? Joyce, you think you'll lose sleep if Jim Bob Buchanon gets his comeuppance once and for all?"

I climbed off the stool. "All I said was that he wasn't going to like it. I have no objection whatsoever to any scheme that ruffles his tail feathers, ladies. In fact, I'll make myself a tissue-paper pom-pom and sit in the first row of the bleachers. I've got a date now, so I'm going to run along and let you all work on the list of all the things you'll have to do. *Ciao!*"

I almost made it to the door.

"Just hold your horses, Miss Social Gadabout," Ruby Bee barked. "You come right back here and explain about this list. I'm sponsoring a baseball team, not going into Starley City to shop."

I held my horses, but also my ground. "Okay, for starters, you need a minimum of nine players, and you've got one. You need uniforms, balls, bats, gloves, bases, a league rule book, a field for practice, and a couple of coaches."

Joyce Lambertino slid off the bar stool, mumbled something about the waxy buildup on her kitchen floor, and escaped past me with the look of a homeowner on Elm Street who's just heard about the newest neighbor.

Ruby Bee and Estelle stared at me, and I stared right back at them as Joyce's station-wagon door slammed shut and the engine growled to life. We continued to stare as tires ground across the gravel parking lot. We stared some more as tires met hot pavement and squealed away.

"No," I said flatly.

"I am your own flesh and blood," Ruby Bee began, but that's all I heard, because I was out of there and fully intending to stay out of there until the Maggody World Series was decided.

Ivy watched Alex as he took the empty crates from the trunk of the car. At times, he was more trying than their son, she thought with a grimace. Send him to the co-op in town for gunnysacks and fertilizer, wait the best part of the afternoon, and watch him return with crates and a stupid grin. He'd probably gotten lost.

His overalls needed patching, his bootlaces needed tying, his hair and beard needed trimming, and she was fairly sure his eyeglasses needed cleaning, because they always did. It was a miracle he didn't walk into a wall more often.

However, when he offered the crates, she wordlessly took them from him and set them down on one of the big plywood tabletops.

"I saw a scissor-tailed flycatcher on the utility wire," he said.

"Through those smudgy glasses? Give them to me so I can wipe them on my shirttail."

"I could see the distinctive silhouette, Ivy. It's the first one I've seen all summer. It was down by the low-water bridge."

"Good, Alex." She plucked his glasses off his nose and began to clean them, not bothering to point out that the bridge was not between their farm and the co-op. "At the rate business is going these days, we may have to fry it for supper. I don't know what's going to happen when that fancy supermarket opens." She stopped as a dusty white Chevy parked in the nearby shade. "Ruby Bee, how are you today? I put aside some particularly fine tomatoes for you. I was going to call you later so you could come by and get 'em."

"I appreciate it, Ivy," Ruby Bee said, more interested in a list she was glancing at. "Isn't Jackie going into the sixth grade this year?"

"He sure is," Alex said. "Hard to believe, isn't it?"

Ruby Bee went between the tables, nodding appreciatively at the piles of vegetables, and cornered Ivy in front of a stack of shallow wooden crates. "There's something I want to discuss with you," she began.

Geraldo Mandozes sat at a small table in the storeroom of the Dairee Dee-Lishus, the bills fanned out in front of him like a deck of cards. Why was business so bad? He ran his fingers through his disheveled hair as he muttered a few choice Spanish curses. The goddamn deli wasn't even open yet, and already he was feeling a squeeze. He was having to throw away more tamales than he sold.

"Yoo-hoo," called a voice from out front. "Mr. Mandozes? Are you home?"

He abandoned the bills and went out to the counter window. "Yes, I am Mandozes. You want to order?"

Estelle hastily looked up at the painted menu above his head. "Why, yes, I believe I'll have a cherry limeade. It's so hot today that my brain is bubbling like a pot of stew."

"You don't want any tamales or some cheeseburgers?"

"In this heat?" Estelle chuckled merrily, then rewarded the foreigner with a right nice smile while he fixed the cherry limeade and put it down on the counter. "Thank you, Mr. Mandozes. I'm sure this will hit the spot. I dropped by earlier, but you were closed up tighter'n a tick."

"I needed supplies, and the wholesaler will no longer deliver such small and insignificant orders."

"Well, imagine that. There's a little something I wanted to ask you, if you don't mind." She hurried on in case he did. "I seem to recall you've got a little boy of about ten or eleven."

"Raimundo is ten," Geraldo said suspiciously. He lit a cigarette and blew a stream of smoke through the screened window. "Has he done a wrong thing?"

"Heavens, no." Estelle took a big slurp of the cherry limeade while she tried to decide how best to continue.

Buzz Milvin popped the top of the beer and grinned at the noise. Weren't nothing finer than to come home to a cool living room, a cold beer, and some peace and quiet, 'cause God knows the factory got louder every day. With the mother-in-law and the kids out back fixing supper, all he had to listen to was the rumble of the window unit. Of course, later he'd have to listen to Lillith bitching at him about smoking too much (he wasn't) and the kids whining about stuff they needed (they didn't), but for the moment he figured he was in heaven, or a damn close fack similar.

The doorbell rang. Buzz put down his beer, climbed out of the recliner, and tried to arrange a neighborly smile as he opened the door.

"Howdy, Buzz," Ruby Bee chirped, the list still in her hand. "Mind if I stop by for a minute?"

"Not at all," Buzz lied. He gestured for her to come in, then sat down on the edge of the sofa. "How're you doing, Ruby Bee? I guess I haven't been over to the bar since Lillith came to live with us a few weeks back."

"And how is that working out?" Ruby Bee inquired politely.

"It's great, just great. Ever since Annie died, it's been

real hard to hold down a job and take care of the kids. Now I don't have to fix breakfast, find their homework papers, and make sure they get out to the bus stop on time every morning. Lillith's a real orderly sort."

Ruby Bee tilted her head and put her finger on her cheek. "Now let me think . . . isn't Martin going on twelve and Lissie just about eleven? One going into sixth, the other fifth?"

"Martin had a birthday last week. He's twelve, and yeah, Lissie's almost eleven. You got a real fine memory, Ruby Bee."

"Thank you kindly, Buzz. I ran into Lissie's teacher at a church potluck awhile ago, and she mentioned being concerned about Lissie. I hope she's doing better these days?"

He gave her a wry grin. "She was out in left field there for a few months, trying to take Annie's place and do all of the kitchen and laundry chores. I was so lost and confused that it took me some time to see what was going on. I think having her grandma living here has helped a lot."

"Left field?" Ruby Bee said brightly. "Funny you should mention that, because there's something I want to talk to you about." She settled into the cushion, giving herself plenty of time to consider her next move. After all, there was a possibility of two recruits and a coach.

Estelle made a check next to the Mexican boy's name, polished off the cherry limeade, and drove over to the Pot O' Gold mobile-home park. She rattled across the cattle guard under the arch, wound through the metal boxes, and parked in a scanty patch of shade under a sickly elm.

Ten minutes later, there was a check next to Earl Boy Nookim's name and she was on her way to Elsie McMay's, where she could expect a glass of iced tea, a homemade cookie, two more players of the grandchild persuasion, and a nice chat in front of the fan.

3

The pigeons at Piazzo San Marco. The glass of Campari and soda beneath a gaily colored umbrella. The day at the Lido. The night Riccardo poled us through the canals, crooning so softly that only I could hear him. After the frivolous lapse in Rome, I'd had to get back on the budget, but on page 127, I'd found a small pensione with a view of the Grand Canal.

However, now it was time to leave the pasta marinara, the straw-wrapped jugs of dark red chianti, the sleek green bottles of mineral water (I was being quite careful not to succumb to any unspeakable maladies that might ruin my tour), the golden glow of Tuscany, and the verdant foothills of the Alps.

I consulted the table of contents and flipped to page 311. Yes, the sun-drenched beaches of the French Riviera were calling me. The glitter of the casino, the yachts, the furs and diamonds. Monte Carlo, where the rich mingled with the commoners and anything was possible.

"You'd just have to think anything's possible these days," Mrs. Jim Bob opined loudly. "Why, the next thing we know, women'll be wearing pants to church and little children will be running wild in Sunday school. Don't you agree, Brother Verber? I mean, what's the world coming to anymore?" She stopped to blot the corner of her mouth with a pristine hankie, then gazed sternly at her companion, who seemed a little distant even though he was sitting not five feet away on her newly re-covered divan. "Don't you agree?" she said, turning up the volume.

Brother Verber looked up with a guilty twitch. "You

know I always agree with you, Sister Barbara. You are the beacon of my flock, the light that shines so pure and bright, it makes the sinners' eyes cross when they face it. And not to mention a most attractive woman."

Mrs. Jim Bob smiled tightly, because, of course, it was all true, what he'd said, but she was keenly aware of the sin of pride—among others—and wasn't about to allow herself to be led astray. "Girls playing with boys! It's a scandal to even think about it."

The images that flashed across Brother Verber's mind had to do with girls playing with boys, but he figured that wasn't at all what she was thinking of, and he whipped out his handkerchief to wipe away the sudden sweat.

"I felt it my Christian duty to have a word with Joyce Lambertino," Mrs. Jim Bob continued, oblivious to his discomfort. "I marched myself up to the door, fully expecting to be invited in for a nice visit, but Joyce wouldn't even let me inside the house. She said the kitchen floor was slippery. I knew better than that, Brother Verber. Better than that."

"You did?"

"I wasn't born this morning. From the way she was blocking the doorway, it was as plain as the nose on your face—which you might want to tend to, by the way—that her house was a mess and she was embarrassed to let me see how slovenly she was. I have always had my doubts about her, what with her wearing her hair like a high-school girl."

Brother Verber tut-tutted, peeked at his watch, and wondered exactly why he was sitting on the newly re-covered divan in Sister Barbara's front room when he could be using the time more profitably. When he'd arrived, he'd hoped for a slice of chocolate layer cake or a warm, fresh cookie, but she hadn't even offered iced tea. He cleared his throat, trying to sound a mite dry, and said, "I'm real glad to hear how you tried to steer Joyce back onto the path of righteousness. Would you mind repeating one more time how she was stumbling into sin?"

Mrs. Jim Bob's nostrils flared, but not so much that

you'd notice unless you were watching real close. "Joyce's husband is coaching the baseball team my Jim Bob organized. She wanted her little niece Saralee to play with the boys. I happened to overhear Jim Bob and Larry Joe discussing it, and I felt it my duty to make it clear that we are not going to have that sort of thing here in Maggody. Some folks have been flirting with sin ever since that wicked, wicked lawyer woman came here awhile back and told wives they could stop fixing biscuits from scratch and start wearing the pants in the family. The next thing you know, we were neck-deep in murder and destruction and the erosion of our Christian values."

"Let us get down on our knees and pray," Brother Verber cut in smoothly. "Just recalling that unpleasantness has opened the door a crack for Satan to sneak in. Ah, could I wet my whistle before we begin?"

"In a minute." She waited while Brother Verber, who was sliding down the edge of the divan, caught himself and got settled back where he belonged. "There is something else I have to tell you about so you can put a stop to it. Edwina Spitz happened to mention that a few weeks ago she was taking her evening stroll down Finger Lane and halted out by the hydrangeas in front of Eilene and Earl's house to catch her breath."

From the intensity of her stare, Brother Verber was aware that some response was required of him. He tugged on his nose for a minute. "I am most glad to hear Edwina's enjoying good health," he hazarded.

"That is not the issue, Brother Verber. I am going to have to describe a very lurid scene now, and I'd like to think you're clear in your mind that I'm only repeating what Edwina told me, and that she was only repeating what she accidentally overheard from behind the hydrangeas."

"It's clear as spring water," he assured her promptly, sitting up straight and preparing his handkerchief. "It's your Christian duty to repeat this to me. No matter how difficult it is, don't try to spare me by skipping anything, Sister Barbara. Not one tiny thing."

Mrs. Jim Bob related the shameful story of Kevin Buchanon and Dahlia O'Neill's disrespectable encounter on the porch swing. Rather than skip anything, she may have embellished it so that he could appreciate just how terrible and depraved and lustful and truly sinful it was.

And he did. She finally took pity on his bright red face and heaving shoulders and went to get him some mint iced tea. When she came back, he'd mopped away most of the sweat and his eyes looked a little less glassy.

"So what are you going to do?" she demanded.

Brother Verber gulped down the tea. His voice still was on the high side as he said, "What do you reckon I ought to do, Sister Barbara?"

"Something," Mrs. Jim Bob replied, her arms locked and her foot tapping away like a woodpecker. "Both of those young people attend the Voice of the Almighty on a regular basis. I know for a fact Kevin has a lapel pin for not missing Sunday school for ten years. Dahlia's granny lets her miss once in a while, but I almost always am obliged to nod to them after services."

"Should I kick them out?" Brother Verber asked, bewildered. "You know, excommunicate them?"

"Excommunicate them out of the church? Of course not! That would not be the charitable, forgiving thing to do, Brother Verber, and I'm shocked you could say such a thing. Who knows what they might do next if they thought no one was minding their behavior, that no one was deeply concerned with teaching them to restrain their lust?"

"I could denounce them from the pulpit, I 'spose. Tell the whole congregation about this shameful scene and ask everyone to pray for their souls right then and there."

Mrs. Jim Bob pondered this one for a second, imagining the two faces when their disgusting actions were aired in front of a good percentage of the town's folks. Reluctantly, she realized Edwina would be in her regular seat at the end of the third pew and would wonder how certain graphic details had crept into the story. "No, we can't have that sort of thing said aloud in the Assembly Hall where God can hear us. We'd be obliged to exorcise the building to get rid of the stench. What you need to do is call them in for premarital counseling, Brother Verber.

Instruct them about how decent, God-fearing, betrothed couples behave. Warn them about going to hell for all eternity if they even think about bestial practices that no good Christian couple would ever engage in."

"What if they won't come?" Brother Verber asked humbly, doing his best not to let his mind stray to his study material under his sofa, where bestiality was almost the order of the day.

"You just tell them that if they won't, you'll be forced to try to save their souls anyways by speaking out during the Sunday service. I do believe you can make them understand, don't you?"

"Oh, Sister Barbara, some days you are a saint just waiting for a halo. I can almost see it now. Praise the Lord!"

She looked down modestly.

Estelle squinted at the list, wishing the light was a little bit better but determined not to pull out her reading glasses and thus give Ruby Bee the opportunity to make catty remarks. "Okay, we got Saralee Chewink, Jackie Sattering, Raimundo Mandozes, Lissie and Martin Milvin, both of Elsie McMay's grandchildren, and the Nookim boy."

Ruby Bee leaned over Estelle's shoulder and carefully counted the names. "We only got eight players. Didn't Arly say we needed nine?"

"Maybe. I used to watch games on television when there wasn't anything else on. You've got your pitcher and your catcher, three base guards, and three outfielders."

"That's just eight," Ruby Bee said, nobody's fool. "We don't supply the referee, do we? Even if we do, one of us could do that part. In fact, it seems real silly to have a child out there telling people what the rules are."

"Hush for a minute and let me think," Estelle muttered.

Ruby Bee went over to the corner booth to make sure the fellow from number four didn't want dessert (he didn't), inquired if he'd enjoyed his lunch (he had), and left him alone to read his important-looking papers.

"Well," she said once she was back behind the bar,

"have you solved the mystery of the ninth player? Are you going to tell me now or shall I wait to read it in the newspaper? Is it gonna be a mystery novel?"

"Aren't we full of ourselves today? I happened to have remembered another position, but if you're more inclined to listen to your jaw flap, then I sure don't want to interrupt you. Go ahead, flap your jaw. It makes a nice breeze."

Ruby Bee stalked into the kitchen, rattled the pots and pans on the stove, ran water in the stainless-steel sink, opened and closed the refrigerator door, and gnawed on her lower lip until it began to smart. None of this took more than a minute, and when she came back out, Estelle was still on the stool, nibbling on a pencil and pretending to study the list.

Ruby Bee grabbed a washrag and began to wipe the spotless countertop. "What other position is there?"

"I beg your pardon. Are you speaking to me?"

"What other position is there?" Ruby Bee repeated, trying not to envision the washrag in Estelle's mouth, which was big enough to hold it without cracking her lipstick.

"Stop short. It's between second and third base."

"Stop short? I've never heard of any position called stop short. You've got it wrong, Estelle. That's downright crazy."

"I do not, Miss Walking Baseball Bible. The stop short is the fellow that hops around between second and third base. He's almost as important as the pitcher."

"How can he be as important as the pitcher? If the pitcher didn't pitch, then the batter wouldn't have anything to try to bat. I suppose now you're going to say this stop short is as important as the batter. I swear, Estelle, you've been sniffing the perm solution too long. As important as the pitcher!"

The fellow from number four came to the register and took out his wallet. "Lunch certainly is a bargain," he murmured.

Ruby Bee glared at Estelle, then managed a pinched smile for the fellow whose name she didn't recall right offhand. "I hope this conversation didn't disturb you."

"Of course not," Lamont lied smoothly, having had more than a little practice in his day. "I couldn't help overhearing bits and pieces, however. I gather you're both baseball fans?"

Estelle glared at Ruby Bee, then fluttered her eyelashes for the fellow, who had attractive silverish hair, a nice face, and drove a late-model black Cadillac. "Perhaps you could settle a small bone of contention for us," she said, still fluttering like crazy to make her request sound more friendly. "You're the fellow in number four, ain't you?"

"Lamont Petrel, and at your service."

Ruby Bee figured Estelle had a gnat in her eye, so she decided to butt in before she made a total fool of herself, which was destined to happen any second. "We were discussing the name of the player what stands between second and third base," she said.

Lamont was watching both of them warily, since neither seemed real stable. "Which team are you interested in? I don't follow baseball religiously, but I might be able to remember a few of the shortstops."

There was a moment of silence.

"Never mind," Estelle said in a funny voice.

Ruby Bee considered saying something right there in front of the fellow, but changed her mind after a quick peek at Estelle's face. "Don't let us detain you from your work, Mr. Petrel."

"Whatever you say," Lamont said, puzzled. "Have a nice day."

"You, too," they said in unison.

Estelle waited until the door closed, then leaned forward and said, "Isn't he opening the supermarket with Jim Bob?"

"Yeah, he stays out back two or three nights a week so he can meet with Jim Bob or go across the street and look at blueprints with those foulmouthed hard hats. The very first day they started that job, there must have been a dozen of them strutted right in here like they owned the place. Let me tell you, I straightened them out quicker than a snake can spit. They don't even look over here when they drive up to work every morning. It's bad enough being driven out of business without having to serve beer and lunch to the people who're twisting the screw in your back. Mr. Petrel's quiet, so I put up with him, and he's real good about paying for any long-distance calls he makes from the room."

"Does his wife ever come with him?"

"Not to my knowledge, Miss Snoopy Bloomers—but that don't mean she isn't home playing bridge or painting her fingernails. Or having her hair done at a fancy salon with one entire wall of sinks and another of hair dryers."

"I was merely inquiring."

"So I heard."

The conversation went on in this vein for a while, but there wasn't really anyplace for it to go, and after a few minutes Estelle picked up the list. "So we got to find one more player. I can't think of anyone, Ruby Bee. We pretty much got every single child in town who was willing to play and wasn't already signed up for the supermarket team. Did you hear they even bought spangely little outfits for the cheerleaders? Red-and-white-striped miniskirts and blue leotards with stars on 'em. Joyce said they were real cute."

"Cheerleaders!" Ruby Bee sniffed at that nonsense. "What featherbrained girls agreed to do that?"

"Some of the high-school girls, I heard. Jim Bob told the boys who're going to work at the supermarket that he'd get them free beer if they could talk their girlfriends into it. Ten minutes later, he had them lined up at the front door for interviews. The front door of his *private* office, I might add."

"No!" Ruby Bee said, shocked.

"It's the gospel truth. Heather Riley told Lottie Estes, in the strictest confidence, of course, so this is just between you and me, that Jim Bob made her stick out her chest and prance around the room like an ostrich. Then he had her sit down right next to him on the cot in his office and asked her questions that had nothing to do with cheerleading—unless that's what they call what goes on in the backseats of cars these days. Heather finally burst into tears and ran out of the room, and now her boyfriend won't even talk to her."

There was a period of relative quiet while the two humphed and snorted.

Ruby Bee finally gave up expressing her disgust and said, "So he's got all the players he needs, a coach, uniforms, cheerleaders, miniskirts, equipment, and heaven knows what else. You know what we got, Estelle? We got eight players." She stuck eight fingers under Estelle's nose to emphasize her point. "We got no coach, no uniforms, no smarmy high-school girls in miniskirts, no equipment, no nothing. We don't have diddly squat."

"I can't argue that one," Estelle said with a morose sigh. "We may have to call those little children and tell them they can't play after all."

"I am not a quitter, Estelle Oppers. Jim Bob is going to be called to explain hisself on Judgment Day just like everybody else, but when he lifts up his squinty yellow eyes, he's going to find Rubella Belinda Hanks standing before him."

"Holding a baseball bat," Estelle added, taken with the image. "Looking at him hard enough to split his britches."

"You can be beside me," Ruby Bee said in a spurt of generosity. "And you know what? When his britches split, it turns out his drawers are red and white striped, and everybody sees it and starts laughing to beat the band. Can you picture the look on his face then?"

That rocked them back and forth until both of them had tears rolling down their cheeks and Estelle nearly wet her pants but managed to hold it. The near-miss sobered her up enough for an idea to pop into her head.

"Stop, Ruby Bee," she said. "An idea just popped into my head. It was exactly like when a light bulb goes on over a character's head in a cartoon."

Ruby Bee wiped her eyes on the hem of her apron and tried to look impressed with all this upcoming illumination. "So what is it, Estelle?"

"It has to do with Arly. We can call—"

"Don't waste your breath. Arly made it real plain that she wasn't going to have one thing to do with any baseball team. She'll have a fit if we so much as throw out a hint in her direction. She may be fond of making jokes

and saying smart-alecky things, but there's something
about her that I can't rightly put my finger on but I try
my best to avoid."

"We're not throwing a single hint in her direction, or
not yet, anyways. Remember Hammet, Robin Buchanon's bush colt that stayed with Arly after Robin was
killed? How old do you reckon he was at the time?"

"Lordy, Estelle, he was such a wild creature that I
didn't want to get close enough to look. He was runty,
that's for sure. Runty and filthy and smelly. And blessed
with his ma's nasty language. Did I tell you what he had
the audacity to say right to my face?"

"More than once. Now what we need to do is find out
where Hammet's pa lives. Why don't you pour me a glass
of beer and scoot the pretzels down this way. This is one
fine idea, if I say so myself."

And she always did, Ruby Bee thought as she pushed
the pretzel basket down the smooth expanse of the bar.

Alex had taken Jackie outside to play catch, which was
somewhat interesting in that Alex couldn't catch a cold,
much less a ball. Neither could Jackie, for that matter,
but he was a docile sort and trudged along rather than
argue.

Ivy was reading a book that would have caused the
good folks at *Organic Gardening* to faint in their compost
piles. "Organophosphate," she read aloud with difficulty.
"Tetraethyl pyrophosphate." She repeated the words
until they had a pleasant rhythm to them and seemed to
roll off her tongue.

Alex wouldn't hear them, because once he understood
what they meant, he'd be as panicky and upset as a
bronco with a burr in its tail. Alex preferred ladybugs
and praying mantises to control the insects that savaged
the gardens every summer. He planted marigolds to fight
the slugs. He constructed quaint scarecrows when a shotgun would have been much more effective.

Alex was in harmony with his environment, Ivy told
herself as she put aside the book. He genuinely liked
the rabbits that gnawed the lettuce, the groundhogs that
wallowed in the squash, the deer that nibbled everything

they could reach over the fence, or everything in sight when they'd knocked the fence down, which they did once a month or so. For all she knew, he had affection for the bugs and slugs and other foul things.

Ivy was more in harmony with the real world of dwindling bank accounts, bills, mortgage payments, supplies, the increase in the electric rate, and all the basically nonorganic aspects of their life.

There wasn't much she could do about the animals that trampled the gardens and enjoyed a well-balanced diet at her expense, but she could do something quite lethal to the ones that traveled on six legs. The insecticide wasn't cheap, but the increase in productivity per acre would more than cover the cost. There was a possibility they could lower prices just a bit, and perhaps keep a few customers.

Alex would protest and perhaps go so far as to forbid it—if he knew, of course. Ivy figured she could send him and Jackie into town on some errand, then waltz out to the garden and orchards to take care of the insects all by herself. Alex could continue to be as organic as he wished, and she could use enough of the organophosphate to at least attempt to be competitive with the supermarket. Or she could sprinkle it on the salads in the deli department and ensure there would be no more supermarket with which to be competitive.

Geraldo Mandozes slammed down the checkbook and leaned back in the metal chair. If business got any slower, he figured he'd have to call it quits and try to sell the damn building and equipment to someone else. But there would be no buyers beating down the door. He'd used all his savings to buy the business and bring his family to this godforsaken place. Geraldo's anger grew hotter than a peck of jalapeño peppers as he remembered how long he'd cooked for other people to save the money.

His tamales really were the best, the very best. It was not fair that this supermarket deli would destroy the Dairee Dee-Lishus as if it were a dry twig to be stepped on.

A mouse darted out from under a stack of dry goods, then froze. *"Vaya!"* Geraldo snarled. The mouse *vaya*-ed back from whence it had come. "This is too much. I got bills, I got payments, I got less customers every day, and now I got mice. I got enough trouble without god-damn mice."

He took the box of poison off the shelf and began to sprinkle it along the baseboards, being careful not to inhale the whitish-gray powder.

Lillith Smew stared in horror at the brown bug scuttling across the kitchen counter. She put her hand on her heart, which wasn't at all strong, and held back a shriek. It was one thing to risk her health, which wasn't at all good, to come live with Buzz and the children and take care of them, but she hadn't bargained on roaches in the kitchen. Why, she was having one of her palpitations right there; she could feel it under her hand.

She forced herself to sit down and try to calm herself so she wouldn't have another heart attack. She'd already had two, even though the snooty young doctor had said they were bouts of indigestion. Lillith Smew figured she knew more than he did, anyway, because she'd spent a goodly amount of time in various doctors' offices, hoping one of them would acknowledge the gravity of her heart condition.

Martin poked his head in the kitchen. "What's the matter, Gran? Are you sick?"

"I saw a roach, Martin. It caused a severe palpitation, and I had to sit down to catch my breath."

"They get to be a problem in the summer," Martin said agreeably. He had big brown eyes, but they never widened in surprise these days, nor did much of any expression ever cross his face. "There's a box of powder under the sink. You want I should sprinkle some around?"

"Oh, Martin, you are such a good little boy. I don't know what I'd do if something happened to you and sweet little Lissie. You'll be my only grandchildren now that your poor mama has gone to heaven." Lillith made a sad face and spread out her arms, looking somewhat like the crucifix at the Assembly Hall. "Come here so I can give you a big hug."

Martin dutifully crossed the room and allowed himself to be crushed. She smelled like medicine, he thought without much interest. She had enough little boxes and bottles to stock a drugstore, and she was always going on about her heart or her blood pressure or her veins or her waves of dizziness or something.

"There's another roach," he said so she'd let go of him. "I better get the poison."

"Then he put his hand on her thigh," Lottie Estes told Elsie McMay, who'd come by to pick up a half-pint of Lottie's blackberry jam, which had won the blue ribbon at the county fair for as many years as Elsie could recall.

They were sitting at the kitchen table, with a plate of thinly sliced pound cake and an open jar of jam handy. Elsie put her hand to her lips. "Did he . . . ?"

Lottie had to stop for a second to compose herself before she could continue. "Yes, Elsie, I'm afraid he did. Now this is in the strictest confidence, of course, and just between you and me, but he did his level best to slide his hand toward . . . Well, to actually touch poor Heather in a very private place that she shouldn't even touch herself, much less allow a man to touch. Heather is a good girl. If she wasn't, she certainly wouldn't have confided in me, her home ec teacher, would she? I don't worry about the ones who share their innermost private secrets with me. No, Elsie, I worry about the ones who don't!"

"Such as?" Elsie said as she spooned a bite of jam on a corner of the cake slice.

"Let me start us another pot of tea and then I'll tell you." Lottie smiled contentedly as she headed for the teakettle on the stove. It was so nice of Elsie to drop by, and even nicer to take such a deeply charitable interest in Lottie's students. And she knew she could rely on Elsie not to repeat a single word.

4

The count had roguish eyes and a dimple. I'd noticed him glancing at me as I sipped espresso on the hotel patio, but I'd pretended to be engrossed in a mystery novel. I wasn't staying at this particular hotel. The less pretentious hotel was perfectly adequate for my basic needs and well within the budget. The concierge (okay, page 314) had suggested I have coffee at one of the more grandiose places on the boulevard that ran beside the beach.

I noted out of the corner of my eye that the count was murmuring to the garçon, who was staring at me. I returned to my novel but allowed an enigmatic smile to dance across my face.

The telephone rang. I looked up quickly, but the count and the garçon were nowhere to be seen. The telephone would have to go, I thought sourly. Sure, this was a PD of sorts and I was its sole P, but that didn't mean I had to answer the telephone as if I was a receptionist in a front office. It occurred to me I could take my radar gun and travel guide and drive down the road a piece to a secluded, shady spot near the skeletal remains of Purtle's Esso Station. Then, if everyone had the decency to observe the speed limit, I could get on with more important things.

I finally picked up the receiver. "*Oui*?"

"Is there someone with you?" Ruby Bee said.

"*Mais non*," I said with a Gallic shrug. "*C'est moi.*"

"You said *we*. Why'd you say that, and what was that other gibberish?"

"A small joke, Ruby Bee . . . a very small joke. What's up? Armed robbery in the bar and grill? Another hostage situation in the motel? Mold on the hamburger buns?"

"I swear, you have been in the dadgum strangest mood lately. I am not the only person in town to have commented on it, either. Ivy Sattering said you were talking to yourself in the launderette, and when you left, you said 'chow' to her instead of 'see you later' or 'have a nice day.' Why would you say something like that, Ariel Hanks? As your own mother, I think I'm entitled to an explanation."

"There's a lot you're entitled to," I said mildly. "Is this display of petty tyranny the purpose of the call? There is criminal activity afoot as we speak, and as the defender of the faith, the protectress of the little people, the—"

"Some days you sorely try my patience. I just wanted to tell you that the bar and grill is closed for lunch 'cause I've been having a terrible time with those big black ants and I'm going to have to seal the cabinets and put out that powder the exterminator left last time."

"Okay," I said. After a distinct lull, I added, "Is there anything else?"

"So what are you planning to do about lunch?"

"I have no idea. What difference does it make to you?"

"Why should it make any difference to me? I was just inquiring, for pity's sake. I didn't ask what time you got home after your date last Saturday night with that state trooper friend of yours, or why it was well after three in the morning—particularly when you told me beforehand that you all were going to the early picture show."

"No, you didn't ask that," I said, totally bewildered. "I'm not sure what I'll do about lunch, Ruby Bee. Maybe I'll pick up a cheeseburger and a lemonade at the Dairee Dee-Lishus and have a little picnic while I lurk for speeders out north of town. Is that all right with you?"

"Hold on a minute." She put her hand over the receiver, but I could hear a muffled conversation. I was about to hang up when she came back on. "No, don't do that. That's a terrible idea, Arly. There's a rumor in town that the Mandozes fellow is using a cheap grade of beef—if it is beef. We can't have you getting sick."

"Why not?"

"Because I said so, Miss Glib Lips. You just go on home and have some soup. That way you won't be courtin' botulism."

"Whatever you say," I said, and hung up before she could say anything else equally peculiar. Ruby Bee and Estelle make me crazy. They always have an elaborate justification for involving themselves in my business, personal and official, and they involve themselves with more enthusiasm and dedication than teenagers toilet-papering a tree. They thrive on cop and private detective shows on television. Estelle once wrote a six-page letter to Tom Selleck pointing out a clue he'd overlooked, but he didn't respond, and after a few months she stopped grousing about it.

The telephone rang, but I managed not to hear it. I picked up my beloved travel guide, went into the back room of the PD (which has exactly two rooms: the front room and the back room) to get the radar gun out of the metal cabinet, and ambled out to the car. Botulism? Beef—if that's what it was?

Shaking my head, I opened the car door. It was very much like opening the oven door to see if the turkey was done. Earlier, I'd cleverly parked the car in the shade and uncleverly forgotten to roll down the windows. The shade was now over by the soda machine next to the door of the PD.

I went ahead and rolled down the window (barn doors and stolen horses here), then decided to go across the road to my apartment, where I could slump in front of the fan and cast enigmatic smiles at the count.

Roy Stiver was sitting in a rocking chair in front of the antique store, watching the traffic and thinking about whatever he thought about. "Yo, Arly," he said as I approached him. "You got yourself an out-of-town visitor. I went ahead and let him into your apartment."

My fingers tightened around the book, but I knew I hadn't quite worked myself up to that stage of schizophrenia, despite the recent exchanges with my mother. The sheriff and/or the friendly state trooper would have hunted me up at the PD. I couldn't think of any other

men who might want to drop in on me. No editorials,
please.

"Who is it?" I asked.

"I reckon it's supposed to be a surprise," Roy said,
cackling like a damn hen. "I knew you wouldn't mind
me using my key, Arly."

"I don't care whether you reckon it's supposed to be
a surprise or not. Who is it?"

"Oops, I think I hear my phone ringing. I've been
waiting all morning for a call from my broker. See ya
later." He pushed himself up and went into his store,
still cackling to himself. I was almost surprised there was
no egg in the cane-bottom seat.

Roy's departure left me with a few options. I could
chase him down to question him further, but I doubted
I'd find out anything. I could stand there at the side of
the highway until I was clipped by a truck. I could go
back to the car, pick up lunch at the Dee-Lishus, and
continue on with my original plan. Or I could climb the
rickety stairs at the side of the building and find out what
the hell was going on. It seemed obvious that Ruby Bee
was behind it, which wasn't much comfort.

I finally opted for the last option. The door was slightly
ajar, and I could hear my television set blaring as I
arrived at the landing. "Glad to see you've made yourself
at home," I called angrily as I banged open the door.

A small figure with stringy black hair was squatting
three inches from the television screen. Several soda cans
were on their sides, as was a box of crackers. He jerked
up in alarm at my voice, then smiled broadly and said,
"Howdy, Arly."

"Hammet?"

"Yeah, it's me. How be ya, Arly? Sure is god-awful
good to see ya again."

I came into the room and sank down on the sofa, wondering if the truck had indeed clipped me and I hadn't
noticed. "Hammet?" I repeated.

He regarded me soberly through small, unblinking,
Buchanon-tinted eyes. "You having a conniption or sumpun? You look whiter'n a dead cow in the moonlight."

"How did you get here?"

"It was real easy. First the social lady called over where I been staying all this time and sez you wants me to visit. I does okay there, mostly, but my stepma said she thought that'd be a right fine idea and had me on the curb when those ladies drove up in a big ol' station wagon. You look mighty funny, Arly. Is your belly achin'?"

"No, Hammet," I said weakly, "I'm a little surprised to see you, that's all. There's something screwy going on here. You said a social worker called your stepmother and said I wanted you to visit?"

"Sure were kind of you. It gits kinda wild sometimes. I got this half-ass brother what sez he's the biggest so I got to mind him, but that's a crock of shit and we get to hittin' and kickin'. Then this snot-nosed sister starts grabbin' on his hair, and he commences to bawlin', and then my stepma gits all het up." He gave me an appraising look. "Ain't easy by any means."

I caught myself grinning just a little bit. "No, I imagine not. So your stepmother agreed and had you all ready when the ladies drove up. Anyone you recognized?" I don't know why I even bothered to ask; I really don't.

"That lady what cooked for us'n and t'other one what hung around all the time," he explained eloquently.

"That's what I thought."

"They was real nice, Arly. They got me stuff to eat and drink in the car, and then they said all about how I could play baseball like those fellows on television. I was aimin' to watch 'em while I waited for you, but I reckon they's at home today."

I closed my eyes and tried not to sigh too loudly. "Oh, they're real nice ladies, Hammet. Real nice. Food, drink, and a promise that you could play baseball."

His smile faded. "Mebbe, they said, jest mebbe. They said nobody was gonna get to play if'n they didn't find someone to coach the team. I ain't ever played baseball, but I think I might like it better'n sorghum on corn bread for supper."

A lot of images went through my mind at that moment. My favorite involved Ruby Bee's staked-out body, sorghum, and an advancing line of big black ants. Hammet, for the uninformed, was one of Robin Buchanon's five illegitimate children. Robin had been murdered while hunting ginseng on Cotter's Ridge. He and I had gotten to be buddies (in our own way) during the subsequent investigation and I'd really become fond of him (in my own way). I'd been downright misty when the social worker took him to his pa's home, but it clearly wasn't possible to insert a small, untamed boy into my lifestyle. We both had realized it wouldn't have worked. However, I'd nurtured a flicker of guilt that was now a full-fledged forest fire.

"Is you okay?" he asked, watching me anxiously.

"I'm fine and I'm glad you're here to visit. Tell you what let's do, Hammet. Let's go down to where the real nice ladies are and have a chat. You can have a piece of pie with ice cream on it."

Hammet bounced up and hooked his thumbs through the straps of his faded but clean overalls. "And see if'n I git to play baseball?"

I nodded grimly and hoped he couldn't see the steam roiling out of my ears. As we walked down the highway to Ruby Bee's, Hammet regaled me with the highlights of fistfights in his new home and I tried to decide what I was going to say to the real nice ladies. Hammet's vocabulary had mellowed greatly since he'd come down from the cabin, and I certainly didn't want to remind him of his innate talent for four-letter words and quaint colloquialisms, most of which concerned farm animals and improbable sexual activities.

There was a CLOSED sign on the door of the bar and grill, but we marched in with no difficulty. The barroom was uninhabited. I told Hammet to pick out a stool, then went around the bar and into the kitchen, where I saw one real nice lady crawling alongside the baseboard and the other watching her. Neither looked especially thrilled to see me.

Ruby Bee got to her feet. "I told you I was closed so's I could tackle these darn ants."

"So you did," I said politely. "I went to my apartment for lunch, just as you suggested."

Estelle and Ruby Bee swapped looks. At last, Estelle

cleared her throat and said, "Hammet's lookin' fine, isn't he? It's astounding how much he's grown in the last year. With clean hair and decent clothes, he looks right smart, doesn't he?"

"Right smart," Ruby Bee said when I failed to respond. "He did so well in school that he's going into fifth this fall. He should be in sixth, but he was ignorant as they come when he started last year. Couldn't even count, his new ma told me. Can you imagine not knowing how to count?"

"I'm counting to ten right now," I said, "but it may not be sufficient. I may have to count to a hundred, or a thousand, or even a million. Did it occur to you to consult me before you invited a guest to stay at my apartment? What if I'd planned a trip or simply preferred to be alone? What if—" I stopped as the door opened behind me and Hammet came into the kitchen.

"Sumpun smells right tasty," he said, sucking in the noxious odor with the style of a seasoned connoisseur.

Ruby Bee put down the box of ant poison and scurried over to him. "I was just telling Arly here how well you've been doing at school. She's real proud of you, I bet. How about some pie?"

We all trooped back to the barroom and Hammet accepted a piece of peach pie, and with an encouraging word from me, a scoop of ice cream on top. I declined the same, mostly because I was so pissed, I wouldn't have accepted a bushel basket of ten-dollar bills from the woman. She could have offered to hang the moon for me, and I'd have suggested an extremely uncomfortable place to do it. Without hesitation.

"So which one of you is head coach?" I said when I could trust myself.

Ruby Bee held up her hands. "I don't know anything about baseball . . . not one blessed thing."

"Neither do I," Estelle added quickly. "Why, I got more confused than a preacher in paradise when I tried to think what they call the players."

I gave them an evil smile. "I'll dash right into Farberville to the Book Depot and buy you a book that'll explain everything."

"Now, honey," Ruby Bee said, "you know I'm too old to teach a gang of children how to throw baseballs and swing bats." She leaned over the bar and put her mouth close to my ear. "Don't forget I'm fifty-two years old. You wouldn't want me to have a heart attack on the field. You'd feel guilty the rest of your life."

I raised my eyebrows and my voice. "Fifty-two, my foot! You're fifty-five if you're a day, and a heart attack's a damn sight cleaner than matricide—which is an appealing alternative at the moment."

"I cannot believe my ears!" Estelle gasped. "Your own mother! Imagine saying such things to your own mother. You young folks have no respect for your elders."

"Can it," I said. "If you've lined up nine players, and I'm assuming Hammet's visit has numerical significance, then you've got eight sets of parents. Surely one of the fathers is a closet jock who'd like to live out his fantasies on the field."

Ruby Bee opened the drawer below the cash register and took out a much-creased piece of paper. "Don't go jumping to conclusions, young lady. For starters, discounting Hammet, we've got six families. Now Saralee is staying at the Lambertinos', and Larry Joe is already coaching the SuperSavers. Joyce has her hands full with the little ones, so there's no way she can coach."

Estelle grabbed the list. "Two of the players are Elsie McMay's grandchildren, visiting for the summer. Elsie's been having real serious problems with swelled-up ankles, so she can't coach."

With a sniff, Ruby Bee retrieved the list. "And that Nookim boy is on the team, and you know perfectly well that his papa's been disabled for a long time and can barely walk. His mama works double shifts at the poultry plant, so there's no way she can do it."

Estelle's snort was on the testy side as she lunged for the list. "We thought we had a good candidate in Buzz Milvin, what with both his kids on the team. But he's aiming to start work at the SuperSaver Buy 4 Less as the night manager, and he said Jim Bob'd fire him in a Noow Yark minute if he found out Buzz was coaching the enemy. He was right worried about even letting the kids play. Ruby Bee had to chew on his ear for a good half hour."

"I'm sure she was convincing," I cut in before Ruby Bee could make a try for the list. "Could we hurry up the pace, please? Hammet's about finished with his pie, and the two of us are not entranced by your long-winded excuses."

"It's okay," Hammet said charitably.

Ruby Bee tried to snatch the list, anyway, but Estelle hung on for dear life and said, "That leaves the Mandozes boy, but I wasn't about to wheedle with his pa. Mr. Mandozes has that fiery Latin temper and a kinda wild look in his eyes when he talks. The only other one is Jackie Sattering, and Ivy was real firm about needing Alex to help on the farm. They're going into apple season, and she said they both work fourteen hours a day this time of year. Besides—"

"Besides," Ruby Bee said, tired of being offstage, "Alex is not what you call athletic. I watched him walk across the yard to get my tomatoes, and I was real surprised when he didn't stumble over his own two feet or drop my tomatoes on the ground. I think Ivy was, too."

I shrugged. "Well, you'll have to keep looking elsewhere. Come on, Hammet, let's go to the edge of town and bust speeders. You can operate the radar gun."

"I gets to shoot 'em?"

"Sort of," I said. I slid off the stool, waited while he wiped his mouth on his sleeve and joined me, and we started for the door—which burst open, almost in our faces. The sunlight blinded me for a second, but as my eyes adjusted, I realized I was nose-to-nose with Mrs. Jim Bob, aka Mizzoner. Mizzoner and I have a mutual loathing society. I'm president this year, but if she behaves, I may pass the honor next year.

"You are just the person I wanted to talk to," she said, advancing on me like a tight-lipped piranha.

"Damn shame, Mrs. Jim Bob. Hammet and I were on our way out to preserve law and order in our cherished community."

Hammet grinned, but he'd encountered Mrs. Jim Bob in the past and had enough sense to maintain a cautious distance. "Yeah, Arly's gonna let me shoot folks what drive too fast."

Mrs. Jim Bob's beady little eyes narrowed. "How amusing I'm sure. No, Arly, your little game will have to wait. I have things to say to you and your mother, and I intend to say them right now." She marched past us to the bar, where Ruby Bee and Estelle hovered uncertainly. "I have heard a most distressing thing, Rubella Belinda Hanks. It smacks of the devil's handiwork, and I'd like to think I was misinformed."

"It's happened before," I said as Hammet and I retraced our steps, curiosity having gotten to me.

"What'd you hear?" Ruby Bee said.

"I heard that you aim to sponsor a baseball team."

"You ain't misinformed yet."

"I also heard that you're intending to allow girls to play right next to boys, and that Arly here is the coach."

Ruby Bee ignored my growl. "You got problems with that?"

"Well," Mrs. Jim Bob continued, her mouth tightening until I wasn't sure how she could spit out the words, "I was afraid of that. You know as well as me that girls aren't supposed to play physical games with boys. It's dangerous for the girls, because they're so much weaker. Everybody knows girls do better at activities like sewing and making little animals out of yarn pompoms. What's worse is that seeing the girls jiggling around gives the boys ideas—wicked ideas about unnatural, sinful things. I know for a fact that Lottie Estes's younger sister's boy, Kyle, went to a coed swimming party, and that very night his ma caught him in the bedroom"—she shot a quick look at Hammet—"doing an unnatural, sinful thing to hisself."

I could see Hammet's mind going every which way. Before he could say anything, I said, "That is absolutely absurd."

"It is not! You can just call up Lottie and ask her. She'll tell you how her sister liked to have cried for an hour on the telephone, and long distance, too—all the way from Enid, Oklahoma. She was sick with worry that Kyle's hands would break out in some kind of rash and everybody would know why. To this day, she frets over his report cards, wondering if his mind is quite right."

"Absurd," I said, still keeping an eye on Hammet, who was mystified but working on it. "Queen Victoria's dead, and we are in the twentieth century, with faint hopes of seeing the twenty-first. Girls have every right to participate in sports. They are not at a major physical disadvantage unless we're talking about weight lifting or wrestling. At this age, girls are better coordinated than boys, which more than compensates for a slight edge in brute strength."

"And nobody said one word about wrestling," Ruby Bee snapped. "I myself would be of two minds about girls rolling around on those mats with boys, especially in that skimpy underwear they wear, but there's nothing wrong with a girl throwing a baseball to a boy."

"Or hitting a ball," Estelle added.

"But they jiggle!" Mrs. Jim Bob said in triumph.

Ruby Bee leaned forward, her face beginning to take on the hue of the contents of the pickled-beet vat. "Not all of them, and the ones that do, why, they jiggle at school, too. They jiggle at the hardware store and at church. They jiggle all the time."

Estelle swept in for the kill. "And if God hadn't meant for them to jiggle, they wouldn't have anything that jiggled, would they?"

Mrs. Jim Bob took a breath and let it out in a martyred swoosh. "I suppose there is nothing wrong with girls having a nice team of their own so they can play other girls. Softball would be better, of course." She glowered in my direction. "And I am aware that Queen Victoria is dead, Miss Chief of Police. You were attempting to make a little joke, weren't you?"

"I was attempting to make you go away, but it didn't work. Come on, Hammet, it's high noon at the O.K. Corral."

Her smile had such a self-righteous air about it that I felt goose bumps rising on my arms. "Let me add one other thing," she said in an appropriately smirky tone. "If you coach this sinful team of jiggling girls and lusty-eyed boys, I shall insist that Jim Bob remove you from your position. He'll have your badge and your gun before you can make one more single smart-mouthed remark."

"You can't do that," Ruby Bee said, horrified.

"We'll just see about that, won't we?" Mrs. Jim Bob nodded curtly at the group, then stalked across the dance floor and out the door, no doubt expecting to be carried heavenward for a round of applause from the saints and angels.

Estelle patted my arm. "Don't worry about her, Arly. She can't insist that Jim Bob fire you just because you're coaching a baseball team."

Ruby Bee came around the bar and started patting my other arm. "Why, that's blackmail. She can't do that."

"She can't walk on water, either, but she'll be the last to admit it," I said. "Just how did she hear about this team and the name of the coach?"

"How would I know?" Ruby Bee said, retreating.

"Because," I said, advancing, "having her tell me I can't coach is about the only incentive that might make me change my mind."

"Is that so?"

"And you damn well know it," I continued. "This is a really cheap trick, and—"

"Yanking his pud?" Hammet said, giving me a puzzled frown. "Is that what she was so all-fired mad about?"

From the expressions on Ruby Bee's and Estelle's faces, I sensed it was time to leave for greener pastures. "Hey, I've got a box with three real bullets in it, Hammet. Let's stop at the PD to play with them before we go after the speeders."

"If'n all he was doin' was yanking his—"

"Ciao," I said brightly.

"You realize you can't repeat a word of this," Elsie McMay began, giving Millicent McIlhaney a serious look. "It was told to me in the strictest confidence, and it can't go any further. You've got to promise me, Millicent."

"I promise," Millicent said obediently. "In fact, let me make sure Darla Jean's still on the telephone. Those girls do nothing but gossip from dawn till dark; you'd think they could find something better to do with their time.

Help yourself to more coffee, Elsie. I'll be back in a minute."

She tiptoed to the top of the stairs. She could hear Darla Jean's voice through the closed door, just bubbling away like a creek, and it wasn't difficult to hear what she was saying, especially if you put your ear against the door.

Millicent was frowning as she came back into the kitchen and sat down across from Elsie. "I swear," she said, shaking her head, "I just don't know what gets into those girls. Sometimes I want to turn Darla Jean over my knee and spank her like she was back in pigtails. She's up there repeating the nastiest stories about folks, and she knows perfectly well that half of what she's saying is nothing more than lies."

"School starts up pretty soon, and she'll be more interested in clothes and football games and the new television shows," Elsie said. Even though there was no need for it, she leaned forward and lowered her voice. "Lottie told me the most horrifying story the other day. I was so upset, I couldn't stop thinking about it half the night. I tossed and turned like I was in a clothes dryer, and my sheets were damp the next morning."

"You'd better tell me, then. It'll do you a world of good to share your burden."

"Remember, this is just between you and me. Not one word to anybody."

"I already promised, Elsie," Millicent said impatiently. "Not one word will ever leave this room."

5

▼

The officially tentative lineup of the Ruby Bee's Flamingos—because, as we've all been told since birth, you can't tell the players without a scorecard:

Pitcher: Raimundo "Ray" Mandozes, the only team member who can throw the ball in the general direction he intends. Ray does not speak any English whatsoever (we're talking *nada*) but did recognize the word *spic* and promptly convinced Georgie McMay of his folly in saying it aloud.

Catcher: Saralee Chewink, the only team member to have caught the ball thus far. Saralee is on the chunky side, with tight yellow braids, glasses, and glittering braces. She spent a good deal of time casting thoughtful looks at Hammet. She persuaded Georgie to avoid sexist slurs in the future.

First Base: Hammet Buchanon, who can neither throw nor catch but has enthusiasm. He actively discouraged Georgie from discussing the delicate issue of illegitimacy in Stump County. Hammet spent most of the first practice blushing whenever he caught Saralee looking at him. There may be romance brewing in the infield, folks.

Second Base: Earl Boy Nookim, who is mute and surly, and simply went to the base (a burlap bag) and stood on it. Why not?

Third Base: Enoch McMay, a runty whiner with a runny nose and a fierce preference for watching television at his granny's house. This preference was aired every thirty seconds or so for two solid hours.

Shortstop: Martin Milvin, who at least put his glove on the correct hand and assumed a professional posture.

He is soft-spoken and very sober, and we can't have anyone playing the vital position on a bellyful of root beer.

Left Field: Georgie McMay, for his own protection. Were it not for the black eye, swollen lip, and twenty excess pounds of adipose tissue, he would not be an unattractive child. Maybe.

Center Field: Lissie Milvin, in hopes nothing will be hit that far. Lissie made a lovely chain of dandelions, and it looked quite striking in contrast with her auburn hair and dark, timid eyes. She caught a tiny purple butterfly, whispered to it, and gently released it. Later she discovered a mysterious hole, but even after twenty minutes of poking with a stick, she could not persuade its occupant to show itself. There is much to occupy Lissie in center field.

Right Field: Jackie Sattering, as above. He has all of his father's clumsiness and none of his mother's common sense. On the other hand, he was as gentle as Lissie with the butterflies and went to extremes not to step on the honeybees in the clover.

Head Coach: Take a wild guess.

Assistant Coach #1: Take another one.

Assistant Coach #2: Ditto.

"Say what?" Jim Bob said, gaping at Lamont as if he were a zoo animal screwing right there in the cage. "That ain't what you said earlier, Lamont. Jesus H. Christ!"

Lamont filled Jim Bob's glass half full of the cheaper whiskey he'd had the foresight to bring, then went over to the mirror and inspected his hair. The motel room seemed a sight more cramped now that the air was thick with Jim Bob's sweat. "I feel real bad, but the boys at the bank dumped it on me this morning, and they call the shots," he murmured as he licked his finger and smoothed down a stray hair. "I'm going to have to do some scrambling of my own, but we're both obligated to come up with whatever cash is required to close the loan next week."

"If I can't?"

"It's explained in great detail in the various documents

that comprise the partnership agreement. You did read it all before you signed it, didn't you?"

"Yeah, but I couldn't make heads or tails of a lot of it. All that shit about parties of the first part and second part and the devil knows what other parts. I thought the money was arranged down to the last penny. Now you're saying we have to pay four points on Thursday. We're talking nigh on to a million dollars. Four points is . . . forty thousand dollars." Jim Bob sank down on the bed and drained the glass.

"But you'll only have to come up with half. Surely that's not a problem?"

"No fuckin' problem at all, Lamont. I got my check-book in my pocket. I'll just write a check for my share. I always keep twenty or thirty thousand bucks in the account in case I want to make a down payment on fuckin' Buckingham Palace."

"And don't forget we have to cover twenty percent of the initial inventory. The wholesalers usually want cash on delivery, but they're giving us a break because of my existing accounts. Your share of that'll be around twenty thousand, too."

"Oh, swell. You do realize I haven't had any income since we started construction six months ago, don't you? I had to get a second on the house just to get along all this time, and Mrs. Jim Bob decided out of the blue to redecorate the entire downstairs. How am I supposed to come up with that kind of money?"

"I'm sure you can think of some outside resources, Jim Bob. After all, we're partners in this venture. You've put as much time and energy in it as I have, and I would be terribly distressed if you were unable to meet your commitments as spelled out in the binding legal documents you signed."

Jim Bob stared at him from under a much-lowered brow. "Just what happens if I can't meet my spelled-out commitments?"

"I'm afraid your interest reverts to me."

"Wait just a goddamn minute! You're telling me I'm fixing to lose my half of the SuperSaver? What about the

Kwik-Stoppe-Shoppe that was demolished? What about my rights there?"

Lamont took a sip of the cheap whiskey, which tasted more like dog piss than bourbon. "I wish you'd gone over all this with your lawyer, Jim Bob. I really do. You owned that property and I owned the adjoining vacant acreage. The titles were merged in order to satisfy the loan people. Your original holding is now an indivisible part of our joint holding."

Jim Bob took a gulp of the whiskey, which he thought was an improvement over that dog piss Lamont usually had in the motel room. "So unless I come up with forty grand, I've lost the Kwik-Stoppe-Shoppe and stand to lose the SuperSaver?"

"This upsets me as much as it does you. We've been in this together since I picked up that piece of property, and I'd like to think we're friends as well as partners." Lamont sighed as he refilled Jim Bob's glass. "If I had enough cash to cover your share, I would, but I'm not in a whole lot better shape than you are. There is one other option that we might consider. I've heard tell of an outfit in Texas with several supermarket chains, and I could try to get hold of them. They might be interested in taking this one off our hands, although I doubt we can get any more out of it than our investment. But breaking even's better than nothing, isn't it?"

"Sell Jim Bob's SuperSaver before it opens?" Jim Bob said, appalled. "But we're going to cut our prices until we run all the competition out of business, and then hike 'em up and have ourselves a little gold mine here in Maggody. I don't want to sell it to a bunch of Texas cowboys. My name's up there on the sign."

"It's up to you," Lamont said diplomatically. "If you can come up with your share of the money by Thursday, then we'll be in fine shape. However, only a minute ago you were saying how strapped you are for cash."

Jim Bob tugged on his chin while he racked his brain. "I think I can get the money. I know a couple of guys down in Little Rock that'll come through for me. Them, and a little I've got tucked away in a safe-deposit box, and maybe I can borrow some from Mrs. Jim Bob's cousin what moved to Peoria. It'll be tight, Lamont, and it would have been a damn sight easier if you'd told me before now. But I can come through and we can keep the SuperSaver."

Lamont drank the last of the whiskey and held out his hand. "Then we're partners, Jim Bob, and that's the best damn news I've heard all day. The grand opening's in a couple of hours. I want you to cut the ribbon, and I want you to be grinning when you do it. You go get yourself all slicked up. I got a few calls to make just now."

Adele Wockermann smiled as best she could, considering that Millicent McIlhaney had dragged her rocking chair so close that she was almost spittin' in Adele's face. "What's that you're sayin'?" she said as she wiped her chin with a tissue.

"Turn up your hearing aid," Millicent commanded. She was beginning to question why she came all the way out to the county nursing home every Saturday morning to sit on the porch with a senile old widow woman who didn't even attempt to show any appreciation. Millicent was keenly aware of her Christian duty, but some weeks it was like pulling ticks off a hound to get through. "Now this is in the strictest confidence, Adele, so don't go repeating it to every Tom, Dick, and Harry."

"Harry who? I don't know nobody named Harry. Are you talking about Horace Wockermann, my grand-nephew? He don't visit since he married that cheap tramp from Starley City. She's too good to visit the likes of me. She probably thinks old age is contagious."

"Just don't repeat this. It seems that Jim Bob Buchanon liked to have molested the Riley girl in his office last week. She was in there for the longest time, then came running out, howling and sobbing, with the buttons ripped right off her shirt. It's amazing she didn't get hit by a truck, she was so upset. Elsie McMay said Lottie Estes got madder'n a coon in a poke when she was telling the story over tea and pound cake the other morning. Isn't it the most awful thing you've ever heard in all your born days?"

"I've ever heard or I've never heard?" Adele began

to rock more vigorously as she picked up a titillating broadcast from her wee friends on the back side of the moon.

Millicent ground her dentures and reminded herself of her Christian duty, although she thought the amount of tribulation might entitle her to cut back to every other week. "You recall when Hiram Buchanon's barn burned a ways back and that little cheerleader came running out with smoking panties in her hand?"

"I reckon I do," Adele said serenely. She did, too.

"Well, this is a sight worse, if you ask me. Now nobody knows much of anything about this Lamont Petrel fellow what's come to town, and that means nobody knows if he's been bothering the girls hisself. With a name like Lamont Petrel, anything's possible, and I wouldn't be a bit surprised to hear that he was the one that did it. But Jim Bob Buchanon's the mayor, so he ought to act respectable. I shiver to think what Mrs. Jim Bob'll say if she ever catches wind of this."

"She passes more wind than she catches. She used to come out here and read Bible verses at me like I didn't attend the Voice of the Almighty Lord Assembly Hall twice on Sundays and every Wednesday night for prayer meeting right up to the day Mr. Wockermann passed away, may he rest in peace. I finally told her that her face reminded me of tadpoles on a mud fence, and after that she stopped a-comin'."

Millicent figured she'd evinced enough Christian duty for the week. "I'm going to run along now, Adele," she said real nicely. "I got to fix my hair and decide what to wear to the grand opening of the supermarket. Maybe I can get a good look at that Lamont Petrel from Farberville. I'll tell you all about him next week, and I'll bring you a box of my chocolate-chip cookies."

"No pecans. You know I can't pass pecans anymore."

Millicent patted Adele's shoulder, then nodded at the nurse's aide who was hovering near the doorway and sailed away, content in the knowledge that she'd kept poor Adele Wockermann apprised of local goings-on. It was real important for the old soul to have outside interests.

*

Ruby Bee had called a secret meeting of the Flamingos, which gave me a breather. Hammet wanted to do nothing else except discuss the first practice, held the previous afternoon in the redolent cow pasture out behind the motel. I wanted to forget it. I wanted to go back to the hotel patio and search for the bedimpled count, but I hadn't had fifteen seconds of peace since my houseguest had been thrust upon me.

I sent him down the road with an admonishment to avoid debating Georgie McMay's prejudices, then went across the street to the PD and shuffled through the mail for an errant one-way ticket to the South of France.

Before I could toss the envelopes in the wastebasket, the telephone rang. I conducted a mental debate, lost, and picked up the receiver.

It was Harvey Dorfer, the county sheriff, who's a pretty nice guy in his rednecked fashion and a true gentleman in election years. Luckily, he is smarter than he looks.

"How ya doing, Arly?" he began affably.

"Fine, Harve."

"I called to see if you wanted a deputy to help you this afternoon. We're real short, but I can scrounge up somebody for an hour or two."

"To do what—answer the telephone?"

Harve exhaled what I knew was a foul stream of cigar smoke. "Traffic control."

"Our regular Saturday-night drunks won't start crashing their trucks until dark, Harve. Till then I think I can handle the traffic by myself."

"Probably so, but I had a request from a county judge to send a deputy over to help you out. It seems he plays golf with that Petrel fellow, and it's what ya might call a small political favor. It's too damn hot to have a county judge breathing down my collar or peerin' too hard at the budget."

It made about as much sense as Ruby Bee's ravings. I rubbed my face, twisted my mouth around for a minute, and finally said, "What's this about, Harve? What do a county judge and someone named Petrel have to do with

me busting speeders on a hot Saturday afternoon? Traffic's usually up on the weekends, but mostly it's tourists
gawking at cows, and people like Raz Buchanon doing
twenty miles an hour toward Starley City to buy chicken
feed and the latest tabloid."

"Go take a look out the window."

"It's your nickel." I put down the receiver and did as
ordered. When I came back, I was almost afraid to pick
it up again. "Good Lord, Harve, there's a damn parade
of cars and pickups out there, and people walking along
the side of the road. Is there an execution scheduled?"

"Where the hell you been all week, Arly?"

I wanted to say France, but settled for a meaningless
mumble involving Ruby Bee, houseguests, and baseball
practice. "So when did you boys put up the guillotine?
Who's the lucky guy?"

"It's the grand opening of that supermarket Jim Bob
built hisself with Petrel. According to them, there's going
to be all kinds of activities and ceremonies and everybody
within thirty miles is coming. Marching bands, ribbon
cutting, all that shit. I'll send Les over before the highway gets so constipated that the traffic backs up to my
office. I plan to go fishing later, and I don't want to be
delayed."

"Send him along," I said with a sigh. "I'll head on
down there and see what all Jim Bob's doing to disrupt
my afternoon. I was planning to go to the Riviera,
myself."

"That the new tavern over in Hasty?"

"Yeah, Harve." I wished him luck with the bass and
the wrasse, hung up, buffed my badge, and tucked in
my shirt. I didn't figure I'd need my bullets to handle
the mob, but I strapped on my .38 anyway, just in case
the bargains addled some brains and we had violence
in the dairy section of the illustrious Jim Bob's Super-
Saver Buy 4 Less.

Edna Louise Skimmer put down the bedpan and stared
at the nurse's aide. "I can't believe it," she said.

Marsha Harrier nodded as slowly as she did everything
else, which meant she wasn't setting any world records.

Her words came out one at a time, like molasses dripping off the edge of the table. "I heard every word of it. I was standing by the door for a breath of fresh air, minding my own business and thinking about this cute little black and yellow bathing suit that's on sale over at the K-Mart in Starley City."

"What did Miz Wockermann say?"

Marsha tried to remember if the loony old woman had said anything worth repeating. About the time Edna Louise looked like she was going to explode, Marsha said, "She was too stunned and sickened by the story to say much. So was I. To think of that fellow taking advantage of all those local girls . . . If something like that happened to me, I would have died on the spot."

Edna Louise sat down next to the bedpan and decided to give Marsha the benefit of her four years of experience as an aide. "You're liable to lose your job if you go blabbing all over town. However, we have a responsibility to our patients to know the reason if they get all upset. Why don't you begin at the beginning and try to finish before the shift is over?"

Traffic was snarly and getting worse. A large area in front of the door was roped off, and those who attempted to step over it were berated by militant high school boys in starchy white uniforms. Ruby Bee's parking lot was filled, as was the motel lot behind it. I could imagine how pleased she was.

I barked at a particularly dim soul who tried to abandon his truck in the middle of the road, and started pointing and waving and making everybody get in gear, so to speak. Those obliged to park a long way down the road weren't real pleased with me, but as we say on the Riviera, *c'est la guerre.*

Forty hellacious minutes later, Deputy Les Vernon burped his siren to force a path to the edge of the SuperSaver lot and came over to join me.

He didn't loom over me, but he had a pit-bull aura about him that promised to be more effective than my winsome demeanor. I left him to it and wandered through the crowd to the front of the store.

Hizzoner and Mizzoner were dressed in their Sunday best. He was slapping backs and acting real genial, but there was something about his production that seemed forced. Every now and then, he shot narrow looks at a silver-haired man in a white suit and string bow tie. I cleverly deduced the recipient of this muted hostility was Petrel.

Mrs. Jim Bob was graciously accepting compliments and kind words with small nods. She could have been in the foyer of the White House, welcoming a select group of politicians' wives for a bridge party.

A big red ribbon barred the entrance. Kevin Buchanon was standing guard beside it, a pair of pruning shears in his hand. His Adam's apple bobbled as always; it was obvious he was taking pride in his assignment to defend the castle. The crowd was swelling as more trucks parked along the highway, and the blistering heat pouring down from above and bouncing up from the asphalt lot was not conducive to a general ambience of goodwill. Men were loosening neckties by the second, and women in panty hose were beginning to sag.

Raz Buchanon, a tobacco-chawin' pain in the rear, was muttering all kinds of rebellious things to anyone fool enough to listen, and Elsie McMay was fanning herself with a creased church bulletin and shrilly demanding to know when they were to be allowed to see the place for themselves. Even Lottie Estes looked mutinous. A bored cameraman leaned against the side of his station's van, and in the front seat a blotchy-faced woman in a sensible suit checked her watch every ten seconds.

Pretty soon, we heard an eerie noise from behind the building, and a dozen or so high-school students in band uniforms came into view, each red-faced and attacking an instrument. I waited to see if Mizzoner would start screeching about unnatural acts, but she produced a pained smile and loyally took her husband's arm. Jim Bob winced. Petrel curled his lip. Kevin snapped to attention and saluted with the shears.

When the band mercifully stopped, Petrel stepped up to a microphone, intoned a few sentences about how pleased he was to serve the community and hoped its citizens could be considered his personal friends, and so on. He then introduced Jim Bob, who reiterated the neighborly sentiments and then introduced Mrs. Jim Bob, who did the same and then introduced Brother Verber, who blessed the building at such length that I started eyeing the crowd, which was milling about and mumbling about hot air and hotshots and that sort of unneighborly sentiment.

Jim Bob wrestled the microphone away from Brother Verber and said, "Amen! There's just one more introduction I want to make afore we cut the ribbon and let you good folks into Jim Bob's SuperSaver Buy 4 Less, where you'll find bargains on every shelf and free refreshments in the international picnic pavilion. I want you all to give a big round of applause for the upstanding young boys of Maggody's championship baseball team. And here they come!"

The band began to play something. A couple of cheerleaders did their best to come cartwheeling across the area in front of the microphone, flashing starlit panties to the spectators' delight. The team, in full uniform from red caps to red-striped socks, marched into view, each looking straight ahead with no-nonsense expressions.

"No, they ain't," howled a voice in the back of the crowd.

"No, they ain't . . . what?" Jim Bob said, shielding his eyes to see better. He must have seen something, because his jaw dropped so far that the sun glinted on a filling. Before he could say anything further, a particularly enthusiastic cheerleader careened into Raz, who fell against Alex Sattering, who flailed his arms before he staggered into a third man, who whammed into Geraldo Mandozes, who snarled in Spanish and shoved him into a blond woman with sunglasses, who smashed into the van and went down like a load of bricks—all to the amusement of the cameraman, who was busily capturing it for the evening news.

Jim Bob sucked in a deep breath. "What ain't they?" he repeated loudly over the riot beginning to foment in front of him.

Ruby Bee (of course; did you even doubt?) pushed

through the crowd, her jaw leading the way. Following
on her heels were the nine members of the Ruby Bee's
Flamingos, each wearing a white baseball cap and a
blindingly pink T-shirt with the team name on the front
and a number on the back. They all looked terrified, and
I didn't blame them.

The sight shut everybody up. Ruby Bee went to the
microphone and elbowed Jim Bob aside. "I want you all
to meet the Ruby Bee's Flamingos. Ain't they something?" When the applause died, she gave Jim Bob a
cool look and said, "And it's going on record now that
this SuperSaver team ain't the town champions until they
win the title, and we aim to challenge 'em to a game to
determine who goes to the tournament."

Jim Bob was way too stunned to say anything. Mrs.
Jim Bob darted to Brother Verber's side to hiss in his
ear. Petrel was observing the scene with a bemused look.
The rabble-rousers on all sides of me, however, thought
the challenge was at least as exciting as the night Hiram
Buchanon's barn burned down, and they expressed their
boisterous enthusiasm by shouting and pushing each
other for a better look.

"Why, that's the Mexican's young'un!"

"There's two gals on the team!"

"Do you see who that one is? That's Robin Buchanon's
bastard. I was real sure he'd gone to an orphanage."

"What in tarnation happened to Elsie's fat little grand-
son? He looks like he done been attacked with a shovel!"

"Imagine picking your nose in front of everybody!
That's disgusting!"

There was a lot of the above in the air, and the unre-
lenting heat was now getting competition from at least a
hundred bodies, some of them obviously unwashed. I
was getting queasy myself and trying to decide what to
do when Kevin scratched his head, took a deep breath,
snipped the ribbon, and yelled, "Y'all can come inside
now!" It was the first intelligent thing he'd done—ever.

Jim Bob came to his senses and growled at the band
to play something. The cheerleaders began to shriek out
entreaties to make that goal and rickety rack, stop 'em

in their track and go, go, go. Once everybody realized there would be no overt violence, they went, went, went.

I hung back until I had some breathing room, then went over to Ruby Bee and said, "Cute. Real cute."

She opted to misinterpret my remark. "Yes, they're the cutest things I've ever laid eyes on. You don't think the shirts are too bright, do you? I had to take what I could get at the sporting-goods store in Farberville and practically get down on my knees and beg to get them to put on the letters right then and there."

"Whaddya think?" Hammet called to me. "Ain't we sumpun?"

"Oh, yes indeed." I turned back and with admirable restraint said, "Do you feel this confrontation is in the best interests of community goodwill?"

Estelle clattered up in a pink shirt, a skirt, and high heels and looked down her nose at me. "I don't see why Ruby Bee has to account to you, missy. You may be the chief of police, but that doesn't mean you're entitled to get too big for your britches."

"Goodness gracious," Ruby Bee said as she fanned her face with her hand, "it must be approaching a hundred degrees out here and I'm feeling dizzy. Let's go see whatall Jim Bob thinks he can give away at this fool picnic pavilion of his." She slipped her arm through Estelle's, gave me a vaguely triumphant look, and beckoned to the flock of Flamingos. "Come along, boys and girls. Maybe there's free soda pop and cookies."

Two seconds later, I had the parking lot to myself. I took a deep breath and counted to ten (in French, no less), called to the deputy that he could leave (no Les?), and followed the crowd into Jim Bob's SuperSaver Buy 4 Less.

The air conditioner was going full blast. The linoleum floor was shiny, the fluorescent lights bright, and the aisles wide enough to accommodate those wandering up and down with awed expressions. The three registers were manned by grim, pockmarked checkers. A ten-foot-square area beyond the last register was enclosed by ply-wood panels; the door had a suspiciously opaque mirror that hinted of covert observation. It was, I presumed, the office.

Jim Bob, Petrel, Mrs. Jim Bob, and Brother Verber had vanished, which was fine with me. I decided to explore the store. I took a hard right and found the produce aisle—and two members of opposing baseball teams on the verge of mayhem. I grabbed Saralee with one hand and a brutish Buchanon mutant with the other. "What's going on?" I demanded in my best cop voice.

Saralee jerked free. "This dumbshit says I can't play ball."

"She's a girl. Everybody knows girls cain't play ball," the SuperSaver muttered. He also jerked free and began to rub his arm. "She oughta stay home and sew doll clothes."

"Take it back, manure mouth," Saralee responded graciously.

"Listen here, you little fat bitch," the SuperSaver began, holding up a fist the size of an early-summer cantaloupe, "you better learn to—"

I blocked his path and glared at him. "Shut up—now." It occurred to me I was glaring up at him. "How old are you, anyway?"

"None of your beeswax, fuzz lady."

"In order to qualify to play in the intermediate league, you're supposed to be entering fifth or sixth grade this fall. Just how old are you?"

He tried to slouch down to eye level. "I be going into sixth grade this fall. If'n you don't believe me, you can call the school and ask."

"He could be telling the truth," Saralee contributed. "It must have taken him three or four years to get through first grade, what with him being such a dumbshit and all. I saw him driving down the highway the other day."

I hushed her and told the boy to drive down the highway right that minute if he didn't want to be charged with terroristic threatening. I could tell the phrase sailed over his head with several feet to spare, but after a dark look at Saralee, he slouched away.

I shrugged at her. "Even though it's illegal, some of

the boys start driving at fourteen or even younger. But he must be six feet tall, for Pete's sake. If he's twelve years old, then so am I. And Ruby Bee's going on twenty-one."

She wasn't interested. "Where'd Hammet go? I was right behind him when we came inside, but then he took off like a hornet flew up his rear."

I suggested we search for him in the vicinity of the free food. The picnic pavilion wasn't difficult to locate; the bodies were packed in and the voices loud. As we approached, a cheerleader bounced up with a platter and invited us to sample a fried chicken wing. Saralee grabbed one. We were again halted by another cheerleader, this time with a platter of sliced meat. The third platter had cocktail wienies in barbecue sauce.

I scanned the crowd for Hammet, Ruby Bee, Estelle, or anyone else of interest. Dahlia O'Neill was of no interest whatsoever, but I watched as she came out from behind the deli case with a platter in each hand and, in the style of a naval icebreaker, forced a path to a picnic table covered with a red and white checked paper tablecloth. She banged down the platters, stopped to wipe her forehead, and trudged back through the crowd. Dahlia usually has a contented expression, verging on bovine, but at the moment she looked royally pissed. I caught myself wondering if she was in a snit because she wasn't in a red and white striped miniskirt, then told myself to stop before I conjured up that image.

Several folks moved over to examine this new offering, and I resumed my search for Hammet, although I wasn't sure I could hand him over to Saralee and still sleep at night. A harried cheerleader rammed me with a platter, gave me a sniffly smile, and offered what appeared to be caterpillar segments in orange oil. I declined, and even Saralee turned up her nose. Another came at us with more chicken wings and a no-nonsense (you'll eat this spinach and like it, young lady) expression. We hastily retreated to the relative safety of a paper-towel display, and the cheerleader veered off at the last second.

Geraldo Mandozes appeared at my side, with Ray trailing along unhappily. "Did you taste the tamales?"

he said angrily. "I took one bite and spit it out. They taste like horse meat and sugary catsup."

"I looked at one," I said.

"But these idiots are stuffing them down like they were genuine Mexican tamales. These tamales, they are terrible. They are so very bad, they will make people sick. But then, when these people get well and want genuine Mexican tamales—genuine because they are made by me, Geraldo Mandozes—they will find a 'Closed' sign on the Dairee Dee-Lishus. I will have gone away to be a migrant worker because I must support my family."

"The samples today may save you," I said soothingly.

"At least they're not giving away free samples from the produce department," Ivy Sattering said from behind me. "Of course, the variety's enormous and the prices lower than anything we can sell for and show any profit. Where do we sign up to be migrant workers, Mr. Mandozes?"

"Do not make fun of me," he growled. He grabbed Ray's shoulder and propelled him into the crowd.

Ivy gave me a wry smile. "Not much of a kidder, is he? Jackie had a great time at practice yesterday, Arly. It's awfully kind of you to let him play, and I hope you don't let Jim Bob make you quit. I heard how Mrs. Jim Bob threatened you."

"I'll do my best."

"I guess I'd better find Jackie and Alex," she said, frowning at the barricade of bodies. "We need to go on home and open the stand in case anyone's foolish enough to stop by for one-hundred-percent organic produce." She followed Mandozes's route and vanished.

I caught a glimpse of Estelle's alpine red hair in the crowd, and a flash of Ruby Bee's tight blond curls, but there wasn't any way to extricate them, so I waited patiently. Saralee wandered away, her eyes glittering as brightly as her braces.

"Do you like our shirts, Miss Arly?" a timid voice asked.

I smiled down at Lissie Milvin. "They're really pink, aren't they?"

"Miss Ruby Bee has one for you, too, but she said she

didn't think you'd want to wear it—" She stopped as her father, brother, and grandmother approached.

"Heard you had a wild practice," Buzz said, grinning at me.

"Some might think so," I said. "Imagine a conversation in which you try to explain that a strike is when you don't strike the ball and the ball's a ball when it's too high or too low, except when it's merely the ball. Is this Lissie and Martin's grandmother?"

"Lillith, this is Arly Hanks, the chief of police and coach of the kids' baseball team. Arly, this is Lillith Smew, who's kindly agreed to keep house for me since my wife passed away."

I took the woman's damp, limp hand, trying not to wrinkle my nose as the sour odor of an old-fashioned pharmacy engulfed me. "Pleased to meet you, Mrs. Smew."

"I can only pray my health is good enough to run the house," she said. "I've had three minor heart attacks in the last year, and I have a recurring problem with shingles. It can be so very painful, you know; I can hardly sleep at night. At my age, I don't need as much sleep as you younger folks, but I have to be careful. The last doctor I saw in Little Rock said I was—"

A bellow from the crowd stopped her. We all swung around in time to see Millicent McIlhaney toss her cookies on Raz's foot. She was bent over, her arms across her stomach, and her face contorted. Raz opened his mouth to protest, but he proceeded to do exactly what she'd done—but on his other foot. Heather Riley, one of the few high-school girls not in uniform, stumbled out of the crowd and followed suit in a series of gut-wrenching spasms.

And before I could stop blinking, faster than a toad in a hailstorm a good half of the fifty or sixty people in the picnic pavilion were retching, groaning, grabbing at each other, staggering into each other, and upchucking all over the shiny linoleum floor of Jim Bob's SuperSaver Buy 4 Less.

For some reason, I doubted this was a scheduled activity of the grand opening.

6

"So what the hell happened?" Harve asked as he fiddled with a stained, splintery cigar butt. His desk was littered with chunks of ash, along with stained manila folders, months of paperwork, manuals, letters, a chewed-up Styrofoam cup, and an ashtray that bore a revolting resemblance to Mount St. Helens. "I had messages every which way when I got back from the lake this morning. I've got the reports from my boys, but none of them can write worth a damn. Their descriptions are on the terse side and limited to one-syllable words . . . like *barf*."

I closed my eyes and leaned back in the chair across from him. The rancid stench of his cigar was doing nothing to ease my uneasy stomach. I gave him a brief rundown on the grand-opening ceremony, and then in elaborate detail described the gruesome scene.

"Lord almighty," he said, looking a little uneasy himself. "I'm damn glad I was out of pocket all day."

"We called every ambulance service in the county, and ended up packing off twenty-three people for suspected food poisoning. Everybody was released within a couple of hours, pea green around the gills but basically okay. I called several of them either last night or this morning. No one suggested we do lunch in the pavilion, but no one reported further symptoms. I talked to a pathologist last night, too. He was amazed at the rapid onset of symptoms, and ruled out botulism, salmonella, and a long list of seriously toxic agents. Other than that, he wasn't much help."

"So we're going to have to rely on tests, huh?"

"Yeah," I said, shrugging. "I've packed off samples to the state crime lab, and the hospital labs are running tests. I've never seen such a vast expanse of vomit, and we're talking slippery, foul, nauseating nastiness. For a while there, it looked like beginners' night at the ice-skating rink. The guy who owns the pool hall twisted his ankle when he fell. He howled about a lawsuit all the way to the ambulance."

"Sounds charmin', Arly. It must have been a real hoot trying to secure the scene."

"Almost as much of a hoot as collecting samples—off the floor, tabletops, and my uniform, which I'm going to burn when I get around to it. I don't know what I'd have done if Deputy Vernon hadn't stayed to have a look around. He managed to get a couple more deputies to help, one of whom had to physically restrain Jim Bob when I ordered all the unaffected customers out of the store and the front door locked. Hizzoner didn't understand why the shoppers couldn't keep on shopping, and the checkers checking and the cash registers ringing merrily. He even suggested the ambulances go to the loading dock in back. He's real big on discretion."

"Within the city limits of Maggody," Harve said, working the cigar from one corner of his mouth to the other. "Or within Mrs. Jim Bob's earshot, maybe."

I wasn't interested in gossip. "Once we got the victims sorted out from those who contributed out of squeamishness, I went to the kitchen. The three cooks had managed to get every last pot and pan washed, so we're going to be forced to rely on our unsavory samples to determine what set everybody off like that." I leaned back in the chair and closed my eyes. "This is going to be a really ripe investigation, Harve."

"We don't have anything to warrant a major investigation, or at least not yet. Sure, twenty-odd people barfed all over the floor and a couple of folks fell, but that doesn't mean we've got ourselves a big-time felony. Could be the deli got hold of some spoiled meat or bad cheese. Offhand, I'd say it was nothing more than an unfortunate incident."

I opened one eye and squinted at him. "Had a call from the county judge, huh?"

He got real busy shuffling folders. "Might have. That

doesn't mean we're not going to carry out a proper investigation and find out exactly what happened. But our hands are tied until we get some answers from the state lab, so there's not much point in sitting on the gate to keep the cows out."

I opened the other eye for a double-barreled squint. "What's that supposed to mean?"

"It means there ain't no call to keep the supermarket closed. It means you might as well let it open for business."

"Another little political favor? Gad, that stinks worse than the floor of the damn pavilion, Harve, and you know it. We don't have any idea why twenty-three people became violently and copiously ill after sampling the food. We've got to wait for the lab results before we let Jim Bob start peddling food from the deli. I've already talked to the state health department, and strangely enough, they expressed the desire to do a thorough reinspection of all the facilities." I stood up, put my hands on the edge of his desk, and leaned over as far as I could bear, in that the ashtray was smoldering. "Yes, it may have been one package of spoiled meat. It also may have been a serious problem with refrigeration or operating procedures. For that matter, it may have been intentional."

"Bullshit, Arly. Are you implying one of the gals in the deli dumped poison in a pot? Why'd anyone risk doing that?"

"We don't know," I growled, frustrated. "And it doesn't have to be one of the cooks in the deli. For one thing, Dahlia was one of the victims, and the other two are from another of Petrel's supermarkets and only there temporarily. They were both terrified they'd be fired. For another, the platters were prepared in the kitchen, then taken out and left on a table; the cheerleaders picked them up and carried them around. Maybe somebody sprinkled something on a platter while it was on the table."

"Like who, for instance?"

I sat back down and thought for a minute. "Well, Jim Bob's always had enough enemies to comprise a Third

World army. There are a lot of locals not pleased about the SuperSaver because they're afraid it will put them out of business."

"Anybody who appears on a regular basis in the Hanks's family photo album?" Harve asked blandly.

I was beginning to regret the conversation. "Ruby Bee was worried that her customers might defect, but so were the Satterings, who operate a small farm with a produce stand, and the Mexican who bought the Dairee Dee-Lishus a few months back. Jim Bob issued himself a permit to sell beer, which may have upset the guy at the pool hall, who does a brisk bootleg beer business despite my continual admonishments. The hippies who own the Emporium may have been concerned that the SuperSaver would carry a lot of hardware odds and ends. It could have been anybody in town, Harve. They were all there."

"Any of those folks you mentioned by name end up in an ambulance?"

"It was an absolute madhouse. Les and I were trying to scribble down names and addresses, and the medics were dragging off the victims before we could do it. Ruby Bee was okay. I think I noticed Mandozes watching the scene with a supercilious look. I didn't see the Satterings, but Les may have logged either or both of them. I'll check with him."

"Good idea." Harve tugged at his lower lip and watched a fly inching toward the ashtray. "Tell ya what . . . the health department boys'll need to inspect the entire store. Even if the deli section gets okayed, it stays closed until we hear from the state lab. But if I don't order you to let the store open within a day or two, I might as well take a one-way hike to the fishing hole and commence my retirement. The county judge is a mean sumbitch with a memory a damn sight longer than a possum's tail."

I wasn't thrilled, but there wasn't much I could do about it. I went to hunt up Les and get his list. None of the names I'd mentioned appeared, but that didn't prove much of anything, because we didn't know if there was anything to prove. After an idle chat with Les about his wife's reaction to his vomit-splattered uniform, I drove back to Maggody for Sunday-afternoon baseball practice.

Kevin had been permitted into Dahlia's bedroom by her granny, who usually was awful strict but was wearied of playing nursemaid by now. His beloved was under a tan blanket; he couldn't help but think of an undulating sand dune in the Sahary Desert as he tiptoed across the room.

"Dahlia?" he whispered.

The dune quivered. "Whatta you want, Kevin Fitzgerald Buchanon?"

"I came by to see if you was feeling better. You looked mighty pale yesterday."

"So would you if'n you'd retched your gut out all afternoon."

He sat on the edge of the bed and patted what he guessed was her shoulder or head or something. "I felt real bad for you, my darling. It must have been about the worst thing what ever happened to you. I brought you a little present."

The blanket edged down until two dark eyes were regarding him in a most unnerving way. "What?"

"A package of vanilla sandwich cookies. I know how much you like 'em, and I was just hoping they might speed you along on your road to recovery." Kevin held his breath until a hand snaked out from under the blanket and snatched the package from his lap. "I guess I'd better let you get some rest now. When do you reckon you'll be better?"

"About the time the preacher finishes the sermon and they lower my casket into the hole. Then everybody throws ashes to ashes and dust to dust down on me and goes away to watch television or have supper, while I just lay there waiting for the worms."

Kevin's stomach began to flop like a crappie in the bottom of a johnboat. "But, sweetness, your granny said you was already feeling better and would be able to get up today. This stomach flu was a terrible thing, what with all those folks retching and upchucking all over the place, but I ain't heard that anybody in town is going to up and die from it."

Cellophane crackled. "That ain't what I'm talking about," came the muffled voice from under the blanket. "I am referring to this humiliating session we got to go to with Brother Verber, that fat ol' pious pig. It's your fault, Kevin Fitzgerald Buchanon, and you know it. On account of how you jumped all over me on the porch swing and tore a hole in my best blue blouse, I got to listen to the preacher go on and on about lust and sin and the fast track to eternal damnation. And so do you."

By now his stomach was flopping so hard, he started to wonder if he had a touch of the same stomach flu that had gripped hold of everybody the day before. "I do?" he croaked.

"Brother Verber and Mrs. Jim Bob came up to me while I was in the kitchen waiting for the pan of tamales to heat up in the oven, and the two of them started lecturing about how I was a lustful slut and you was some kind of sex maniac. All I could do was stare. Before I could even think what to say, she was telling me how the whole town knows you and I was fornicating on the porch swing, and he was all the while sermonizing about going to hell in a hand basket. Then she got all priggy and said we got to have some damn fool premarried counseling session or we're going to be the stars of next week's sermon."

"Oh my gawd . . ."

The blanket flew back and Dahlia grunted and struggled around until she was sitting up. Her eyes were almost invisible under her lowered brow, and her mouth was screwed up something fierce. Her words came out like bullets that pierced his heart. "This is all your fault. What do you aim to do about it?"

"Maybe I can talk some sense into them," he said, scooting back so far that he almost toppled off the edge of the bed. "They ain't got no call to tell us we have to go to this counseling session. I'll tell them that to their faces."

"What are you going to tell your ma and pa next Sunday morning when Brother Verber starts naming names from the pulpit of the Voice of the Almighty Lord Assembly Hall? What am I supposed to tell my granny?

She's scrawny as a free-range chicken, but she packs a mean wallop when she gets het up."

Kevin breathed in and out for a while, his Adam's apple rippling and his palms getting so sweaty that he had to wipe them on the sheet. He couldn't think of a single thing to say, which was probably just as well.

"Now to which base do we throw the ball?" I asked patiently. I was on the pitcher's mound (a clump of weeds), with those players who hadn't found something more interesting to do. "There's a runner on first and the ball is hit to Martin. He stops it and then . . . ?"

Hammet waved his arm. "Home plate. We don't want those dumbshit sumbitches to get a score. Long as we got the ball at home, ain't no way they can sneak in."

I pretended to consider his reply. "That's true, Hammet; the opposing side cannot score if our catcher has the ball at home plate. But we also need to make outs. Everybody think. Where can we most easily make an out?"

"Home plate," Saralee said promptly.

"Why?"

" 'Cause none of them can catch the ball except me. Ain't no point in throwing it at them if'n they're gonna miss it. You could walk over and hand it to Enoch, but he'd drop it like it was a hot potato. Earl Boy'd throw it back at your face." She took off her glasses and cleaned them on her shirt, then settled them back in place and studied Hammet, who promptly turned petunia pink and began to shuffle his feet in the weeds. "I don't know about him," she added pensively. "He's kind of mysterious, ain't he?"

"About as mysterious as a skunk squashed on the highway," said Georgie, snickering. "You can smell it a good mile away, and you just about puke when you get too close."

Saralee and I were hanging on to Hammet for dear life—Georgie's, anyway—when Buzz Milvin picked his way through the cow patties. "Howdy, Arly," he said. "Everything going well?"

I hissed a warning into Hammet's ear, and when he

relaxed, I left him in Saralee's custody and went over to Buzz. "Everything's just dandy. Have you decided you want to coach? I've got a ton of work at the PD and I'd truly appreciate some relief. The bats and balls are in that bag and—"

"Sorry," he said, grinning at me. "I have to run over to the factory in Starley City to pick up my final paycheck and I just stopped by for a minute. How are my two doing?"

"Martin's giving it his best, although he hasn't quite yet figured out what to do with the ball if it lands in his glove. He is not alone." I looked over Buzz's shoulder at Lissie, who was sitting under a scraggly oak tree at the far edge of the pasture. She glanced up at us, then quickly looked back down at the daisies in her lap. "Lissie's not especially motivated," I added, shrugging, "but she's not alone, either."

Buzz located her and let out a piercing whistle. "Lissie, get over here! No, you leave those fool flowers alone and get over here right this minute!"

"She's not a problem, Buzz," I protested. "Enoch and Georgie are a lot more interested in picking their noses than catching fly balls, and Jackie Sattering won't even stand up unless I go out there and pull him to his feet. Our pitcher speaks no English, and our second baseman has yet to speak at all. Our catcher and first baseman are both contenders in the local Golden Glove competition."

"Lissie can try," he said as she came slowly toward us, her head drooping like the one daisy in her hand. She stopped several yards away and continued to stare at the ground. Buzz snorted and said, "What's this I hear about you not playing baseball, young lady? Didn't I tell you I expected you to try your best? Didn't we go outside after supper most every night last week and practice throwing and catching?"

"Yes, Pa," she whispered.

"Do you recollect that talk we had about team spirit?" Buzz continued relentlessly. "Do you?"

"Yes, Pa," she repeated, still not looking up. "Can I go now?"

"I'm not through with you. You're supposed to be

minding Miss Arly. If I hear about her getting any sass from you, you can expect to be real sorry. Do I make myself clear?"

"Yes, Pa." She gave me a dark look, as though I was responsible for her father's tirade, then she trudged back toward the outfield.

"I'll play catch with her tonight," Buzz said to me.

I managed a tight smile. "Well, I've got to get back to practice. We're going to see if anyone can hit the ball."

"I appreciate what you're trying to do, Arly. You must have the patience of a plow mule to put up with this bunch of misfits."

"They're trying," I said, still annoyed. "It's supposed to be fun, you know, not some obligatory experience in the back pasture of hell."

He held up his hands. "You're right, and I apologize. It disturbs me when Lissie acts like a baby, but I suppose she's entitled to act however she wants. It's been real hard on all of us since Annie died. She was in the hospital nearly three months, and that wiped out my savings account. I've been working as much overtime as I can get, and the kids had to grow up way too fast."

"But things are better with Lillith around to take care of the house," I said.

"A hundred percent. There wouldn't have been any way for me to spend half an hour after supper playing catch if Lillith wasn't here. I would have been washing dishes and fretting about bills. With her Social Security check added into the budget, I don't have to worry about putting new shoes on the kids a couple of times a year or having to sign them up for free lunches at school. Milvins don't take kindly to charity."

"How's the new job at the SuperSaver?"

Buzz licked his lips and looked away for a minute. "It'll work out okay," he said at last. "It won't be the hardest thing in the world to show Kevin Buchanon where to mop, or tally the register receipts and have the cash ready for Jim Bob to take to the night depository. At least I don't have to drive over to Starley City every morning at sunup and drag home eight hours later."

"Did Jim Bob say anything about when the SuperSaver would be open?" I asked delicately.

He gave me an amused look as he lit a cigarette. "Yeah, he did. This ain't a direct quote, but it had something to do with when a certain chief of police stopped behaving like a pedigreed bitch in heat and saw fit to take down the goddamn police tape that was put up Saturday. Lordy, that was something, wasn't it?"

"Yes, indeed," I said, struggling not to visualize it.

"Any idea what caused everybody to start . . . ?"

"No, we'll have to wait for the lab results. The sheriff seems inclined to dismiss it as an accident, and he's apt to be right. I surely don't want it to turn out to be someone's idea of a prank."

"You mean like when a couple of years back someone poisoned bottles of aspirin and two or three folks died?" he said, bewildered. "I saw something about it on the news."

"Let's keep our fingers crossed that it can be explained by sloppiness in the kitchen or sour milk." I did not need rumors flying around the town like ravenous mosquitoes. I didn't need a baseball team, either, but it seemed I had one. I reminded Buzz of my immediate concern and waited until he waved at his children and left.

Then, with a bright smile and an omniscient sense of utter futility, I told everyone to gather at home plate— a burlap bag—to learn how to hold a baseball bat.

Brother Verber flipped to the next page and let out a low whistle of disbelief. Was this the sort of depravity he could expect to hear about in the counseling session? Why, it was enough to make a grown man cry. He studied the slightly blurred photograph for a long while, then reluctantly decided there weren't no way three people and a German shepherd could all fit on a porch swing. Besides, he figured Eilene Buchanon would have been real suspicious if Kevin had gone out to the porch wearing nothing except a leather mask and handcuffs, no matter how he tried to explain it. Furthermore, if he remembered rightly, that particular Buchanon family didn't even have a dog.

But it was important to be familiar with this variety of perversion. There wasn't any doubt in his mind that the O'Neill girl was a slut, and only the Good Lord knew what all she and Kevin might have done.

They were going to have to confess to every last lustful encounter so he could judge the level of depravity and determine how best to make them repent, Brother Verber thought as he blotted the saliva on his chin with a handkerchief. Every last lustful encounter, from the first timid kiss to the very last sweaty, fiery, wild-eyed, groanin' and moanin', steamin', mindless act of passion. On their knees and in detail.

He turned to the next page, just in case.

Emotions were still in high gear on Monday morning. Mrs. Jim Bob twitched her foot angrily as she stared at her husband across the breakfast table on the sun porch. "I don't know when I've ever been so embarrassed in all my days," she said, not for the first time. "Do you realize Eula Lemoy is in my Sunday-school class? How am I supposed to face her next week after what happened?"

Jim Bob was pretty sure a gremlin was residing in his head and setting off firecrackers every few seconds. His hand shook as he tried to gulp down the last of the coffee in his cup. It was colder than a well digger's ass by now, and tasted like raw sewage. He choked it down anyway and opened his mouth to offer a rebuttal.

"I have never been subjected to this kind of public humiliation before," she continued. "All of my friends were there, as were the many, many people in the community who look up to me for moral and spiritual guidance. And what happened? You have to go and poison them. You might as well have driven a stake through my heart. How can I face Eula, or Lottie, or Millicent, or any of my dearest friends ever again as long as I live?" She snatched up her napkin and dabbed her eyes.

"I didn't poison anybody."

Mrs. Jim Bob flung down the napkin. "Oh no? Then how are you planning to explain that ghastly scene in the pavilion, when everybody turned green and started throwing up? If that wasn't because of poison, then I'm not president of the missionary society for the third year in a row!"

"Nobody knows what happened." He hesitated for a second, a little surprised he'd gotten a few more words in. When she merely glowered like a jack-o'-lantern, he added, "I'm meeting with the health department first thing this afternoon so's they can take another look at the equipment. All the girls in the kitchen have their certificates of clean health. There ain't no way anyone's going to blame this on us."

"*Us*? All I see is you, Jim Bob. I don't happen to see Mr. Lamont Petrel sitting in a chair beside you, willing to take his fair share of the blame. You look mighty alone right this minute."

"I told you already that I don't know where Lamont went. When everybody started whooping and shrieking in the pavilion, I left Lamont in the office and went back to have a look-see. By the time I got back to tell him what all was going on, he was gone. I haven't heard a squeak from him since Saturday afternoon. It's been close to forty-eight hours by now. I called over to his house, and his wife said she'd give him a message when he showed up."

"I think it's perfectly clear what happened," Mrs. Jim Bob said briskly and with an air of complacency that sent a shiver down Jim Bob's spine. "Mr. Lamont Petrel is responsible for the poisoning. A guilty man always flees the scene of the crime. The fact that he was scared to stay around proves it. Do you want to call the sheriff or shall I?"

Jim Bob waited while the shiver ran its course all the way down and out his tailbone. "Now, we don't have any account to call the sheriff, Mrs. Jim Bob. We don't know for a fact that Lamont dumped something into the free samples. He sure didn't have any reason to do it. The SuperSaver's lost two days of business already, and today's half-shot. The last thing either of us wants is a passel of bad publicity . . . but we sure as hell got it."

"There will be no profanity in this house," Mrs. Jim Bob said promptly but without heat, preoccupied with how best to pass along the information that Lamont Petrel—rather than her husband—had done his cold-blooded level best to poison every last soul in town. Eula was home and she could be trusted to spend the afternoon on the telephone. Lottie Estes had mentioned having a few teachers from the high school over to admire her chrysanthemums, and they'd linger to chat over coffee.

It simply needed a touch of orchestration, and by prayer meeting on Wednesday, Mrs. Jim Bob told herself smugly, there wouldn't be more than a scant handful of folks who would not have heard the truth, presuming Eula, Lottie, and a few others could be prevailed upon to do their Christian duty.

Despite the fact the gremlin had advanced to bottle rockets, Jim Bob could see what was going on in his wife's mind. He considered restating his argument that Lamont had no motive, then decided he didn't give a damn if Lamont's name was dragged through the swamp in a gunnysack and tossed to the hounds afterward. Lamont wanted to take the SuperSaver away from Jim Bob; let him take the blame along with it. If he had the sense God gave a goose, he sure as hell wouldn't show up to defend himself anytime soon.

"I got to make a call to the bank," he said, and hurried into the house. When he spoke to the loan officer, the gremlin had moved on to dynamite, but Jim Bob managed an oily tone of concern as he explained the closing of the loan would have to wait until his partner was available. And, no, he couldn't say when that would be. He didn't say he hoped to hell it wouldn't be anytime soon, but he thought it.

Hammet was madder than a bobcat in a trap, but I felt no remorse. Joyce Lambertino had called early in the morning and asked if he could spend the day at her house playing with Saralee, and I'd readily accepted on his behalf. I'd ignored all his protests, even the explicitly colorful ones, insisted he put on clean overalls and wash behind his ears, and then pretty much booted him out the door. He'd cussed up a storm all the way to the corner, bless his little heart. I felt like a proud mom on prom night.

But *zut alors*, it was time to go to the PD and then *à* Paris, to drift along the Seine in a gaily decorated boat, a glass of champagne in hand and glittery lights of the Left Bank reflecting in my eyes. My tiny hotel was nestled amongst the lights, with its French Provincial furniture and cozy sitting room. A continental breakfast was included in the rate. Lunches would consist of fresh bread, a slice of pâté, and a bottle of vin ordinaire. I was *sans souci*, or at least I was right up until the front door of the PD opened.

It was my amiable state trooper, Sergeant John Plover, who had a slightly crooked nose, a decidedly crooked smile, freckles, and blond hair that on occasion demanded to be ruffled. He and I had gotten off to a rocky beginning, but once he conceded I was a functional professional rather than a silly girl playing police officer, we settled into a casual relationship that waxed and waned with the moon.

"*Bonjour*," I murmured.

"Whatever." He took off his sunglasses, perched on the corner of my desk, and said, "What's this I hear about half the town being poisoned?"

I raised my eyebrows. "What exactly is the *bon mot* at the barracks, Sergeant?"

"The word at the barracks, Chief, is a four-letter word, perhaps too uncouth for your sensitive ears."

"I'm touched by your gentlemanly concern. I feel quite sure no four-letter word has been uttered aloud within the city limits of my domain, unless, of course, it was the night Hiram Buchanon's barn burned. From all reports, things got way out of hand."

"The word is B-A-R-F, all caps and in a boggling quantity. From what I heard, half the town was doubled up on the floor of that new supermarket, begging for death. Luckily for them, everybody survived. I presume you didn't—"

"Sample the canapés? No way, José. We won't know what happened until we get some test results from the state lab. Harve's determined to write it off as an accident, but I'm not so sure. How'd you hear so quickly?"

"Corporal Anderson was off duty Saturday afternoon,

and it seems his cousin's boy is on some baseball team that was included in the opening ceremonies. Anderson's presence was deemed a familial obligation, since he's got a camera."

"Did you drive all the way out here to discuss barf?"

Plover removed himself from my desk and sat down in the ratty chair I keep to discourage visitors. "No, I just thought it was interesting—a typical Maggodian sort of madness. Let me know what the lab reports indicate, will you?"

"You'll hear it more quickly on the barracks grapevine," I said lightly. It was, after all, my jurisdiction and therefore my case. If I wanted the cavalry, I would send for it. "If you didn't come to tease me about that, then what is it that has propelled you to the boonies?"

"Well," he began, then stopped. He studied the floor, the ceiling, the wall above my head, and the mess on my desk. The air conditioner sputtered as always, but not loudly enough to fill the sudden vacuum of silence. "Have you had lunch?"

Fantasies about French bread and pâté were inadequate to sustain me for any length of time. "No," I admitted, "but I was thinking about it. You buying?"

"I might."

We drove to Ruby Bee's in his real, live official vehicle. I tried not to be too envious of such things as a working radio and a working air conditioner and all kinds of mysterious buttons and knobs that no doubt worked also. He parked between two semis and we settled in a booth.

The proprietress came over with menus, looking a lot more cheerful than I'd seen her for several weeks. "We haven't had the pleasure of your company for a while," she said to Plover. "How've you been keeping youself?"

"Fine," he said, smiling back at her.

"Me, too," I said, although nobody had asked. My smile may have lacked warmth. "I missed you and Estelle at the practice yesterday afternoon. I called here and at your unit several times, but all I got was a busy signal. It's hard to get much accomplished when my major concern is keeping everybody off each other's throats."

Ruby Bee's expression was that of a puppy that'd been kicked across the room. "Why, land sakes, Arly, you know I'd have given my right arm to get out there yesterday to help you, but business has been real brisk these last two days and it's all I can do to sit down and rest my feet for a minute."

She had a point. The bar stools were all occupied by neckless hulks, and most of the booths by more of the same. The whiny country music from the jukebox was almost drowned out by the babble of the troglodytes and the clatter of utensils.

We were given menus and told to holler when we made up our minds. Once she was out of earshot, I leaned forward and said, "Okay, why are you here?"

The infamous kid with his hand in the cookie jar couldn't have looked more uncomfortable. Plover again found many things to study, none of them remotely in the direction of yours truly. When I kicked him under the table, he cleared his throat and said, "How's the meat loaf? I don't think I've ever tried it."

"The meat loaf is heavenly. You're here on official business, aren't you?"

"What was that bit about baseball practice?"

"You're not going to like it when I stand on the table and scream at you. Just tell me why you're here, okay? Then I'll tell you about baseball practice and we'll both be fully informed."

"I'm getting to it," he said, suddenly obliged to start rereading the menu. "Let's wait until we order."

"Let's not." By this point, my voice was beginning to compete with the general racket surrounding us, and more than one asphalt cowboy was glancing at us and most likely hoping for an old-fashioned public brawl between the sexes. The CBs would sizzle all the way to the Missouri line and on into Illinois and Indiana.

He winced. "Okay, okay. It . . . ah, it seems we've once again lost someone in Maggody."

"What?"

"We had a call from Muriel Petrel. She said her husband came here Friday evening to prepare for the grand opening on Saturday. She thought he'd be home that night or at least the following day, but she hasn't seen him or heard from him for the last forty-eight hours."

"That's Jim Bob's partner," I said, frowning at him.

"I came out to find out when he was last seen and to ascertain if he could still be in town. His car's parked out back in front of his motel room, and his suitcase is in the room."

I was fighting to control both my eyelids and my jaw, but I wasn't having a helluva lot of success. "Did you talk to Jim Bob?"

"He said he didn't see Petrel after the minor problem arose in the pavilion. Said he left Petrel in the office, looking at the initial inventory invoices. When he returned thirty minutes later, the invoices were in a neat pile and the office was empty."

I finally got hold of myself and glared across the table. "So you're supposed to breeze into town and question everyone who might have knowledge of Petrel's whereabouts. Did it occur to your lieutenant to consult the local police department?"

"I'm consulting it right now. The issue of jurisdiction's tricky. Petrel lives in Farberville, and the missing-persons report was filed initially with the local police department there. They told Mrs. Petrel to call us."

"But you've already begun talking to witnesses," I said coolly. If my air conditioner had worked better, I could have worked myself up to coldly, but it had been one long, hot summer. "Who else has been contacted?"

"Mrs. Jim Bob said Petrel had poisoned everybody for his own dark purposes and fled the county, if not the country."

"Does she have any evidence?" I asked.

"What do you think?" Plover put his hand over mine and tried to smile guilelessly. "Petrel probably forgot to mention a business trip, that's all."

"And walked to the airport?"

"Hell, I don't know. It hasn't even been seventy-two hours yet, so I'm just poking around. Maybe he has some phobia about barf and went stumbling into the woods.

Maybe he hitched a ride to an unknown destination because . . . because Mrs. Jim Bob's correct and he poisoned everybody for his own dark purposes."

"In your dreams," I said glumly, shaking my head. "Harve's probably right about there having been some weird accident during the food preparation, but I'm staying on it until I'm satisfied. After all, it cost me a perfectly good uniform. Even my badge stinks, which could lead to all kinds of complex philosophical questions about the role of enforcer in an evolving society, were we so inclined. However, I'm more inclined to meat loaf."

7

"He raped her right there on the sofa bed in the office," Edna Louise Skimmer whispered to Barbie Buteo, her second cousin once removed on her mother's side, who lived in Emmet but got by every now and then for a nice visit. They were obliged to whisper due to the kids being in the next room.

"No?" gasped Barbie. "Did she go to the emergency room at the hospital?"

Edna Louise tried to remember what all she'd heard at the county nursing home several days back. "I don't think so," she admitted with a trace of regret.

"Does her pa know about it?"

"Oh, no, and this is strictly between you and me, Barbie. One of the aides just happened to have overheard a conversation on the porch and passed it along to me, but I can't afford to lose my job for repeating gossip, even if it's the gospel truth. I wish I could tell you more about whatall he did, but I can't say another word." She rolled her eyes and zipped her lips to emphasize her point. "You do understand what I'm getting at, doncha?"

"I won't tell a soul," Barbie vowed solemnly, going so far as to draw an X on her chest. "Cross my heart and hope to die. I just can't believe everyone's gonna let that slimeball do you know what to a local girl and not even make him say he's sorry or offer to replace the shirt he ripped off her."

"It was awful," Edna Louise said. "The girl was hysterical when she came stumbling out of the office, and she nearly got herself run down on the highway by one of them tractor trailers. A neighbor happened to be driving by, and she put the poor little thing in her car and got her home afore anybody else saw her. We have no way of knowing if she was the only one—or only the first one."

Barbie peered around the corner to make sure all seven of the children were safely engrossed in cartoons, then leaned across the table and shook her head. "You know what I think, Edna Louise? I think they ought to tar and feather that fellow and escort him right out of town on a railroad tie. What'd you say his name was?"

"Petrel. Lamont Petrel." Edna Louise said this very firmly, because she was very sure.

After lunch, Plover said he wanted to question the owner of the Flamingo Motel about Petrel's disappearance. I offered to assist and was told my presence would not be required. I pointed out she was my mother and was told that was the problem. I mentioned that I was the chief of police and was told everybody already knew that.

So I may have been in a snit as I slammed the door on my way out of the bar and grill. As I stalked up the highway toward the PD, I may have been thinking of a whole lot more devastatingly clever things I should have said, and that may have been why Jim Bob had to bellow like a bullfrog to get my attention.

I shaded my eyes and looked across the highway. "What do you want?"

"The inspectors from the health department are here and they want to talk to you," he yelled. "Have you gone blind and deaf, Chief Hanks . . . or just plain stupid?"

"It's the heat. If I had a decent air conditioner in the PD, I wouldn't be reduced to a mindless mass of indeterminate gray matter," I yelled back, not in the mood for Hizzoner's particular brand of humorless humor any more than I was in the mood for a certain state trooper's "Don't worry your little head about it" attitude. I hate that.

"The inspectors have to talk to you, and they want to do it sometime before the sun sets in Hawaii. If you can't cross the street by yourself, I'll come hold your damn fool hand."

I waited until a truck rattled by, then took my own

sweet time going across the road and the parking lot.
Two men were waiting with Jim Bob under what shade
there was beside the door of the SuperSaver. Despite the
fact that one was tall and the other short, one rosy and
the other anemic, one with a nice smile and the other
with stained, crooked teeth, they had a certain sameness
that bureaucracy demands and therefore begets. Neither
looked especially impressed with me, but frankly, my
dear, I didn't give a rat's ass.

"This is Chief Hanks," Jim Bob muttered. "She has
to hear how you inspected the store and didn't find dead
mice in the vents or bug spray in the icebox."

Tweedledee bobbled his head and assured me everything satisfied current state regulations. Tweedledum
bobbled his head and rumbled an agreement.

"Then we're not to worry about the twenty-three people who had to be taken away by ambulance?" I asked
blandly. "It was just . . . one of those pesky little things
that can happen to any of us?"

This time Tweedledum bobbled his head and reassured
me all the facilities looked shipshape to him. Tweedledee
bobbled his head and rumbled an agreement.

"Good grief," I said to Jim Bob, "where'd you buy
these two? Do they work part-time as dashboard figu-
rines? You know, with one of those wiggly plastic hula
girls between them and a pair of foam dice dangling from
the rearview mirror, you could have yourself a real
nice—"

"Thanks, boys," Jim Bob cut in heartily. He slapped
them on their backs and told them how very deeply he
appreciated them having to come all the way out to Maggody to satisfy some meddlesome cop who had nothing
better to do than stand around in the hot sun and make
smart-alecky remarks.

He kept it up until they drove away, then looked at
me with one of his smirkier smirks. "I do believe you've
been informed that once the state health inspectors have
been here, I can reopen the store?"

"But not the deli until we hear from the lab."

"Fuck the deli. Just get all that tape out of here and go
find something useful to do for a change. You're running

behind on speeding tickets this month, and I'd be real sorry if the town council had to unplug that air conditioner of yours in order to cut down on expenses. Then you'd really have something to bitch about, wouldn't you?"

With a parting smirk, Hizzoner went into the store. Apparently, he'd been confident of a favorable report from the health department, because several high-school boys drove up and headed for the front door. I decided the orange tape gave the place a festive air, and went back across the road. This time, no one offered to hold my hand, but I did it just the same.

At five o'clock Monday afternoon, roughly fifty hours after twenty-three people had been removed from the premises in ambulances, Jim Bob's SuperSaver Buy 4 Less reopened for business, although without a marching band, dignitaries, careening cheerleaders, or any fanfare at all.

At 5:10, the first customer of the day, Raz Buchanon, bought a tin of chawin' tobacco, a tabloid that claimed Elvis was not only alive but had endured a series of sex-change operations to protect his anonymity, and two gourmet frozen dinners (breast of chicken à l'orange with vegetable-rice medley). If you don't understand why he bought two, don't worry about it. If you do, try not to dwell on it too much.

At six o'clock, the small patch of gravel in front of the Satterings' produce stand was as vacant as a dead man's eyes. Ivy figured she knew why, but she told Alex to wait there on the off chance there'd be a customer. She went into the house and combed her hair, then drove into town to compare tomato and snap-bean prices at the SuperSaver.

At 6:15, Geraldo Mandozes banged down the counter window of the Dairee Dee-Lishus, banged into position the CLOSED sign, banged his car door shut, and drove over to the SuperSaver to see whether the shits were selling tamales that tasted as if they were made of dog meat and catsup.

At 6:20, Eula Lemoy told Millicent McIlhaney that

Lamont Petrel had tried to poison every last soul in town and was now hiding out in a brothel in Little Rock or maybe Pine Bluff.

At 6:30, Barbie Buteo told her husband, R.T., that some fellow in Maggody had raped half a dozen high-school girls. This is hardly vital to the plot, but let it be noted that R.T. spent a goodly portion of the ensuing evening (and of his paycheck) at the Dew Drop Inn on the south side of Emmet, which isn't too far from Maggody.

At 6:45, Ruby Bee and Estelle got so tired of standing on tippytoes in front of the kitchen-sink window, trying to see who all was going in and out of the SuperSaver, that Ruby Bee taped up the CLOSED sign on the door of the Bar & Grill and the two went over to identify the traitors by name, rank, and serial number, if nothing else.

At 7:13, Hammet Buchanon hit a baseball for the first time in his life. It rolled between Martin Milvin's feet, bounced over a clump of Johnsongrass, flattened a honeybee on a black-eyed Susan, and came to a stop not too far in front of Georgie McMay. After a moment of thought, Georgie hurled it as hard as he could at Earl Boy Nookim's head, but it soared over him and hit Ray Mandozes in the back. The subsequent exchange of expletives, some in Spanish and some in English, evolved into an epic brawl.

At 8:55, Dahlia sauntered real casual like past the end of the last aisle and ducked into the employee break room because she wanted to have a few words with Kevin before he started work. He came in shortly afterward and they commenced a conversation interspersed with jabbing fingers and more than a snively tear or two.

At nine o'clock, Buzz Milvin discovered the two in the break room and told Dahlia to run along home and Kevin to get to work and do something about the smell lingering in the general area of the picnic pavilion. When Kevin looked blank, Buzz told him where to find a bucket and mop, then went to the third aisle for a jumbo bottle of Lysol. He assumed Dahlia left through the back door.

At some moment during the next hour, Hammet Buchanon stopped complaining about what a dopey, cross-eyed calf Saralee Chewink was and fell asleep in front of the television. Saralee herself went to sleep on a roll-away cot in the Lambertinos' family room, thinking about what a mysterious fellow Hammet was. What she really meant was enigmatic, but that was a word decidedly outside the limited scope of her fourth-grade vocabulary. Also safe in bed for the night, Jackie Sattering told his pa how he'd caught a monarch butterfly in right field. Alex shared his excitement. In the tiny bedroom of a rusty mobile home at the back of the Pot O' Gold, Ray Mandozes was awake in the top bunk, imagining himself a courageous toreador and Georgie McMay a trembling, drooling, bowlegged toro. Olay, as they say in Maggody.

At ten o'clock, Enoch McMay was conversing in his dreams with Gilligan and the Skipper. Georgie McMay picked at a scab on his lower lip. Earl Boy Nookim caught a lightning bug and squished it in his fist, and only went inside the mobile home not too far from the Mandozeses' when his ma threatened to whup him if'n he didn't.

At pretty much the same time as above, Lillith Smew ordered Martin Milvin to turn off his light and go to sleep if he knew what was good for him. She checked on Lissie, who was curled up tightly around her rag doll and breathing evenly, then went into her bedroom and sat down to rub liniment on her knees. All this cooking and cleaning was getting to be awful hard on her, she thought with a grimace. Buzz and the children didn't appreciate how she sacrificed herself day and night for them. Her daughter had been properly sympathetic, but she sometimes wondered whether Buzz even listened when she discussed all her recurring symptoms of heart trouble, shingles, rheumatoid arthritis, failing eyesight, palpitations, dry mouth, and other equally life-threatening conditions. She put away the liniment and opened the first bottle of pills in the long row.

At 10:30, all the way over in Farberville, Sergeant John Plover picked up the telephone receiver, dialed five or six numbers, then sighed noisily (which didn't matter, since he lived alone) and told himself to let his favorite chief of police cool off for a day or two. Also in Farberville at that time, Muriel Petrel plumped her pillow, gazed at the unoccupied twin bed, and considered calling her sister to have lunch the next day, since she wouldn't have to be home to fix something for Lamont. There was that new place with tables on the patio that sounded real nice.

At 10:35, Estelle Oppers tried to warn Tom Selleck not to get in the convertible with the bleach-blond floozy, but he didn't pay her any mind and got right in. Estelle figured he deserved what he was gonna get before the next commercial (it was a rerun and she knew for a fact he was going to be mighty sorry, even if he didn't know it).

At 10:36, Ruby Bee read the last page of a mystery novel about a deranged, tattooed serial killer who murdered seven beautiful models before the quick-witted police detective tracked him down in a seedy bar in Miami and shot him deader'n a doornail. As she reached for the light, she thought she heard footsteps outside. It took a good five minutes before she found enough courage to go over to the window. All she saw was the parking lot, and it was empty. She stayed at the window for a minute, because it looked kinda shimmery and romantic in the moonlight, like a lake.

And at the end of this busy day in Maggody, perhaps even as early as eleven o'clock, everybody and everything had pretty much shut down except for the night shift at the SuperSaver. Jim Bob had come in and disrupted the scheduled routine with a lot of nonsense, but he was long gone. Buzz was driving to Starley City, the two canvas money bags on the seat beside him. Kevin was supposed to be setting out cans of pork'n beans, but he wasn't.

The only other light worth mentioning was in the apartment above Stiver's Antique Store: Buy, Sell, or Trade. It was a small yet adequate reading lamp beside the bed.

*   *   *

It was nearly noon by the time Hammet and I headed for Ruby Bee's for lunch. Because the SuperSaver was open and, based on the number of cars and trucks in the lot, doing a brisk business, I was on the leery side as we went into the bar and grill.

Ruby Bee gave me a calculating look as I hopped up on a stool, but merely tossed me a menu and asked Hammet if he'd like a cheeseburger and glass of buttermilk.

"Yessum," he said.

"Business seems normal," I said as I debated between pork chops and pot roast with gravy.

She busied herself cleaning up after one of her sloppier customers. "For the time bein', I suppose. I saved some lemon icebox pie for you and Hammet. Earl Buchanon liked to burst into tears, but I told him no siree Bob, this is for Arly and her little friend what plays on the Ruby Bee's Flamingos. How's that coming, by the way?"

This display of nonchalance and maternal charity wasn't fooling me one whit. "If I had an assistant coach to sit on Georgie McMay's head, I might make some progress. As it is, no one knows the difference between a dugout and a hole in the ground."

"Ain't that a shame." She stayed busy for a minute, but I could almost hear the corroded gears grinding in her head. "I hope you all will do me proud at the game. I was thinking Estelle and me might go into Farberville and buy some little trophies to give to everybody at a party after the game Thursday. I was of a mind to serve hot dogs and corn chips, but Estelle says everybody likes hamburgers better. What do you think, Arly—hot dogs or hamburgers?"

"I think you think I didn't hear what you just said," I said promptly. "Or perhaps you think I think the Ruby Bee's Flamingos will master the rudiments of the game in two days and be ready to take on a team made up of jockstrapped giants. That leads me to think you're out of your ever-lovin' mind."

"I think hot dogs sound swell," Hammet contributed, then caught my look, slithered off the stool, and went over to the jukebox to ponder the selections.

"But the Starley City tournament starts Saturday,"

Ruby Bee said in a low voice, keeping an eye on those on nearby stools in case they were SuperSaver spies in denim trench coats. "We got to prove my team's the champions if we're going to represent Maggody at the tournament."

"We may lead the league in cow-patty hurling and nature study," I began, then stopped as the telephone behind the counter rang.

Ruby Bee answered it, and, after a moment, whispered, "It's Eilene Buchanon. She's looking for you."

"Oh," I whispered back as I took the receiver. "What's up, Eilene?"

"Arly? I think you'd better come over here as soon as possible. I got something you need to see."

"Can you tell me what this is about?" I asked, more concerned with the pork chop versus pot roast dilemma.

"I don't think I better say any more on the telephone."

I said I'd be there shortly, then handed back the receiver to Ruby Bee and told Hammet to wait for me. Ruby Bee was frowning, but she had enough sense not to ask me anything. I was puzzled by Eilene's insistence that I come to her house. Although she's got two strikes against her (she's married to a Buchanon and is Kevin's mother), she always seemed a reasonable sort.

I drove down Finger Lane and parked in the driveway. Eilene met me at the screened door and said, "Thanks for coming, Arly. I wasn't sure what to do, but I figured I'd better do something before Earl gets home from work this evening." She ushered me through the living room to the kitchen, where she pointed rather melodramatically at a chocolate cupcake on the table. "That's the culprit."

Nothing in my training had prepared me to arrest a cupcake, or even interrogate it. In that it was nestled in the remains of a cellophane wrapper and had a squiggly line of white icing across its top, I deduced it was store-bought. In that they tended to come in two's (à la Noah's ark), I furthermore deduced one was missing and was either ingested or had fled the scene of the crime.

I straightened up and said, "What's this about, Eilene? I know these have enough sugar in them to levitate a nursery-school class, but that's not enough to press charges against the bakery."

She wasn't smiling. "Look at that little silver dot on the side," she said. "You recognize what it is?"

I examined the culprit more carefully. "It looks like a pin head."

"And it's attached to the rest of the pin. There was one in the other cupcake, too. I know this because I bit into it and scratched my tongue. Luckily, I had enough sense to spit it out. If I'd swallowed it, the Lord only knows what damage it would have done further down the road."

I stared at her for a minute. "A pin in the cupcake?" I said, not sounding especially bright. "Someone put a pin in one and you took a bite and hurt yourself?"

She stuck out her tongue and pointed out a ragged red scratch along one side. "Ith thill bleeding," she said.

I sat down and studied the second cupcake. I suspected I already knew the answer, but I went ahead and asked, just for the hell of it. "Where did this package come from, Eilene?"

"Kevin brought it home this morning from that supermarket where he's working. When he went in last night, I gave him a grocery list. It didn't have cupcakes on it, but he decided on his own account to get a few other things. I had to take the cupcakes away because he's not allowed to have chocolate on account of breaking out."

"I suppose I'd better talk to him," I said. Eilene told me he'd gone to Dahlia's house. I asked her for a bag, scooped up the evidence, and went to find him.

Dahlia and her granny lived out past Raz Buchanon's place. The porch didn't look strong enough to support her granny, much less Dahlia. However, I traversed it without trouble and rapped on the door. I wasn't surprised when Kevin opened the door, but I certainly was when he yanked me inside and said, "Thank God you're here, Arly! We got to do something fast! Dahlia's been poisoned!"

I dashed past him and found the object of his affection on her hands and knees in a tiny bathroom. She regarded me over her shoulder, then jerked back in time for a brief episode of severe gastric disorder.

Kevin shook my arm. "Should I call an ambulance?"

"Shut your mouth," Dahlia said before I could answer. She backed out of the bathroom to the hall, where she had room to get to her feet, and proceeded to do so, albeit ponderously. "I must've told him twenty-seven times it's just another touch of that stomach flu. I ain't about to go off to a hospital again. I liked to have rolled right off that narrow ol' bed they made me get on last time. And the nurses were the snottiest people I've met in all my born days."

"But, beloved," Kevin protested, "what would I do if'n anything happened to you?"

"Visit that fat, pious pig by yourself, that's what."

"You're awful pale."

"You're plain awful, acting like you did and tearing a hole in my best blue blouse."

"I told you I was sorry."

"You can be sorrier than an undertaker for all it matters to me."

"Both of you hush," I said. "Kevin, did you bring Dahlia anything from the supermarket—such as a package of cupcakes?"

His jaw dropped and his Adam's apple shifted into fifth gear. "I paid for everything I took this morning. You can ask that checker with the black ducktail if I didn't pay for everything."

"That's not the question. Just answer me before I shake it out of you."

"I brought my sweetheart a peace offering," he mumbled.

Dahlia had her hand on her mouth and she was beginning to look a little bug-eyed, but she managed a nod. "Kevvie brought me a package of those little gold-colored sponge cakes. He knows they're my favorite."

I realized time was of the essence. "You ate them?"

"I didn't stick 'em in my ears." Her cheeks bulged, as did her eyes, and she pushed past me to fall to her knees in front of the commode. The entire house shook; we're talking six or seven point something on the Richter.

Not wishing to invade her privacy, I grabbed Kevin's elbow and hauled him to the front room. It took a good while to get his story, what with Dahlia appearing and then thundering away every three minutes or so, but after a half a dozen more episodes, she seemed to recover and admitted that the sponge cakes hadn't been up to snuff but that she'd eaten them anyway. Kevin assured the both of us he'd taken them and the cupcakes off the shelf beside the checkout counter, and no, he hadn't examined the wrappers, but why would he do that?

When I left with the cellophane wrapper safely stashed in a small plastic bag, I knew there was something going on at the SuperSaver that was at best malicious and at worst murderous.

Once I got to the highway, I debated whether to go directly to the SuperSaver or stop by the PD and call Harve first. I opted for the latter, and found Sergeant Plover seated in my chair, behind my desk, talking on my telephone. There was a scratch pad in front of him and a much maligned expression on his face.

"Yes, ma'am, I'll give her the message," he was saying as I came inside. He wiggled his eyebrows at me, listened for another minute, and said, "Yes, ma'am, as soon as possible. I do understand the urgency, but Chief Hanks is out on an investigation at the moment. I'm just helping out for the afternoon. No, I don't know where she is. Yes, ma'am. Goodbye, ma'am."

"Now what's going on?" I demanded.

"You're asking me? How in blazes am I supposed to know what's going on in this bucolic bedlam of yours? I came by to see if you were still in the mood to rip my ears off. The telephone started ringing, and I've been taking calls for a good twenty minutes."

I tried not to wince. "Any messages of interest?"

He came around the desk and put his hands on my shoulders. "I didn't mean to insult you—okay? You're a very efficient chief of police."

I ducked out of his grasp and took possession of my chair. "As much as I'd enjoy remaining in a foul, immature, unprofessional snit, I've got too many other things to worry about for the time being." I glanced at the names on the scratch pad in front of me: Ruby Bee, Lottie Estes, Millicent McIlhaney, Perkins (who, like his eldest daughter, has never been honored with the usage of a first name, if he has one), and someone named Barbara Buteo. "Anybody report an emergency?"

Plover looked at me. "Your mother said the big game's at three o'clock sharp, and she and Estelle will do everything possible to get to help out at practice this afternoon. The next three callers presumed you might be interested in their gastrointestinal upheavals. The Buteo woman said she'd call back, because what she had to say was too delicate to discuss with me."

"You're not going to believe this," I said, not too sure what I myself believed. I told him where I'd been the last half hour or so and what I'd learned about the goodies from the shelves of Jim Bob's SuperSaver Buy 4 Less.

"Holy hell," was all he could say when I had finished.

"It sounds as if we'll be there shortly," I said. I rubbed my face, then called Harve and reiterated the facts, along with the presumption that three of the previous callers had suffered ill effects also.

"But I got the report from the health department right here on my desk," Harve said unhappily.

"This doesn't have anything to do with the inspection, and the deli's closed. Unless you think Eilene Buchanon stuck a pin in a cupcake to add a little crunch, you'd better take my word for it and back me up when I go close down the SuperSaver in five minutes," I said. "State Police Sergeant Plover from the barracks in Farberville is here in my office. Jim Bob won't be able to ignore him, but I've got to have your okay on this, Harve."

Harve told me to do whatever I had to do and he'd get himself organized and be there shortly. Plover offered to drive. As we went outside, I asked him if he'd encountered a similar problem before.

"We've never seen any product tampering in this area," he said, opening the car door for me as if we were heading out for dinner in a prefeminist (read: prehistoric) era.

I managed to close it all by myself. "But it's been in

the news within the last two or three years," I said. "Do you honestly think someone's so opposed to this new supermarket that he would stick pins in cupcakes and dribble some substance on the packaged desserts and on the free samples the other day?"

"A substance like syrup of ipecac?" Plover put on his sunglasses and assumed the stony demeanor of a state trooper.

"Why'd you say that?"

"Because I called my ol' poker buddy at the state lab earlier. You won't get the report until late this afternoon, so I came out here to tell you what he told me."

I sank down in the seat and turned the air conditioner on high. "Ipecac is used primarily to induce vomiting in the case of accidental poisoning by a noncaustic substance," I intoned. "Third week of emergency first aid at the academy. The one thing it's not is an ingredient in chili sauce. Mandozes said something to me about the sauce tasting like sweet catsup. Ipecac has a nauseatingly sickly sweet taste to it." I switched the air conditioner back to low, partly out of a heightened awareness of the need for global energy conservation and partly because I was shivering like a dashboard hula girl.

8

Jim Bob was not a happy camper by any means. He sputtered threats and cursed steadily as Plover and I rounded up all the shoppers, ordered them to abandon their carts in mid-aisle, and sent them away bereft of bargains. The four employees gathered near the office door, awed equally by Plover's commando tactics and Jim Bob's command of the viler side of the King's English.

Once the door was locked, I went over to Jim Bob and said, "Go right ahead and call the sheriff. I've told you I cleared this with him beforehand. He's busy having his men question everyone who called to report nausea and pins, but he'll be here shortly. You can't keep selling merchandise until we figure out what in blazes is going on."

"I cannot believe this shit," Jim Bob groaned. "We open Saturday at two o'clock and at three we're closed down tighter than a rabbit's ass. We reopen not even twenty-four hours ago, and now we're closed down again. Is this some kind of friggin' conspiracy to keep the SuperSaver closed until we go broke? You working for somebody, Chief? Somebody who doesn't like the competition, for instance?"

"Shut up," Plover said as he came around the corner of the office. He looked at the huddle of high-school boys. "You all came to work yesterday afternoon and again this morning at seven, right?" They nodded. "Anyone missing who worked yesterday?" They shook their heads. "Go wait at the picnic tables in the pavilion. Someone from the sheriff's department will be there before too long to take your statements."

They reluctantly went toward the back of the store, leaving Jim Bob to grouse without an appreciative audience. When he lost momentum, I told him we'd have to question the night staff, too, since Kevin had bought the cupcakes and sponge cakes on his way out the door shortly after seven o'clock that morning.

I followed him into the office enclosure and waited impatiently as he threw papers here and there and made several graphic comments about my lineage, among other things. He at last found a notebook, opened it to the page with the schedules, and tossed it to me. "Are you saying one of these people diddled items on the shelf to try to kill half the town?"

The list was distressingly short: Buzz Milvin and Kevin Buchanon. I frowned at it for a minute. "No one else came into the store last night after it closed at nine o'clock?"

Jim Bob sat down at the desk and took a bottle of whiskey out of a drawer. "Nobody had any cause to. You'll have to ask Milvin."

"I will, but he can wait for the time being. According to the schedule, he's supposed to total the receipts and count the cash. Is there a safe here?"

"It hasn't been installed yet. I came by at ten-thirty to verify the figures and take the cash to the night depository at the bank in Starley City," he said, his face turning pale. He took a drink from the bottle, but it didn't seem to help. "I ended up sending Milvin to the bank because I was in a hurry."

"In a hurry to get home?"

Pale turned to outright pasty. "I had an appointment somewhere else. In Farberville."

"At eleven o'clock at night?"

"Yeah," he muttered. "Business."

"With Lamont Petrel, perhaps?" I said, wondering why he looked as if he was about to pass out. "As you know, he disappeared three days ago and the state police are conducting an investigation. In your statement to Sergeant Plover, you said you had no idea where Petrel is. If you had some sort of secret meeting with him last night, you'd better say so now."

"It wasn't with Petrel. I was . . . interviewing a checker." Several inches of whiskey gurgled down his throat.

"Oh, were you? She must be some potential checker to warrant the drive to Farberville that late at night. I'll have to have her name and address so I can verify this."

"This doesn't have anything to do with sticking pins in cupcakes—and you damn well know it!" he roared, a little of his customary charm returning along with his circulation. "If you know what's good for you, Chief Hanks, you'll just worry about whoever it is trying to ruin my store and stop pestering me. I got every right to do interviews when and where I choose."

"And I have every right to question everybody involved and verify stories," I said, taking an inordinate pleasure in the sweat popping out on his forehead like crystal zits. "Her name and address?"

"I don't reckon I recall offhand."

"I reckon you'd better try harder."

A loud rapping on the glass door interrupted any reckoning about to take place. I stuck my head out the office door, saw Mrs. Jim Bob arguing with Plover, and turned back with a bright look. "It's your wife. I suppose we could wait until she comes into the office, but it's your choice."

The whiskey bottle went back into the drawer. "Cherri Lucinda Crate, and she lives in that apartment house across from the airport. Top floor at the far end." Jim Bob tried to give me a nice smile, but his heart wasn't in it and the curl of his lips reminded me of an animal that'd been dead in the woods for several weeks. "Ain't no cause to go bothering her, though," he continued in a low voice. "She doesn't know anything about this."

"I should say not!" Mizzoner snapped as she came into the office. "I explained at great length to Eula Lemoy and to Dahlia O'Neill's granny that I for one cannot be held responsible for whatever funny business is going on in this store. Although I must say I fail to see anything funny about it." She turned on me with the fury of a goose defending its nest. "I want you to arrest Lamont Petrel, and I want you to do it before he poisons the remaining members of the missionary society. This has got to stop."

I agreed, pointed out the slight difficulty in arresting Petrel at the moment, and left the two alone for a cozy chat. Plover was unlocking the door for Harve, Les Vernon, and two other deputies. We went down to the far end of the checkout counters, where Mrs. Jim Bob's shrill voice was less deafening.

Harve gave me a disgruntled look. "We talked to this last bunch of victims. All the tampered products were purchased this morning from the display by the register next to the office." He scratched his head as he consulted a tattered stenographer's notebook. "We've had six reports thus far, and I'll call the dispatcher shortly. There haven't been any complaints on cupcakes and sponge cakes or anything else purchased yesterday evening, but that may not prove anything. The puke-provoking packages could have been put on the shelf last night or this morning."

"Kevin left the store at seven-fifteen," I said. "That narrows the time frame just a bit."

"There were a lot of folks in the store last night. As soon as we've interrogated the checkers, I'll get the list to you and you can start working on it. Les, you check the cake packages on the shelf for prints."

I felt slightly better that the perp list was now expanded to include more names, especially since I'd eliminated Kevin from contention and couldn't come up with a motive for Hizzoner, despite my best efforts. I suggested we examine the remaining stock for suspicious seals, and we fanned out for what became a tedious two-hour marathon of studying the underside of candy bars and corn-chip bags for telltale smears of glue—all without putting our own prints on top of someone else's, and as it turned out, all for naught, since none of us found anything.

We regrouped at the last register to listen to Deputy Vernon. Three packages of cupcakes had been pierced through the cellophane with straight pins. Two packages of cream-filled sponge cakes had been resealed, and sloppily at that. To our collective disappointment but not our great surprise, there was nary a print on any of the items.

Harve pointed at the beads of glue on one of the packages. "I'd bet my new weedless bucktail jig it didn't come this way from the factory."

No one took him up on it.

Plover offered to send the evidence to the lab, since he seemed to get better service than Harve and I did. Harve thanked him effusively (the primaries were coming up fast), and went to call the dispatcher for an update on the upchuckers.

I walked out to the parking lot with the amiable state trooper. "I won't fall over backward if the lab finds ipecac in the sponge cakes," I said, squinting as the sunlight pounded down on us. "I wish I knew what the hell was going on. First some unknown party dumps an unknown quantity of the damn stuff in the tamale sauce and takes down twenty-three innocent grazers. Petrel disappears, but it takes a stretch to see him as the perp. He and Jim Bob both have an interest in the store's success, not its failure—and a lot of folks won't be shopping within five miles of it. The picnic pavilion might as well stay closed; no one's going to patronize it anytime soon."

"Heard anything about Petrel?" Plover asked quickly, then winced as if he'd stepped on a live coal and said, "Just asking, Chief."

I told him about Jim Bob's trip into Farberville, but added that I had a feeling Cherri Lucinda Crate would eventually, if somewhat unwillingly, back his story. "Nobody even saw Petrel leave the office? What about the checkers and customers in the front of the store?"

"They all went to the back of the store to watch the show," he said morosely. "There was a ten-minute interval during which Petrel could have ridden out the door on a pink-polka-dotted mule."

He told me he'd be back shortly and drove away. As I started for the door, Deputy Vernon came out and said, "Harve says there's still no answer at Buzz Milvin's house. He wants you to run up there and see if the guy's scrunched in a closet counting up his victims on his fingers and toes."

"The stuff may have been tampered with before he came to work at nine," I said.

"Harve had a chat with the employees, and they finally produced a half-assed list of customers what came in last evening after six. Lots of folks, including"—he gave me an odd look—"Ruby Bee Hanks, Estelle Oppers, Buzz Milvin and his mother-in-law, and a dozen or so more."

"Mandozes, the Mexican guy?"

"I think so. Anyways, Harve says for you to go see if you can hunt up Milvin and bring him back for questioning."

I tried to assign Buzz a motive as I drove down the road to his house, but I was as bereft of inspiration as I was of cool air from the piss-poor air conditioner. I parked beside Buzz's truck and went to the front door. I rang the bell, and when there was no response, I went around the side of the house to see if they might be having a barbecue or something.

As I swung around the corner, I almost crashed into a small figure under an open umbrella. "Lissie," I said urgently, "where's your pa?"

"Napping."

"What about your grandmother and Martin?"

"They're napping, too. I wasn't sleepy, so I got Roxanne"—she held up a rag doll—"and we decided to go for a walk all the way up the road to the mailbox. I made her a raincoat and a rainbonnet. See?"

There was an icy rock growing in my stomach, and growing damn fast. I briefly glanced at the doll wrapped in clear plastic and said, "Good for you. I need to talk to your pa now."

"Please don't tell Pa where I went, Miss Arly. He likes me to stay close to the house, but sometimes Roxanne and I get bored with the same old yard. Pa says not to talk to outsiders, too. I suppose it's okay to talk to you."

Humming tunelessly, she went past me and vanished around the front of the house. I continued to the back door, knocked on the glass, and then ordered myself to try the knob. I had a real bad feeling about it.

"Anybody home?" I yelled as I stepped inside. The kitchen was clean, with dishes drying on the rack and the dish towels neatly hanging from plastic hoops. I repeated my question, listened for a reply, then went along a dark hallway to the living room.

Buzz Milvin was lying in a recliner. His eyes were closed, and had it not been for his wheezy breathing and gray skin, I might have thought he was, as Lissie had told me, sleeping. I hurried over to him and shook his shoulder. "Buzz? Buzz? Are you all right?"

He mumbled something and his head flopped to one side. A trickle of saliva ran down his chin, and his breathing seemed to worsen. I went back to the kitchen and called the sheriff's office. The dispatcher promised to send an ambulance immediately. I glanced in at Buzz, who hadn't moved, and went on down the hall to several closed doors.

I recoiled from the odor as I opened the first one. It had the sour pharmaceutical smell I'd noticed when I first met Lillith Smew, but something had been added that made it even less tolerable. The woman on the bed was motionless. Unlike Buzz, her chest did not jerk up and down as if responding to jolts of electricity. Her skin was grayer than his, and her tongue protruded between slack lips. Death had voided her bowels.

I gulped back an acid taste, shut the door, and went on to the next one. It was the children's bedroom. The bottom bunk bed was vacant, but a hand dangled over the rail from the top bunk. I approached the hand, and again heard labored breathing.

"Martin?" I croaked.

"Yeah?" he said so softly that I could barely hear it. "That you, Gran?"

"It's Arly. I've sent for the ambulance. Someone will be here to help you in a minute." I squeezed his hand, more to comfort myself than him, and said, "What happened, Martin?"

"Where's Gran? I wanna talk to Gran."

"I'll listen," I said, straining to hear him with one ear and the ambulance's siren with the other. "I'll listen to you, Martin. What do you want to tell Gran?"

"That I wasn't lying."

"Of course you weren't lying." I jiggled his hand.

"Lying about what? You can tell me; I know you won't lie to Gran or to me, Martin."

"What's the matter with my brother?" Lissie asked from the doorway.

"He's sick," I managed to say calmly. "So are Gran and your pa. I sent for an ambulance."

"Why's everybody sick?"

Martin groaned from the top bunk. I wiped the sweat from his forehead, murmured to him that I was there, and looked back at Lissie. "I don't know why everybody's sick. Do you?"

She began to shake her head, and continued to do so as the ambulance arrived out front. For all I knew, she was still at it as I ran to the front door and barked at the medics to bring two gurneys. There was no need for hurry with a third.

Ruby Bee closed the front door and went back across the dance floor to the bar, where Estelle and Hammet were sitting in gloomy silence. "I jest can't figure out what all's going on over there," Ruby Bee muttered, mostly to herself, since the other two had given up trying to provide answers. "First Arly and that nice state trooper come screeching up like there's an armed robbery in progress. The next thing, Hiram, Perkins's eldest, and a few other people come barreling out the door and looking mighty frightened. Then we get the sheriff and some of his boys. Before you can say boo, everybody's coming and going every which direction like they was driving those awful bumper cars at the county fair carnival."

Hammet sighed. "I wish Arly'd get back. It's nigh on time fer baseball practice. I got a hit yesterday—a real hard one that liked to have made that Martin kid squeal like a pig getting his dick chopped off."

Estelle rolled her eyes and sighed herself. "You already described it, Hammet. I'm sure it was a real hard hit. I do believe we've already heard enough about where it bounced and any sound effects that may have occurred thereafter."

"I can't for the life of me figure out what's going on

over at the SuperSaver," Ruby Bee said. She shoved a basket of popcorn under Hammet's nose. "Here, eat some more of this. It'll keep your strength up for practice—if and when Arly shows her face. She left you here a good three hours ago. If that ain't irresponsible, then I don't know how to make biscuits from scratch. I'm her own mother, and—"

The whining of an ambulance siren cut her short. The three looked at each other as the sound increased, peaked in an ear-splitting shriek as it passed the bar, and abated as it continued down the highway.

"Lord a mercy," Estelle gasped. "Do you think something's happened to Arly?"

"There ain't no reason to think that," Ruby Bee said with a look of warning in Hammet's direction. "Maybe Arly was sent out to investigate an accident on that bad curve just past the Voice of the Almighty Lord Assembly Hall."

Estelle leaned forward, beckoned for Ruby Bee to do the same, and whispered, "If there's been a wreck or something, then somebody probably called over to the sheriff's office. Why don't you see if you can find out anything. Go on, I'll handle Hammet." She sat back and smiled at him. "Tell you what, I've got a nice shiny quarter that'll pay for three songs on the jukebox. You can go right over there and pick out what you want to hear."

"I don't wanna hear some dumbshit song," Hammet said, his face wrinkled up like a Pekingese. "If'n Arly's hurt, I gotta go help her."

He jumped down from the stool and ran out the door before Ruby Bee or Estelle could open their mouths. He was a good ways down the road and still going full steam before either of them made it to the door to yell at him. And by the time a truck piled high with chicken crates moved out of the way, he was long gone.

Ruby Bee started for the telephone. "He'll be all right. He knows his way around town by now. I'm going to call LaBelle over at the sheriff's and ask her real politely if she knows where I can find Arly. If that doesn't work, I think I'll mosey on over to Jim Bob's SuperSaver and pick up a package of paper towels and a few other things."

"You got three cases of paper towels in the—" Estelle squared her shoulders and nodded. "I think I might go with you to keep you company."

Brother Verber folded his hands in his lap and gazed sternly at the sinners sitting right there beside each other on chairs he'd brought over from the dinette. He gave them a minute in case they wanted to take off repenting without any prodding on his part, then said, "I am deeply troubled, deeply troubled indeed. Y'all have been coming thrice weekly to the house of the Lord under false pretenses. People what come to the house of the Lord thrice weekly ought to do so without carrying a heavy, burdensome load of sin in their hearts."

Dahlia stared at the wall above his head. "I ain't done nothing," she said flatly.

Kevin twitched as Brother Verber's eyes bored into him. He wished he was almost anyplace else except in the hot, stuffy mobile home parked next to the particular house of the Lord under discussion. Mopping floors was better'n this, he thought glumly. Mopping floors weren't half so bad as being told he was some kind of pervert and sex maniac. However, he couldn't think of anything to say, so he settled for a gulp and a shrug.

"The only way," Brother Verber intoned, "the only way to cleanse yourselves of this sinful, disgusting lust that's sucking on your souls like a tapeworm is to repent. If you don't repent from the beginning and in detail, well . . . Satan's just waiting around the corner, hoping for two new workers in the eternal furnace. I ain't here to pressure you all, though; you can make up your own minds. Maybe you want to shovel coal into Satan's furnace for all eternity while little red devils poke you with pitchforks till you scream."

"I ain't done nothing," Dahlia repeated. She elbowed Kevin so forcefully, he nearly jumped off the chair.

"Me, neither," he added hastily. "We was sitting on the swing talking about our new jobs at the supermarket, that's all. Anybody what says different is lying—and that's a sin, too."

He was pretty impressed with his speech, but he could tell just from looking that Brother Verber wasn't. In fact, the more he looked, the more he could see the fat ol' pious pig cranking up to spew out all kinds of stuff. And although Kevin knew there hadn't been any fornicating on the porch swing, he didn't much want to discuss various incidents over the last two years. The outhouse, for instance. The back room of the Kwik-Stoppe-Shoppe, on numerous occasions. Once, while Dahlia sat on the stool behind the counter and he'd . . .

Kevin all of a sudden realized that he was about to get hisself in deeper shit, because the same devil that had tormented him on the swing was back for another visit. "I have to go to the men's room," he said in a strangled voice (although it wasn't his voice that felt like it was being strangled—not by a long shot).

Having been prepared for a detailed description of lustful abandon, Brother Verber was unprepared for this and he began to blink like an addled calf. He may have been staring at Kevin, but his mind was in the bathroom. To be precise, it was in the wicker basket beside the commode—along with two insightful issues of his study material. After a minute, he said, "Right now, we'd better get down on our knees and pray for the salvation of your souls. This ain't the time for wordly concerns, not with damnation seeping into the room like swamp gas."

"I got to go."

Dahlia snorted under her breath, but she didn't say anything and Kevin repeated his plaintive request once again. Brother Verber stood up and went down the hall to the bathroom, hoping for a chance to relocate the well-worn June issue of *Kittens and Tomcats* and the July issue of *Rubber Maid*, but Kevin was so close behind him, he could feel hot breath on his neck.

"Let me see if the hand towels are clean," Brother Verber said. He stepped inside and closed the door. The room was small and short on hiding places. If he put the magazines in the one cabinet, Kevin might poke around out of idle curiosity, especially if he had business that might take a while.

He waited for a bolt of inspiration, but when nothing struck, he jerked open the window and dropped both issues out. Then he folded a damp towel so it'd look fresh, ascertained there was ample toilet paper, and opened the door.

"Don't be all afternoon in here," he said grimly. "We got some serious praying and repenting to do."

Kevin hurried past him and locked the door. Brother Verber returned to the living room and told Dahlia he needed to step outside for a minute. He didn't have a handy explanation, but she sat in the chair like a great pink Buddha and didn't so much as turn her head. Once outside, he hurried to the back of the mobile home.

The bathroom window was open, of course, and from inside he heard a curious moaning sound that made him wonder if he needed a plumber. He stopped worrying about the sound when he looked down at the patch of brown grass below the window, where there should have been two magazines. He'd dropped them out the window less than a minute earlier. He'd heard them flutter like pigeons.

Brother Verber looked around wildly. Across the street at the Emporium, one of the hippie women came out the back door and dropped a bag in a battered garbage can. She didn't appear to notice him, though, and he figured she couldn't have gotten to the mobile home and back inside the store in that short a time.

A truck towing a horse trailer came down the county road, braked momentarily in deference to the stop sign, and pulled onto the highway. A drunk stumbled out of the pool hall, but it was a good block away and the drunk wasn't exactly leaping like a ballerina.

Clasping his hands over his belly, Brother Verber looked skyward. "Why me, Lord?" he said. He waited for a reply, but he didn't hold his breath or anything.

Lissie and I were sitting on the porch steps when Harve and Les Vernon drove up. I told Lissie to wait there,

then went over to the car and gave Harve a rundown on
what I'd discovered and what I'd done thereafter.

"Jesus H.," he said, taking off his hat to run his hand
across his carefully oiled hair. "The little girl's okay?"

"She seems fine. The medics said Buzz was critical.
They were more optimistic about Martin, the boy. His
color was quite a bit better, and he was semiconscious
when they put him in the ambulance. The coroner's on
his way with Plover and a couple of men to take prints
and photographs."

Harve got out of the car and stared at the house. "Did
you look around at all?"

"I didn't see any half-eaten sponge cakes, if that's
what you're getting at. Damn it, what's going on in this
town? Have we got a maniac on our hands? Maggody's
not big enough to have a resident maniac. Don't try to
tell me—"

Harve hushed me and herded me away from the porch.
We hissed at each other until Plover drove up, followed
by other official vehicles. He issued orders, then joined
us. "Do you want to come inside?" he asked me.

"I want to crawl under my covers," I said in all sincerity. "No, I've seen enough to hold me. You all can go
look for cellophane wrappers and fingerprints and whatever it is you think you'll find."

"We'll need you to wait."

"I'll wait." I went across the yard and sat down in the
grass, battling to maintain a professional composure. I'd
seen nasty things in my life—and some of them in a
shabby little town where, in theory, nothing ever happened. When something happened here, however, it happened with an intensity that made it a hundred times
worse. A corpse in Manhattan was a corpse. In Maggody,
it was someone's mother, someone's child, someone who
lived next door or sang in the choir. It had a name. The
violence wasn't isolated in a Bowery doorstep. It was a
blister that enveloped all of us; we couldn't dismiss it as
an inexplicable act of greed, or lust, or rage.

My eyes were closed and my shoulders trembling when
I felt a small hand on my knee. "Don't cry, Miss Arly,"
Lissie said softly. "When I cry, Pa says all it does is make

my nose turn red. He says it don't help to act like a baby and that I have to be a big girl now that Mama's in heaven."

"I'm sure your pa loves you very much," I said, aware of the incongruity of a police officer being comforted by a ten-year-old child whose father might be dead within the hour. There was a bright yellow dandelion near my foot. I picked it and handed it to her with a weak smile.

She searched my face for a long while, then crawled into my lap and put her thumb in her mouth. I wrapped my arms around her, and the two of us rocked back and forth in the grass.

9

Lissie couldn't stay at home, so I told her to wait by my car and went into the house. One of Plover's men was taking photographs of the recliner. The coroner was in Lillith Smew's room, pronouncing the obvious to Deputy Vernon, who looked ill. In the kitchen, a trooper with an exceedingly grim expression was removing items from a garbage can and placing them on the table. Plover and Harve muttered to each other as they examined the items.

I kept my eyes averted from the bunk beds as I packed a few things in a small suitcase. I told Plover I'd be back, then put the child in my car and drove toward the Lambertinos' to see whether she could stay there for the time being.

"Where'd they take Pa and Martin?" Lissie asked.

"To the hospital."

"Why didn't they take Gran, too?"

I glanced at her, but she looked only mildly curious. "I'm afraid Gran was too sick for the medics to help her," I said gently.

"Is she gone to heaven with Mama?"

"Yes, she has."

"Oh." Lissie leaned down and pointed at the battered police radio. "What's that thing do?"

As I explained what the thing was supposed to do but rarely did, I pulled into the Lambertinos' driveway and cut off the engine. "Lissie, I need to ask you some questions. Is that okay?" She nodded, still frowning at the radio. "We think that Pa, Gran, and Martin all ate or drank something that made them sick. You're not sick, so you obviously didn't have whatever they had. Can you think what it might have been?"

"Huh-uh. Does the siren work?"

"Upon occasion," I said, watching her closely. "Let's talk some more about what happened today. Were you awake when Pa came home from the supermarket at seven?"

"Yeah, I woke up real early like I always do, but I didn't get out of bed right away. I read a story to Roxanne, and then we made up our own stories."

"So you and Roxanne made up stories?" I said encouragingly. "Then what did you do? Did you have breakfast?"

She nodded, but her forehead was wrinkled and her lower lip was extended. "I didn't make up the stories. Roxanne did. I just listened." She held up the doll as if to verify the statement.

"Fine, fine. And then you went to the kitchen, right? Was everybody having breakfast?"

"Is this where I'm gonna stay until Pa and Martin get back? I don't think I want to stay here, Miss Arly. Saralee might hit on me, and she's mean."

"Mrs. Lambertino won't let Saralee bother you." I reminded myself of the necessity of eliciting information, and let an authoritative edge creep into my voice. "Lissie, you do understand that I'm the police chief and I have to find out what happened at your house today. You need to help me. Once you've done that, we can talk about the radio or anything else you want. Okay?"

"Okay, Miss Arly. Gran fixed me cereal, but she was grouchy, so I ate real fast. Then Pa came in and she said she wanted to talk to him in the back room. He said he had a gawdawful headache, but she said they was going to talk right then."

I nodded. "Good, Lissie. Did they talk?"

"In the back bedroom. I couldn't hear much, but I think they were both mad at Martin. He came in from the backyard, and pretty soon Gran came out and told Martin to go talk to Pa. I finished my cereal and went into the living room to watch television."

"Did Martin tell you why Pa and Gran were mad at him?"

She shook her head so vaguely that it seemed to drift back and forth. "I watched television all morning. Gran came in and looked hard at me, but all I was doing was sitting in Pa's big chair with Roxanne. Martin went back outside, and I think Pa went to bed on account of how he had to stay awake all night."

"You're doing great, Lissie. What about lunch?"

"Martin and me had canned spaghetti and leftover corn bread. Gran fixed it, but she said she wasn't hungry. While we ate, she talked on the telephone about how people were getting sick from something. I think she was talking to somebody named Eula, 'cause she said, 'land sakes, Eula,' and 'I can't believe that, Eula.' Pa came out later and had a baloney samwich and a beer."

In that I didn't know what poison had been used, I didn't know how long it had taken until the symptoms became serious. Breakfast seemed innocuous, and Buzz and Martin had eaten different things for lunch. According to Lissie, Lillith hadn't eaten anything. I scowled at myself in the rearview mirror, then tried to smile. "I want you to do something for me, Lissie. Close your eyes and try to think if your pa brought home a bag from the supermarket."

She obediently scrunched up her eyes. "No," she said in a faraway voice, "he just came in and said he was tireder than a fiddler's elbow at a barn dance. Then Gran started in on him and they went to the back bedroom."

"Did you see anyone have something to eat or drink after lunch?" I asked without much hope.

"No, but everybody was fumin', so I stayed in Pa's chair until he told me to go outside and play. I wanted to watch television some more, but he said the noise was giving everybody a royal pain." She began to squirm on the seat. "It's awful hot sitting here, Miss Arly."

"You're right," I said as I took her overnight bag from the backseat. "Let's go talk to Mrs. Lambertino."

Joyce wasn't thrilled, but after I explained the situation, she agreed that Lissie might as well sleep on the other roll-away cot and keep Saralee company.

"Saralee's not here," she added as she took the bag from me and sent Lissie inside. "She went to practice about half an hour ago."

"Practice," I said hollowly, having been preoccupied with more important things for most of the afternoon. "There's no way on God's green earth I can get over there, not even for a minute. I don't suppose there's any way you can . . . ?"

"The baby's teething and has been howling nonstop for three days. Larry Junior's running a temperature, and Traci's acting like she's coming down with something, too. I'm smack in the middle of fixing supper. Larry Joe's off practicing with the SuperSavers, so he won't be home for another hour. I'm real sorry, Arly, but there ain't no way."

I asked if I could use her telephone and then dialed the number of Ruby Bee's Bar & Grill. It was answered with alacrity. "Arly? What in heaven's name is going on? Is it true half the folks in town have been poisoned, including the entire Milvin family? All four of them found dead in their beds?"

"Calm down," I said through clenched teeth. "The grapevine's a little ahead of itself. Yes, there have been a few isolated . . . problems with items purchased at the SuperSaver. The Milvin family seems to have gotten the worst of it." I stopped for a moment, puzzled. "Where are you getting your information, Ruby Bee?"

"Here and there. In fact, Estelle heard a most astonishing story from Perkins's eldest, who cleaned at Mrs. Jim Bob's this afternoon. I'll be the first to agree that Perkins's eldest may be a few logs shy of a rick, but Estelle said she said Mrs. Jim Bob said—"

"Stop! I don't have time for this—now or ever. Can you and Estelle handle practice for me?"

"Baseball practice?"

"No, parachute practice. The plane's waiting for you out front."

She sputtered for several seconds before she said, "You know I have an aversion to heights. My eyelid starts twitching when I have to ride an escalator. Now why would you think I—"

"Of *course* I'm talking about baseball practice. I've got to go back to the Milvin house. Have Hammet go to my apartment and get the equipment bag, then trot yourselves out to the pasture and make sure everyone survives. Don't worry about teaching anyone to do anything. Just tell them to play catch for an hour."

"But I have to keep the bar open."

"Then tell Estelle to do it. You'll only have seven players today, since neither Milvin child will be there. But the rest of them are probably waiting by now, and you're liable to find fresh blood on home plate if you don't get over there—now."

"But what if they start acting up? What if they ask me about how to play or bat?"

"What if you had wheels? Then you'd be a tea cart, right? For Pete's sake, Ruby Bee, I've got other things to do, and unless you want Georgie McMay's untimely demise on your conscience, you'd better get over to the field." I hung up on her and shrugged at Joyce, who was trying to pretend she hadn't been listening. "I think it's different in the major leagues."

"Me, too," she said. She promised to call me if Lissie remembered anything of importance, and I drove back to the Milvin house.

Brother Verber was sweating like a roofer in August, but it wasn't because of the paltry confessions he'd wrung out of Kevin. Even if he'd been paying attention, hearing stories about a few smooches and a bizarre-sounding encounter in an outhouse (of all the dadgum peculiar places) wasn't going to begin to compete with his study material. Which brought to mind a serious problem, and in spite of himself, Brother Verber let out a groan that sounded like a Greyhound bus belching carbon monoxide.

Kevin stopped in mid-confession. He glanced at Dahlia, who hadn't moved in so long that he was beginning to worry, then he looked back and said, "Are you all right? You look mighty sickly."

"I am wrasslin' in my soul on your behalf," Brother

Verber snarled. "If you weren't such a revolting, perverted sex fiend, none of this would have happened."

"You mean we wouldn't be here?" Kevin said, his
voice cracking in bewilderment.

Brother Verber couldn't explain exactly, so he nodded
and pursed his lips as if he was thinking real hard. "Just
get on with your disgusting story, and don't take all day
about it. I got better things to do with my time than to
listen to you snivel about every little peck and every little
pat on the fanny."

"But you said to tell about all that and not skip anything," Kevin pointed out, now so befuddled that he
wouldn't have known which end of the fork to scratch
his head with. It was out-and-out mystificating, trying to
figure out what he was supposed to say and what he
wasn't and why Brother Verber kept looking out the window like he thought there was more sex maniacs loose
on the grounds of the Voice of the Almighty Lord
Assembly Hall.

"There was the time we went for a walk out to Boone
Creek," he suggested, then waited to see if it qualified
or not.

Brother Verber shook himself like a wet dog in a snow-
storm. "Okay, okay, let's hear it. But if you're going to
describe nature, you'd better make sure you're talking
about the birds and the bees. Otherwise, I'll be sorely
disappointed, Kevin Buchanon. I may be so sorely disappointed that I'll be obliged to send you away and get to
work on my Sunday sermon."

Nervously wetting his lips, Kevin again peeked at
Dahlia. She didn't so much as quiver, so he took a deep
breath and said, "It was a right pretty evening. The birds
was chirping, but I ain't sure we saw any bees. Dahlia
had fixed us a nice picnic supper. Deviled eggs, if I recollect rightly, and pimento cheese sandwiches with the
crusts trimmed off and double-fudge brownies with icing.
The dogwoods were beginning to bloom, and you could
smell the sweet evening air like it was perfume."

He continued along these lines, working himself into a
veritable poetic frenzy that would have irritated Brother
Verber, had he been listening.

*   *   *

Mrs. Jim Bob rang Eilene's doorbell, her foot tapping steadily and the corners of her mouth veering downward with each passing second. "This is most inconsiderate," she said under her breath. She'd driven all the way over to have a talk with Eilene, and now it looked as if Eilene had just gone on her merry way without worrying one bit about keeping people standing on her front porch as if they were peddling burial insurance.

When Eilene opened the door, she didn't appear to appreciate how much she'd vexed Mrs. Jim Bob, who was in the midst of a trying day. "We're having supper," she said with a vague look toward the kitchen.

"I heard about the pin in the cupcake," Mrs. Jim Bob said briskly. "I came over here to talk to you about it. Shall we sit in the front room or out here on the"—she glanced at the porch swing and shuddered—"I believe the front room will do nicely."

"For a minute." Eilene opened the screened door without noticeable enthusiasm and gestured for her visitor to come inside. Once they were seated across from each other, she said, "What have you got to say about the pin?"

Mrs. Jim Bob realized Eilene was not going to be an easy row to hoe, not with her sitting there like she was a judge facing a common criminal. "I heard how you scratched your tongue," she began, sounding as solicitous as possible.

"On a cupcake that came straight from Jim Bob's SuperSaver Buy 4 Less."

"That doesn't mean Jim Bob had anything to do with it, Eilene. Use your head; why would Jim Bob want to make everybody mad at the SuperSaver?"

"I don't know, but he's doing a real fine job of it," Eilene said unhelpfully.

Mrs. Jim Bob regretted not wearing her white gloves, since she always believed they gave her an authoritarian air. She went ahead and waggled her finger anyway. "Now, let's not go leaping to wild conclusions. Jim Bob didn't put pins in the cupcakes or poison in the sponge cakes . . . but I know for a fact who did!" She waited for a moment, but Eilene didn't budge, so she had no choice but to lift her chin and plow ahead. "It was Lamont Petrel, that fellow from Farberville who was Jim Bob's partner. You may not have heard, but he fled the scene of his crime right when everyone started getting sick in the picnic pavilion. His wife called the police yesterday to report him missing."

"I heard. Doesn't mean he did it."

"Then why did he run away? You just tell me that, Eilene Buchanon."

"I don't know why he ran away, but he doesn't have any more reason to poison everybody than Jim Bob has. You yourself said he's a partner." She stood up. "If that's all you got to say, then I'll be getting back to the supper table. My tongue's so sore, all I can have is liquids. Earl says we ought to get ourselves a lawyer on account of my injury."

Mrs. Jim Bob stood up, too, but her knees felt like gelatin and she had to hold on to the arm of the sofa until she got herself steadied. "I cannot believe my ears," she said coldly. "Neighbors don't treat each other like that, and it's hardly the Christian thing to do. You and Earl have been upstanding members of the Voice of the Almighty for years, and I'd like to think you're above spite and malice."

"I am—but my lawyer ain't." Eilene smiled as the blood drained from her visitor's face.

The troopers and the coroner were gone, as was the body and what scraps of possible evidence anyone had found. Les Vernon was in Harve's car, talking on the radio to the dispatcher. Plover and I sat on the green metal glider on the Milvins' porch. Harve had pulled over the matching chair, fired up a cigar butt, and was now making notes on a legal pad.

"Lemme see," he muttered, "the kid said none of the victims ate the same thing at any of the meals, and she didn't notice much of anything all day due to the television set being on. That right?"

"She also said her father didn't have a bag when he came in this morning," I said slowly. "If what we have is related to the product tampering at the SuperSaver, then we missed something in the search. These people didn't eat sponge cakes—unless they ate the cellophane wrapper, too. Besides, I'm guessing those were doctored with syrup of ipecac, just like the tamale sauce. Everybody we've heard from recovered within a few bouts of . . . unpleasantness."

Plover nudged the glider into motion and said, "We've got three episodes of poisoning—Saturday at the grand opening, sometime late yesterday evening or night, and whatever happened here today. The first two have an unmistakable resemblance, since Arly's apt to be correct about the substance on the sponge cakes. We don't know if this is related or not."

"Buzz got off work at seven," I said, frowning. "He's the night manager. Who relieved him?"

Harve flipped back a few pages. "Jim Bob. He and one checker showed up at seven, and then the other three boys came in after a while."

"Kevin paid a checker with a black ducktail for his bag of groceries," I continued. "Why don't we find out if Buzz happened to buy anything?"

Grumbling, Harve went into the house. Plover and I sat in silence, although not of the companionable variety. I was thinking about what might happen to Lissie and Martin if their father died. The officers who'd searched the house had found no reference to any other relatives; at the moment, Lissie was the official next of kin. Plover seemed to be entertaining equally glum thoughts.

Harve looked a damn sight more pleased when he came back to the porch. "That was sharper than a hornet's behind, Arly. The checker said Milvin bought a magazine and a package of dessert cakes on his way out. Didn't want a bag and just stuck them in his coat pocket."

I took a deep breath. "You might send a man over to the Lambertinos' to collect Lissie's doll's rainbonnet. It was made of cellophane."

"This is a goddamn mess," Harve said. "And I'm handing it over to you, Plover, all officially and wrapped in cellophane. We don't have the manpower to handle this kind of investigation. I'll assign Deputy Vernon to assist you, and there's no way short of incarceration to keep Arly out of it."

"It's my turf," I muttered.

Ignoring me, Plover said, "I'll get Anderson on the paperwork as soon as I get to the office. As for the local chief of police, I tend to agree with you. I suppose we'd better have another run at the sponge-cake display. Maybe we'll get lucky and find one package with one print."

"Maybe," Harve echoed.

As we walked toward our respective vehicles, I looked at the dandelion. It already had wilted.

On the way back to the supermarket, I swung through the motel parking lot so I could check on practice in the field out back. Petrel's car was still in front of number four, but I barely glanced at it.

Ruby Bee and Estelle stood next to the fence, neither one doing much of anything. Georgie and Ray were exchanging blows by the burlap bag designated as third base. Enoch was pensively picking his nose as he watched. Earl Boy was on second base, pounding his fist into his glove as if he was hoping to be invited to join in the fun. Jackie and Saralee were chasing butterflies out by the fir trees.

I backed out before assistant coaches number one and number two spotted me and threw themselves in front of the car. I drove across the street and parked next to Plover's car. The SuperSaver was dim except for a light in the office area, and the deputy outside told us Jim Bob had left a few minutes before.

I told the deputy to stay put. Plover and I went inside and continued into the office. While he called the hospital to find out if the initial analysis of the contents of Milvin's stomach had suggested sponge cakes, I leafed through various papers and documents on the desk. One notebook seemed to contain a variety of lists, notes, and cryptic reminders such as: cheap whiskey, stock boys—9, call KPIG, qt, close Thursday, 12, and a lot of squiggles I couldn't decipher (which isn't meant to imply I was having mind-boggling success with the ones I could).

"Look at this," I said to Plover when he'd completed his call. "It's Petrel's personal notebook."

"I don't suppose it has anything about an appointment in Des Moines Saturday afternoon?"

"No, but it has a schedule of sorts, I think. If one were to interpret this as a continuing story line, he was going to buy cheap whiskey for the stock boys at nine, call the television station but quietly, close the store Thursday either at noon, midnight, or on his way to the twelfth green."

"Fascinating," Plover said. He sat down and held out his hand for the notebook. I resisted the urge to put it behind my back, having given up my childish ways several hours ago.

"Just remember who found it," I said in a display of maturity.

"That's fascinating, too, because I searched the office late yesterday afternoon and it wasn't here."

In a display of increased maturity, I merely gave him a dirty look as I said, "You searched the office and didn't invite me along?"

"You were at the practice field, although it looked more like tackle football than baseball. That little girl with the yellow braids is fearless, isn't she? I watched for a while, but I could see you were having too much fun to be interrupted. Please may I have the notebook?"

I handed it to him, then went around to lean over his shoulder. "The first four notes seem to deal with the grand opening on Saturday. Booze, stock boys, media. But he wouldn't need to call the media on the QT, would he?"

"Maybe he intended to close the store on Thursday on the QT," Plover suggested. "Of course, with the ipecac in the tamale sauce and the pins and poison in the cupcakes, it might be challenging to keep things quiet for a week."

"What did the lab report?" I said, losing interest in Petrel's hieroglyphics. "Did it confirm our theory about the sponge cakes?"

"They didn't have anything on the contents of the boy's stomach, but they had done some preliminary analysis of Milvin's, since he was first to have his stomach pumped. We were on the right track but in the wrong lane. There was a small quantity of sponge cake and cream filling, along with tinted coconut flakes."

I went over to a display shelf and pointed at the cellophane-wrapped mounds. "I went through these earlier, and I didn't spot any evidence that the seals had been opened."

"So your prints are all over them?"

"I was careful, but I can't swear I didn't touch one," I said levelly.

Before he could come up with a smart-assed comment, various official cars promptly pulled into the parking lot.

I gestured at the latest arrivees. "The cavalry has arrived. I'm going to take another look at the deli."

"I'll let you know if we turn up any prints on the coconut-cake packages."

"I'm sure you will." I went through the picnic pavilion, around the corner of the deli counter, and into the kitchen area. Most of it would be visible from the front, I realized, so it would be impossible for a nonemployee to sneak to the stove and sabotage a pot of tamale sauce.

Everything had been put away. The counters were as spotless as Ruby Bee's, and the spice bottles above the stove were neatly aligned. I examined each one, just in case, but they were all innocuous. I tried to remember what I'd learned in the emergency first-aid course. Ipecac came in one-fluid-ounce bottles, small enough to be concealed in one's hand. But one fluid ounce wasn't going to take down twenty-three people.

However, I thought as I roamed around the kitchen, picking up utensils and replacing them, opening and closing cabinet doors, we'd only been offered samples. Each tamale had been sliced into half a dozen pieces and then speared with a toothpick. Dahlia'd brought out platters and put them on a picnic table. A cheerleader had picked one up to circulate, and I was fairly certain I'd seen another go by with a platter of ugly orange tidbits. We weren't necessarily dealing with a vast quantity of sauce requiring a gallon of ipecac, especially not with the power of suggestion murmuring to slightly queasy stomachs. If one of the cooks had stirred the sauce three or four times, she very well could have dumped enough ipecac into it to set off a chain reaction in the pavilion.

But why? Two of the cooks were temporaries from another of Petrel's stores. Dahlia had looked angry, but she'd also chomped into a tamale herself and ended up in an ambulance. Dahlia was stupid, but not that stupid. Or that wily.

It would be risky to approach the untended platter and sprinkle the contents of a small bottle on the tamale slices, but not impossible. I'd noticed Ruby Bee and Estelle in the vicinity; Mandozes had headed that way, as had Ivy Sattering and several dozen other people.

I stopped cold and forced myself to evaluate the possibility that Ruby Bee—my mother—would do something that drastic to put the picnic pavilion out of business. You may be shaking your head, but I wasn't. Ruby Bee'd once gotten so ticked off at Eula Lemoy that Eula had been besieged by a nonstop parade of cemetery-plot salesmen and vacuum-cleaner demonstrators. After several weeks, Eula actually came over and offered an apology. She retracted it when she started receiving somewhere in the range of a dozen magazines a week—invoices attached—and the solicitous attention of bicycling missionaries, not to mention Cheese of the Month Club selections, records, books, and telephone calls from asthmatics who'd read her personal ad in a porn magazine. It took most of a year for the dust to settle outside Eula's mobile home. Ruby Bee never admitted anything, but she had an aura of complacency most of that very same year.

So it wasn't incomprehensible that she might have wanted to make a public statement about the deli, I thought with a shrug. But she wouldn't have put pins in the cupcakes, much less used the substance that I was assuming had resulted in Lillith Smew's death.

I didn't know much about Mandozes, but he had been angry at the opening. Ivy had joked about becoming a migrant worker. Her smile had lacked depth, though, and her voice had been too tight. It wasn't impossible to imagine her or Mandozes adding a few packages to the display. But would either of them see the SuperSaver as such a threat that he or she would be willing to kill?

I gave up and went to the front of the store. Plover was talking to a fellow trooper who was putting away bottles of black powder and wispy brushes.

"Corporal Anderson, Chief Hanks," Plover said as I joined them.

Anderson nodded at me, then said, "Prints all over the display shelf, naturally, but I suspect they'll match with those we'll have to get from the installation crew and the stock boys. I pulled up two partials from this package; from their position, I'd guess some customer picked it up and changed his or her mind."

I made a face at Plover. "Unless a law-enforcement agent of some species picked it up earlier when we searched for tampered packages."

"Yours are on file," Plover said. "We'll keep them in mind."

Anderson finished packing his equipment and picked up the case. "The rest of the packages are all clean as a whistle, thanks to automation in the factory, and the seals look okay. I doubt any of them have been tampered with."

"Well, shit," I said, eliciting a frown from Anderson. Once he'd moved away, I perched on the checkout counter and said, "Then how did Buzz happen to buy the only one laced with the mysterious poison? Do we have anything on the ducktailed kid?"

Plover beckoned to a sheriff's deputy (we were still an oddly homogenized group) and asked him to find the deputy who'd interviewed the employees. We twiddled our thumbs and gazed blankly at tidy rows of candy bars until Les Vernon arrived.

"Yeah, I took their statements," he said. "That kid smelled okay. We ran background checks on all of them, and he was one of three that doesn't have a track record. The others have a smattering of minor-in-possession, driving without a license, busting heads after football games, that sort of thing. It's hard for our youth to find ways to amuse themselves out here. But that kid in particular seemed clean. Lives in Emmet, a cousin of Jim

Bob's, planning to work full-time until school starts and then cut back for football. And cut his hair.''

I threw up my hands, literally and figuratively, and went to the office to call the hospital. Buzz Milvin was critical but stable. Martin Milvin had been moved to a semiprivate room and was upgraded to resting comfortably. I called Joyce and learned that although Saralee had come home with a bloody nose, she and Lissie had eaten supper and were out doin' something. A baby screamed incessantly in the background.

My stomach rumbled, but I wasn't about to snitch a candy bar from the rack. I told Plover I'd start questioning people the next morning, and also inquire whether anyone had seen Petrel after three o'clock Saturday afternoon. As I walked across the parking lot, I realized I was two meals short and very confused. If the checker was clean, which I supposed he was, then he didn't set out the poisoned package for the first customer to pick up. Buzz wouldn't have done so and then eaten one later in the afternoon. It occurred to me that Kevin might have noticed something. Yes, a long shot, and apt to be as successful as teaching a turkey to sing.

Hammet and his companions were hunkered down way in the back corner of the baseball-practice pasture, hidden for the most part by a scraggly mess of stunted firs and prickly blackberry bushes.

Their expressions ran a broad gamut, from shock and incredulousness to straight-out disgust. Eyes widened from time to time, and jaws were going up and down as if they were chewing big wads of bubble gum.

"I cain't believe that," Hammet gasped.

"I don't even wanna look."

"I may just puke. Look at that calf slobber all over them."

"That one's homely enough to crack a mirror, fer chrissake. Why'd anyone want to put whipped cream there?"

Hammet bravely turned the page.

10

Ruby Bee's was sparsely populated, which was fine with me. I waved to a couple of people in the front booth, then stopped in the middle of the dance floor as I caught sight of the occupant in the last booth, way back in the corner where it was almost too dark to read the menu. Jim Bob was slumped down so far, his head was barely even with the back of the booth, and he appeared to be having a dispirited conversation with three beer pitchers and a bowl of pretzels.

As far as I could tell, he was doing all the talking, but you never know.

Ruby Bee hissed at me to get myself over to the bar. I sat on a stool beside Estelle, who was hunched over a glass of sherry and snorting under her breath.

"Where have you been?" Ruby Bee snapped.

"I'm surprised you don't know every single place I've set foot in today," I said. "What's the matter—grapevine let you down? What a shame."

"Don't get prissy with me, Miss Mute Mouth. You sailed out of here a good seven hours ago . . . and you didn't have the decency to warn me you wouldn't be back until late. Then you had the audacity to order me to go watch those youngsters beat each other up. Then you hung up on me just like I was trying to sell you vinyl siding."

"All true." I nudged Estelle. "Have fun at baseball practice?"

She took a deep drink of sherry, and in a voice more suited to a heavy smoker on a respirator, said, "I think you're right about them not being ready to play on Thursday." She pulled back her cuff to show me a red, crescent-shaped indentation. "You see that? Teeth marks. All I was doing was trying to pull them apart, and now I most likely need a tetanus shot. My legs look like I was stomping purple grapes to make wine."

I was about to show her the bruises on my shins when something struck me. I'll readily admit I don't have a great memory and the cliché about out of sight and so on has some personal applications. While living in Manhattan (the cat-burglar capital of the world), I'd dialed 911 once when I'd heard someone trying to get into my apartment, but at the last second remembered I was married and what's his face not only lived there but also had a key. During my senior year in high school, I dropped Ruby Bee off for a doctor's appointment in Farberville, bought a fashion magazine at the drugstore, and was home reading on the sofa when I realized something was amiss(-ing). I never attempt to introduce anyone to anyone. I check myself in the mirror when leaving, not out of vanity but out of concern I might have forgotten to button my shirt or put on my badge.

"I drove by the field," I said carefully, "to make sure you two were there. I told you to expect seven players, but I saw only six. Where was Hammet?"

Ruby Bee fluttered her hand. "He . . . he had other things to do, I guess. Maybe he got busy."

"What other things?"

Estelle snorted. "Other things. He had other things to do, that's all."

"He left under his own steam," Ruby Bee added. "He was right upset about you abandoning him, if you must know."

"Is he at my apartment?" I asked.

"Why don't you call and find out for yourself." She flounced away to a safe distance, muttering something about someone's inability to keep track of her own houseguests.

I went over to the pay telephone and called, but there was no answer. My palms were wet as I replaced the receiver, and my legs weren't at their best as I went back to the bar. "Listen, you two, I want to know where Hammet is. We've got a maniac running around town;

for all I know, Hammet got hold of a bad sponge cake
and is retching his guts out in a ditch somewhere, or even
worse. Someone's playing hardball, and I'm not talking
about kids in a cow pasture."

Ruby Bee's defiant expression slipped. "Is it true what
I heard about Buzz Milvin's mother-in-law?"

"Heard what from whom?" I said.

She fiddled with her apron for a minute, shooting desperate little glances at Estelle, who managed not to
notice. "Well, I just happened to call over to the sheriff's
office, hoping I might find out where you were, and
LaBelle may have said something about the ambulance
and all. When I happened to call back later in case she'd
heard from you, she told me Buzz and Martin were at
the hospital and poor Mrs. Smew was headed for the
morgue."

I poked Estelle's arm. "Okay, let's get all the gossip
out in the open. What did you say Perkins's eldest said
Mrs. Jim Bob said—or something like that, anyway? Go
ahead, spit it out. I'm as ready as I'll ever be."

"Mrs. Jim Bob took a message for Jim Bob from some
bank in Little Rock or Hot Springs; Perkins's eldest
wasn't real sure which. I don't know why she'd get the
two mixed up. They don't sound the least bit alike, you
know. If it was Springdale or Springfield, I could see
why—"

"It doesn't matter," I cut in. "Mrs. Jim Bob took a
message from a bank. Did he bounce a check?"

"No, but after she hung up, Mrs. Jim Bob said a four-
letter word, slammed down the pencil, and went upstairs,
sizzling like a slice of bacon on the grill. Perkins's eldest
couldn't help but be curious, so when the coast was clear,
she took a peek at the pad of paper by the telephone."

"And?"

"And Mrs. Jim Bob had written the number twenty
thousand and there was a dollar sign in front of it."
Estelle pulled me closer, and with a narrow look at the
back booth, she whispered, "The other thing she wrote
was the word *Thursday,* and it was underlined three
times! Do you want to know what I think?"

I shook my head and went to the back booth, where

Jim Bob was still mumbling away to his inanimate and therefore captive audience. "I have a question," I said as I sat down across from him.

"Get yourself an encyclopedia. Get a whole damn set of 'em."

His breath smelled so bad that I was surprised I couldn't see it. I exhaled vigorously and said, "The answer won't be in an encyclopedia. Are you and Petrel supposed to close some kind of loan Thursday—something to do with the financing for the supermarket, for instance?"

"Goddamn permanent financing, but none of your goddamn business." He hiccuped loudly and gave me what he probably thought was a sneer, although gravity was doing strange things to one of his eyelids and his lower lip.

"And you're supposed to come up with twenty thousand dollars?"

"That ain't the half of it." He hiccuped again. "Mebbe it is. Yeah, the half of it."

"More than twenty thousand? Forty thousand, for instance?"

"Thought you had questions, Chief. Sounds like you got answers, so why don't you remove your butt from the seat and mosey back to the bar?"

"But I do have a question: Is the closing at noon?"

"How the fuck do I know," he said petulantly. After a couple of near-misses, he got hold of a pitcher and filled his glass with what was apt to be flat, tepid beer. "Go ask Petrel; he's the big-shot businessman—except when the shit's in the fan and we can't stay open long enough to play a tune on the cash register, much less make any money." His eyes turned watery and he slid into good old-fashioned maudlin drunkenness. "Petrel really screwed me. He screwed me to the wall and kept on goin'."

I wasn't accustomed to hearing Jim Bob's confidences, but I was game. "How'd he do that?"

"He tol' me we was set just right on the loan, that we'd waltz right in, scribble our names, and be done with it. Then, as sure as I'm sitting here getting stewed to the gills, he ups and says we got to pay points."

"Hmmm," I said, shaking my head at the treachery. "I can't believe he'd do that to you. Imagine him saying you had to pay points."

"Points and payments and payroll. Piss on it. God-damn toad sucker ought to be shot."

"Hmmm," I said again, determined to remain sympathetic until I figured out what we were talking about. "What happens if you can't pay the points, Jim Bob?"

He gave me an exasperated look. "Well, whatta ya think happens, fer chrissake? I win an all-expenses-paid trip to fuckin' China. All the rice I can eat. A little squinty gal to tiptoe on my back every night."

I refilled his glass and tried to sort out his remarks from the hyperbole. "If you can't come up with your share of the points, can Petrel force you out of the partnership?"

"Why doncha ask him—if you can find him?" He snickered for a moment, then went blank and gradually slithered out of view, as if he was being sucked into a pit of quicksand.

I went back to the bar, wishing I could ask Lamont Petrel a whole lot of things. I hadn't done a blessed thing about a decent meal, but I had some more pressing problems to deal with, such as mass poisonings and a possible murder. A lost houseguest. A lengthy list of witnesses to be interviewed. An ulcer if I didn't watch it.

Ruby Bee came out of the kitchen with a small bag. "I made you a cheeseburger," she said. "And Joyce Lambertino called a minute ago and said Hammet was in the backyard with Saralee and Lissie Milvin. She'll send him home directly, she said."

"Thanks," I said as I took the bag. "You don't happen to have a bottle of syrup of ipecac handy, do you? Considering the day, I'm liable to get a bout of heartburn tonight."

"I don't have whatever you said, but I got plenty of milk of magnesia and that's always been good enough for me."

I looked at Estelle. "You have any ipecac at home?"

"Never heard of it," she said without missing a beat. "I favor those powders you mix that taste like fruit drinks. I'll be glad to run home and get you a grape or cherry flavor if you want."

No, it wasn't nice. It was sneaky. But I was convinced neither of them knew what syrup of ipecac was and therefore hadn't sabotaged the tamale sauce or the sponge cakes. On that bright note, I said good night, detoured past the back booth to listen to Jim Bob's snuffly snore, and walked up the highway to the PD.

My travel book was in the top drawer, and I managed to eat my cheeseburger in a quaint café on the Left Bank, gazing at Notre Dame, sipping inky espresso, and allowing myself to be a pedestrian in the human race, if only for a few minutes.

I then bid adieu and took out a notebook. Deputy Vernon had given me a list of all the people who'd come by the SuperSaver when it had reopened the previous day. We'd agreed the list was likely to be incomplete, but business had been desultory and the checkers had not been checking their little brains out as they'd done at the one-hour grand opening. All the reports of tampered products had arisen from items purchased Tuesday morning, but those who'd been there Monday evening needed to be questioned.

I drew lines through all the names of subsequent victims, although I didn't erase them. I crossed off Kevin and Dahlia, Buzz and Lillith Smew, Mrs. Jim Bob, Raz Buchanon (because I couldn't produce a motive, no matter how farfetched), Darla Jean McIlhaney (same problem), and all employees.

This left a more manageable list. Ivy Sattering had sniffed around the produce section and left without buying anything. Ruby Bee Hanks had bought a box of Ant B-Gone, accompanied by the always-opinionated Estelle Oppers, who'd taken the opportunity to comment that the picnic pavilion stank worse than a buzzard's roost. Mandozes had demanded to know when the deli would reopen and had become agitated when no one seemed to know. There were a couple of unfamiliar names, and several vague descriptions along the lines of "man in Pro

Bass cap," "woman wanting fancy toothpicks," and "pregnant lady with screaming baby."

I was staring at the list as the door opened and Hammet came into the PD.

"Howdy," he mumbled as he sat down across from my desk.

"I heard you missed baseball practice. What've you been up to?"

"Nuthin' much. Can I play with the radar gun?"

I looked more closely at him. "Your knees are caked with mud, Hammet. What have you been up to?"

"Nuthin', I said. Saralee and Lissie and me played tag, and Saralee knocked me down and sat on me and wouldn't lemme up till I said she was prettier'n a pink flower on a store-bought cake. She's got to be the dumbest girl that ever was born. Fractious, too. Somebody oughta sit on her head, and in a hog waller."

"She's not a delicate little debutante," I said mildly. "Did Lissie tell you what happened at her house and why she's staying at the Lambertinos'?"

He gave me a funny look, then got up and wandered into the back room. "Yeah, she told me and Saralee some stuff, but we had to swear we wouldn't tell anybody."

"I was there," I said to the empty doorway. "It won't be a secret for long, not with the tongues waggling all evening."

"I swore I wouldn't go spouting off about what all she told us 'cause of it being a secret. We had to spit in her hand and everything. Does this stupid-lookin' thing work?"

I had no idea what he was looking at, but I went for the percentage answer. "Probably not. Tell you what, Hammet, let's pick up Lissie and drive to the hospital in Farberville. Martin's out of intensive care, and I need to talk to him. You two can say hi and then go to the cafeteria for a soda."

"Naw, I think I'll go read or sumpun." He still had the funny look on his face as he came back into the front room, but it had such overtones of stubbornness that I decided not to press my invitation.

I called Joyce, who had a quick talk with Lissie and reported back that she seemed tuckered out something awful and needed to get to bed early. It wasn't sporting, but I asked if Larry Joe had said anything about baseball practice.

"He's pleased with the team," Joyce said. "Half the boys can knock the ball over the back fence, and one of 'em has a curveball good enough for the minors. Larry Joe says you can't even see the kid's fastball; it goes by like greased lightning."

"That's great," I said with a wince, and hung up before I heard about the scouts coming to town to recruit the whiz kid. I dropped Hammet off at the bottom of the stairs to my apartment, told him I'd be back within an hour or so, and headed for Farberville.

At the front desk at the hospital, I asked about Buzz's condition and was told he was stable. I went to the pediatric wing and was told that Martin was asleep and could not be disturbed unless I had a court order and a battalion to back it up. Having neither, I meekly inquired about official visiting hours, went back to my car, and drove out of the parking lot.

As I headed out of Farberville, I realized I could save myself a trip the next day. Jim Bob's potential checker lived across from the airport, and I was in the landing pattern, so to speak.

The parking area was a weedy expanse of gravel, with a few dented cars and a pickup truck set on concrete blocks. A large metal dumpster was filled to overflowing; the smell of rotting garbage and stale whiskey competed with the fumes from heavy traffic on the highway. The two-story building was in need of paint, new railings, screens, and trash disposal—or perhaps demolition. There were half a dozen units on each story, some with battered mailboxes beside the door and others without. Most of the tenants who'd settled for the Airport Arms Apartments had little hope of mail, not even the sort addressed to Occupant.

I went up the creaking stairs and down the balcony to

the last unit. If the doorbell worked, I couldn't hear it, so I knocked on the door.

"Yeah, what?" a female voice called.

"I'm a police officer, and I'd like to have a word with you," I answered in polite professional lingo.

"Bugger off. I'm washing my hair."

"In the living room? Look, I'll have to ask you a few questions sooner or later, and it will save us both time if we do it now. If I have to come back, I'll have time to think of a lot more questions, ma'am." Not true, of course. Jim Bob's whereabouts after he'd left the Super-Saver the previous evening were of no importance (except to Mrs. Jim Bob—but not necessarily), and I really wasn't sure why I was standing in front of a blistered apartment door when I could be drinking espresso and gazing at Notre Dame. "Let's just get this over with," I added.

The door opened to a slit, and a heavily lined eye regarded me. "Yeah, go ahead."

"Are you Cherri Lucinda Crate?"

"I ain't Mrs. Santa Claus. She lives up north somewheres."

"Could I step inside, Ms. Crate? I don't want to disturb your neighbors."

"They ain't the kind to be easily disturbed. What do you want to know?"

I felt rather silly conversing with a disembodied eyeball, but I was certain I wasn't going to be invited in for tea and cookies. "Could you please describe what you did last night from approximately eleven o'clock on?"

"You're kidding, ain't you?" she said, laughing. "You planning to write a porn novel or something?"

"That's not what I meant," I said coolly, although I was grateful for the darkness hiding my face. I rephrased the question. "Did you have a visitor last night? If so, what was his name and how long did he remain here?"

"I didn't see a living soul last night. I watched a movie and did my nails. See?" The door opened wide enough for a hand to slink out. The bright red talons would have shamed an eagle.

"A witness in a murder investigation told me he came here last night. Are you denying his story?"

"Whose story?"

"Listen, Ms. Crate, as much as I'd like to stand here half the night and exchange witticisms with you, I've got other things to do. Either answer my questions or be prepared to file your nails in a nasty little cell."

The eye blinked several times. Finally, the door opened and the woman came outside, closing the door behind her. She wore a flimsy white peignoir that was stained around the collar and had seen better nights. On the other hand, her body was voluptuous enough to distract all but the keenest observers. Her heavy-handed makeup extended to red lipstick, pink blusher, and penciled eyebrows that gave her a faintly startled look. Her hair was hidden by a terry-cloth turban that reminded me of some of Estelle's more fanciful styles.

"Can we get on with it?" she demanded.

"I'd love to get on with it. Tell me about last night and I'll let you get back to washing your hair."

She patted the turban and shrugged, sending ripples all the way down to the bottom hem. "Well, I was just getting ready to wash it when you interrupted me. I like had the shower on and was getting the shampoo out of the cabinet. Whatta ya want to know, honey?"

"Did you have a visitor last night?"

"No. As sure as a goose goes barefoot, I was here by my lonesome all night." She looked down at her bare feet and giggled. "As sure as we all go barefoot, I guess."

"Jim Bob Buchanon didn't come here sometime before midnight?" I asked, wishing the light were better so I could observe her reactions more accurately.

"Jim Bob? I haven't seen him in a coon's age. How's he doing, by the way? Still strutting around like a banty rooster?"

"Not at the moment," I said. "But you're willing to swear under oath that he wasn't here, right?"

She held up two fingers in a mock scout salute. "Jim Bob didn't show his little bulldog face last night. I watched a movie, did my nails, and went to bed like a good girl. By that, I mean all by myself. I read the Bible, said my prayers, and went to sleep dreaming about a gold Le Baron convertible."

Her voice was a sugary drawl, and she was doing her best to be an ingenuous ingenue doing her damnedest to help the police. I nodded and waited until the deafening roar of an airplane taking off abated. "But what about your remark earlier about me doing research for a porn novel? Your version of last night's hardly hot copy, Ms. Crate. It won't even sell at Times Square."

"Just a little joke, honey. I always like to kid with the cops." She wiggled her fingers at me and went inside. The lock clicked into place.

I went down to my car, but as I glanced up, I saw a curtain in her window fall back and a shadow move away. I drove back to Maggody on automatic pilot, trying to decide which of the two had lied. Jim Bob had crawled way out on the limb—and had encountered a polecat. He must have figured I'd check with Cherri Lucinda, if only to have it to dangle over him during town council budget sessions. It was a damn odd lie, if indeed it was a lie. But why would she lie about it?

I'd made no progress as I parked behind the antique store and went upstairs. As I reached for the door, I heard a muted gasp and a scuffling noise, but when I got inside, Hammet was sitting contentedly in front of the television. The fact that the screen was blank was a bit suspicious.

"I'm back," I said lamely.

"Did you visit with Lissie's brother?"

"No, he was asleep and the nurse wasn't about to allow me to wake him. Have you had supper?"

"Miz Lambertino gave us some stuff. Tuna fish all yucked up with peas and goop." He yawned, reached for the button on the television, and realized his mistake. "Guess I dun already turned it off. I'm so worn out, I must've been sitting here like I was deaf and dumb and too slow to whistle."

I'd had my fill of lies for the day. "No, you were doing something else when you heard me outside. What, Hammet?"

"Jest sittin' on my hindquarters. I weren't doin'

nuthin', nuthin' at all. How come you're all the time
trying to make me say things and saying I tell you lies,
'cause I don't tell no one lies—except for the school-
marm, but she's fat as a sow and a hunnert times
stupider."

"Calm down," I said, bewildered. "I didn't say anything about lies. Let's go to bed, shall we?"

He slunk into the bathroom and slammed the door. I
had no idea what was wrong with him, but he hadn't
been off the mountain all that long. His mother had been
the orneriest mountain woman to ever make moonshine
and turn tricks in the Ozarks. For the first ten years of
his life, Hammet had never seen a book, watched television, or uttered a sentence that could be repeated in
church. His hair had been cut with a pocketknife. His
clothing had come from cardboard boxes left at the edge
of the yard by timid do-gooders from charitable organiza-
tions. He'd shared a straw pallet with his siblings and
fought with them over food. Wolf cubs probably had easier lives.

"You've come a long way, baby," I said to the closed
door.

Brother Verber was crawling around under the mobile
home when he saw feet. In that the feet were shod in
sensible heels and walked with a missionary's determina-
tion, he was pretty sure he knew what all there was ankle
upward. Rather than emerge to greet his caller, he scuttled into the shadows.

Mrs. Jim Bob rapped on the front door. "Brother
Verber, it's Sister Barbara. Are you in there? I got something to discuss with you."

He shrunk farther into the shadows, where it was
damper but darker and therefore muddier but safer. He
felt as if the shower'd turned icy cold and he was buck
naked in the spray. There wasn't any way she could
know, he told himself. There wasn't any way anybody
could know, not even Kevin and Dahlia, who'd looked
a little confused when he'd ordered them to go pray for
their forgiveness—somewhere else.

Her knuckles hit the door with such insistence, he

could feel the mobile home vibrating. "Brother Verber?" she repeated stridently. "Brother Verber . . . ?"

He put his knees right up to his chin and closed his eyes. He didn't bother to ask for divine guidance.

The next morning, I drove to Dahlia's house. She was sitting on the porch, a glass of tea and a box of cookies nearby, but her hands were folded in her lap and her eyes were vacant.

"I need to ask you a few questions," I said as I opened the gate and went up the sidewalk.

"Okay," she murmured without looking up.

I sat on the edge of the porch and took out a notebook and pencil. "Let's start with the preparations for the grand opening on Saturday. When did you"—I consulted my list—"Erma Jean, and Feebie start fixing the food that was later passed out as free samples?"

"The night before. We went in at five and cooked till ten or so. There was some stuff that had to be fixed the next morning, like the ham rolls and cheese squares. That Petrel fellow was real strict about when we was to do what."

"What about the tamales?"

"I didn't do the tamales," she said dully. She took a cookie from the box, studied it for a moment, then put it in her mouth and chewed pensively. "I fried chicken wings until I was ready to scream. That's what I did. Everyone said they was real tasty. Did you try one?"

"I'm afraid I missed those. Who did the tamales? Erma Jean or Feebie?"

"I think it was Erma Jean. She opened the cans, cut them into pieces, and put them out nice and neat in a roasting pan. The sauce was simmering on the stove. The first thing next morning, she dumped it on the tamales and put the pan in the oven to heat up."

"So the tamale sauce was in the refrigerator all night?"

"She didn't take it home with her, if that's what you're asking."

"Did anyone come into the kitchen the next morning?"

"Nobody." This time Dahlia managed to transport

three cookies to her mouth. Once she'd dealt with them, she said, "Can I ask you something, Arly?"

"Sure," I said, hoping it was relevant to the case but not optimistic.

"Is it blackmail when you tell someone they have to do something or you'll make them regret they was ever born?"

I perked up. "It could be, Dahlia. You'll have to tell me more details before I can be sure."

She sighed morosely and dipped back in the box. "I don't reckon I can. It's mighty personal, if you know what I mean."

"But I don't know what you mean," I said, trying not to sound too eager. If someone had coerced her into dumping ipecac in the tamale sauce, I didn't want to alarm her into silence. "If you'll give me a hint, I'll try to help you. Blackmail is illegal. If you've been forced to do something out of fear, then it's not really your responsibility. You're a victim."

"I am?" Her lips formed a tight circle and began to pucker in and out as she thought. Both cheeks and several of her chins inflated until I was worried about an explosion. "You're saying I'm a victim, right? I don't have to pay any mind to their threats? You can put them in jail?"

"Who're we talking about?"

"I can't say just now," she said, relieved enough to take a handful of cookies.

"Does this have anything to do with the problems at the SuperSaver?" I persisted. "If it does, you've got to tell me, Dahlia. You heard about Lillith Smew, didn't you? What may have started as a prank has taken a serious turn, and whoever's behind it has to be stopped."

All this sincerity wafted right over her head. She shook her head (chins and all) and said, "I can't say no more."

I lacked the physical superiority to shake it out of her, and I'd lived in Maggody long enough to learn the futility of arguing with certain people. There are some horses you can't even lead to water. "Let's go on to Monday evening," I said. "You went by the store to talk to Kevin. Did you see anyone else?"

"I saw Buzz Milvin. He came to the back of the store and was right unfriendly. He told me to leave, so I did."

She was trying to sound haughty, but it didn't ring quite true. Watching her closely, I said, "Right away?"

Dahlia picked up the box of cookies, squeezed it so hard that I could hear crumbling inside it, then put it down and let out another sigh. "I may have detoured to the break room for a few minutes. Kevin and I had things to discuss."

"Wedding plans?"

"Not hardly."

There was something wrong with the story, but I couldn't quite get hold of it. Dahlia's veiled remarks about blackmailers—"them"—should have made some sense, should have done something besides confuse me all the more. But if her mind moved, then it did so in deeply mysterious ways and she wasn't about to offer me a map. I thanked her for her invaluable assistance and drove back to the PD to make a few notes.

"Now this is just between you and me," Barbie Buteo said over the telephone to Joyce Lambertino, who was stirring eggs with one hand, buttering toast with the other, and keeping an eye on Larry Junior, who was feeding the baby pieces of cereal.

Holding the receiver with her shoulder wasn't making life any easier for Joyce, but Barbie had called long distance and it wouldn't be polite not to listen. "What's between you and me?" she said, doing her best to sound intrigued.

"You got to promise not to tell another soul. This was told to me in the strictest confidence—and it could cost someone her job."

"Then don't tell me." Joyce tossed pieces of toast to Saralee and Traci, dumped milk on Lissie's cereal, and snatched up Larry Junior's glass of orange juice just as the baby lunged. "Maybe I ought to call you back," she added.

"It's about that Petrel fellow. I just wanted to warn you to lock all your doors and windows, Joyce. I know

Larry Joe's gone all day, and I hate to think you and the children would be at the mercy of a madman."

The glass slipped out of Joyce's hand and splattered the floor in a yellow-orange explosion that delighted the spectators. "Mommie did a boo-boo," Larry Junior cackled. Saralee, Lissie, and Traci giggled, and the baby threw a handful of Cheerios in the air. Everyone thought it was festive, except for Joyce, who'd turned rigid and was gulping like crazy.

She snapped at Larry Junior to clean up the mess, then took the telephone and moved around to the far side of the refrigerator. "What on earth are you talking about, Barbie?" she whispered. "Petrel is Jim Bob's partner, isn't he?"

"I wouldn't know about that," Barbie said. "I'm only telling you this for your own good, Joyce, 'cause we were best friends in high school and I'm worried about you. The police arrested him for raping a bunch of girls, but he escaped from their clutches and is hiding in Maggody somewhere, waiting for a chance to brutalize some innocent girl or housewife. That kind don't stop until someone puts a bullet through their hearts—if they have hearts, anyway. He's an animal, a crazed wild animal out there watching and waiting."

Joyce looked out the kitchen window at the tire swing, the sandbox with its collection of plastic trucks, buckets, and shovels, Larry Junior's deflated basketball, and the usual crap she saw every day through that same window. A robin hopped across the yard and a squirrel was hanging from the bird feeder. Their dog, a scrawny tan mutt with a fondness for plastic trucks, lay on his side in the sun. It looked pretty normal, and it was hard to think of a rapist squatting behind the forsythia bushes.

"He is?" she finally said about the time Barbie was starting to get alarmed.

11

When I got to the PD, I called Harve to see if he'd heard anything from the state lab on the second and third incidents of poisoning. He hadn't, but the lab moved exceedingly slowly and neither of us bothered to feign any surprise.

"You working on the list of witnesses?" he asked.

I told him what Cherri Lucinda Crate had said the previous night on the balcony of the Airport Arms Apartments. "It's screwy," I added. "I can't think of any reason either of them would bother to lie about it."

"Folks lie all the time," he said succinctly.

"I know they do," I said, sighing, "but usually for some perceptible motive. Jim Bob's whereabouts at eleven o'clock Monday night aren't relevant—or at least I don't think they are. What may or may not have happened in her apartment is only of prurient interest."

"Guess you better run it by him again, tell him what the gal said and ask him what all he's got to say. Hold on a minute, Arly, I got to see a man about a horse."

I leaned back in my chair and propped my feet on the desk. If the V formed by my feet was the gizmo at the end of a barrel, I'd have a clean shot at my visitor's seat across the room. I twitched my feet for a minute, frowning, then let it slide and picked up the notes I'd written after talking to Dahlia. Almost all the scribbles had question marks at the end, and when Harve came back on the line, I went over them with him.

"So the sauce could have been spiked Friday night or Saturday morning," I said. "But according to Jim Bob's statement, the SuperSaver was uninhabited that night because there wasn't any cash in the registers. Dahlia and the other two cooks showed up early in the morning and were in the kitchen until the tamales were taken out to the pavilion."

"Which puts us right back where we were. Unless you want to pin it on the cooks or a cheerleader, one of the folks in the area went over to the table and dumped ipecac on the tamales. And unless we got a copycat, that same person got nastier and nastier till the Smew woman died."

"Damn it, I wish we knew what was in that coconut cake," I said. "At some point Monday evening or during the night, someone must have set the tampered cakes out where they'd be the easiest to pick up."

"Weren't many folks there during the night," Harve pointed out. "You'd better look harder at those who came by before the SuperSaver closed and had reasons to resent it."

Like Ruby Bee. "Wait a minute," I said, getting so excited that my feet nearly slid off the desk. "According to Jim Bob, the regular schedule calls for Buzz Milvin to come in at nine, total the register tapes, and count the money. Jim Bob verifies it and takes the money to the night depository in Starley City. But something changed Monday night, and Jim Bob sent Buzz with the money and then went to Cherri Lucinda's apartment or not, depending on whose story you believe."

"So the store was empty for what—about an hour?"

"Not exactly," I said slowly, "but I think it's time for a long talk with Kevin Buchanon. Dahlia hinted at dark secrets. Kevin will spill the beans if I have to handcuff him and hoist him into the sweet gum tree in his backyard."

Harve chuckled and wished me luck.

I called the hospital and learned that Buzz was out of immediate danger but still hooked up to various support systems and unable to have visitors. Martin Milvin was fully conscious and would be released after twenty-four more hours of observation. I wanted to pass along the news to Lissie, but Joyce's line was busy and I was primed to tackle Kevin Buchanon.

He was sitting on the porch swing, looking as distracted as Dahlia had earlier, although he wasn't shoveling cookies into his mouth. "How's it going?" he asked as I came onto the porch.

"Not well," I said. "You've heard that Buzz and Martin Milvin were poisoned and Lillith Smew may have been murdered?"

"Yeah, my ma heard something from somebody last night when she was swapping recipes. Buzz is a pretty good ol' guy for the most part, and I feel real bad for all of them."

I gave him an icy look. "Then maybe you'll cooperate? I don't know what you and Dahlia have been up to, but I want to hear the truth—and I want to hear it now."

His face turned splotchy and he began to gulp loudly. He grabbed the arm of the swing, staring at me as if I'd announced I'd come to arrest him for murder and execute him on the spot.

"Calm down," I said, retreating to the edge of the porch and hastily assessing my chances if I stepped back into the azaleas. "I just want to know what happened Monday night, that's all."

"That's all?"

I nodded. "That's all, Kevin—unless you're in the mood to confess to serial murders or unsafe sex."

Apparently I'd said something else wrong. A gurgling noise came from his throat, as if it had been slashed. "You're one of them," he gasped, pointing a trembling finger at me. "I didn't think you was like them, but now I know. All you folks do is gossip and tell tales and turn innocent stories into big fat lies!" He covered his face with his hands and moaned, his shoulders jerking and his feet pounding on the porch in an unsteady cadence.

Eilene came to the screened door. "Morning, Arly. What on earth's the matter with Kevin?"

"I don't know," I murmured to her. "I made a small joke, not very funny, and he suddenly . . . went to pieces and . . . I don't know what to tell you, Eilene. I didn't mean to upset him."

She came out onto the porch and rapped him on the head. "Stop this nonsense at once, young man. Do you want someone walking by to hear you carrying on like this? After what happened last week, I'd like to think you'd be a little more worried about making a spectacle of yourself."

Kevin moaned loudly. Anyone walking by would be more likely to wonder if the family had adopted a terminally ill coyote.

"Did something happen last week?" I asked. I couldn't see how it related to my investigation, but the intensity of Kevin's reaction was curious.

Eilene gave me a bright smile, but she sounded embarrassed as she said, "Just a little problem between Kevin and his fiancée. Kevin's pa had a word with him in the woodshed afterward, and I don't believe there'll be any more of that."

"Good," I said vaguely. I told Eilene to tell Kevin I'd come by later when he was more in the mood to discuss Monday night, then went to my car and pulled out into Finger Lane.

And saw the brick pillars on either side of Hizzoner's driveway, a *J* and a *B*, both beckoning to me. If I couldn't get anything out of Kevin—except a primitive display of histrionics—then it might be a good time to have a run at Hizzoner . . . in his own home and, with any luck, his own wife at his side.

The investigation hadn't progressed, but I discovered I was in a much better mood as I drove up the winding road to the pretentious redbrick house on top of the hill.

I rang the doorbell several times. I was about to leave when Hizzoner opened the door, said, "Wait, I'm on the telephone long distance," and slammed the door.

I walked up and down the porch until he returned five minutes later. "I've got some questions," I said, wondering if he remembered our conversation the previous night at the bar and grill.

"So do I," he said. "I wish to hell you'd tell me where Lamont Petrel is. If I don't get forty grand to the wholesaler by tomorrow, he'll slap a lien on the store and we won't be able to close the loan. Then the folks with the construction loan'll get antsy, and gawd only knows what they'll do. I can come up with my share, but I sure as hell can't cover the whole ball of wax. I'm having to make payroll out of my pocket as it is, because the SuperSaver gets closed down every time I turn around to piss downwind."

He was upset, but not especially at me, which was a refreshing change. I almost felt a twinge of guilt as I said, "My questions have to do with your purported visit to Cherri Lucinda Crate Monday night at eleven."

He grabbed my arm and pulled me off the porch and away from the house. "What's purported about it?" he said in a low voice, keeping an eye on the front door.

"I questioned her last night, and she said she was alone Monday night, doing her nails and watching a movie. She said she hadn't seen you in a long time, and even asked how you were doing."

"That little bitch! She knows damn well I was there. Are you sure you questioned the right person?"

"Airport Arms Apartments, top floor on the end," I said, shrugging. "She said she was Crate, but I didn't demand to see her driver's license."

"Blond hair and two-inch fingernails?"

"She had a towel on her head, so I didn't see her hair. I did see the fingernails, though. They were rather striking."

"That's her." Jim Bob began to pace between the shrubs, his brow wrinkled and his mouth twisted to one side. "And she said she hadn't seen me anytime lately, did she? I've got a hundred witnesses who could say different. Jesus H. Christ, I dunno what the hell's going on. Maybe I'm going crazy, what with the bank breathing down my neck like a slobbery dog, and the wholesaler whining, and Petrel off somewhere working on his tan or screwing some waitress while I get all the shit."

"You have no idea where he is?"

"If I knew where he was, I wouldn't be neck-deep in shit! I'd be dragging him back so we get this straightened out." He banged his fist against his palm, no doubt wishing Petrel's face was available.

"The state police will find him eventually," I said. "But I have to know what happened Monday night. Why did you send Buzz to make the deposit?"

"What the fuck difference does it . . ." He stopped

pacing and looked down at the lawn for a moment, his eyes narrowed with thought. "Petrel's car still parked at the Flamingo Motel?"

"As far as I know." I waited for him to continue, but he gave me a studiously flat look and I couldn't for the life of me guess what he was up to. "Does that tell you something?" I said at last.

"Yeah. He didn't drive it away. Listen, I got better things to do than stand here answering a bunch of dumb questions. I sent Milvin to Starley City 'cause it was too damn much trouble to go myself. I don't know why Cherri Lucinda said I wasn't there, but it's not a big deal one way or the other. I didn't stick pins in the cupcakes. Run along and do something useful, Chief. Peel dead animals off the highway or bust one of the kids for smoking pot. Better yet, see if you can teach that runty team of yours how to play baseball. The game's still on, ain't it?"

He strutted across the porch and went into the house. I'd had such impressive success with my three witnesses that I knew absolutely nothing I hadn't known before, except that Dahlia and Kevin had had a spat, Jim Bob was in financial trouble if Petrel stayed gone, and the game was still scheduled for Thursday afternoon.

Heather Riley gaped at Darla Jean, her jaw going up and down as if she was chewing taffy. "Say that again," she said in a stunned voice.

"Now I'm only trying to talk to you for your own good, Heather, 'cause it's not healthy to keep stuff like that bottled up inside you. It'll give you ulcers, and your grades will go down and you'll get kicked off the pom-pom squad."

"Just repeat what you said," Heather commanded.

"I heard Elsie McMay tell my ma about what that horrible man did to you," Darla Jean said, worried that she ought not to have brought up the subject if Heather didn't want to talk about it, after all. But she had, so she plunged ahead and explained to Heather about hearing that she'd been raped by Lamont Petrel and run down by a truck and been so traumatized that she hadn't told anybody.

Heather hugged herself as she listened to the story, and when Darla Jean ran down, she merely said, "So I'm traumatized, huh?"

"It's most likely caused amnesia. That's my opinion, 'cause I saw a show on television where the exact same thing happened. Staci said she thought maybe you just wanted to spare Beau Swiggins from having to beat the guy up, but Rene and Debbi and Melanie all agreed that was stupid, because Beau's bound to find out sooner or later."

"Beau doesn't know?"

"Of course not, Heather! You think we'd talk about you behind your back?"

"Is he still dating that Janine from Emmet with the big boobs and fat ankles?"

"Yeah, but Billy Dick said he asked if you've dated anybody since you two broke up. I'm not supposed to tell you this, but Billy Dick said Beau said he'd beat the shit out of anybody that even asked you out."

"Is Janine putting out for him?" Heather asked. When Darla Jean nodded, she said, "All the way?"

"But I think he still loves you. He's just going with Janine to get back at you for not being a cheerleader for the SuperSavers. Billy Dick shared the beer with him, but it wasn't the same, I guess."

"I guess not," Heather said distractedly. The lurid story had upset her initially, along with the knowledge that every last soul in town—except for Beau, apparently—had been discussing it nonstop. Somehow Jim Bob putting his hand on her knee had now escalated into some guy named Petrel raping her on the office floor and leaving her traumatized to the point of amnesia.

She considered the possibility that she had been raped and then blocked it out, but decided that was nonsense because she remembered every last second of the tacky interview. She'd stomped out of the office and was stomping home when she ran into Miss Estes, who'd noticed Heather's red cheeks and mentioned the risk of heatstroke and so had ended up hearing about Jim Bob.

And Beau was doing it with Janine, who'd do it with her pa and all her uncles if they asked nicely. It wasn't Beau's fault he was going with a slut who probably flopped down on her back, spread her knees, and told him it was open house.

He'd been pissed when she refused to be a cheerleader, and he'd even said she was just a prude and a cockteaser who wouldn't prove that she loved him by taking a blanket to a particular place beside Boone Creek where a lot of love was proved on a nightly basis and quite a bit more on weekends.

But how was he going to feel when he found out she had been raped and was currently amnesiated? Awful. He'd feel downright awful and be sorry and beg her to go steady again.

"Are you okay?" Darla Jean asked. "You have the funniest look on your face. Are you beginning to remember?"

Heather massaged her temples and, without a whole lot of effort, assumed a bewildered expression. "I think I am, but just bits and pieces. It's kinda like a puzzle with a whole lot of pieces missing. The trauma's still there, just like you said, but I'm in a foggy tunnel and it's dark and I can't quite make out anything."

Darla Jean was impressed. "That's spooky, ain't it? Can you remember what he did when he threw you down on the floor? Did you cry or kick him? Did it . . . hurt when he . . . did it?"

"It hurt something terrible. It was the worst thing in my entire life, and I'm just going to have to face it before I develop ulcers." She looked down at her bedspread while she did some more remembering. "I struggled with all my might. I yelled and kicked, but he held my wrists in one hand while he ripped off my clothes with the other."

"Oh, my gawd," Darla Jean said. She sat down next to Heather and patted her knee. "Then what happened?"

"I cried out for Beau," she said simply. "It was silly, of course, 'cause there weren't no way he could hear me and come save me from being brutalized by that monster."

"He's gonna absolutely die when he hears that. It's gonna cut his heart in pieces like it was a buzz saw ripping into a log."

"But we can't let him find out. You've got to swear to keep this between you and me, Darla Jean. Beau'd get so upset, he'd go kill the guy, then he couldn't play football and maybe get a college scholarship. It'd ruin his life."

"I won't tell a living soul," Darla Jean vowed, almost in tears from hearing all this nobleness and sacrifice. She knew Billy Dick would be just as touched, although she'd have to make him swear not to repeat it to anyone, ever. Especially not to Beau.

"That was Joyce," Ruby Bee said as she replaced the receiver and gave Estelle a grim look. "She called to warn me because that fellow stayed here and might come back. I saw him the other night, you know. Well, at least I heard him creeping around outside, but it was too dark to do more than catch a glimpse of him."

"And that makes about as much sense as turkey potpie," Estelle said in that snooty voice Ruby Bee couldn't stand. "Warn you about what fellow?"

"Lamont Petrel," Ruby Bee said in her unfriendly voice, which she knew Estelle couldn't stand. "Joyce called to say Petrel is on a rampage raping women all across the county. She thinks she saw somebody in the backyard way out by those forsythia bushes by the fence. She's locked in the house and calling to warn everybody."

"Does Arly know? It seems to me she's the one who ought to be doing something—if the story's true. I for one am not sure. Lamont seemed like a real gentleman to me. When you introduced us, I thought for a second he was going to kiss my hand like they do in movies about foreigners."

"Now who's talking turkey potpie?"

"Well, Miss Mind Reader, it's a relief to know you're keeping track of everything I think. Why doncha tell me what I'm thinking now? Go ahead; I'll think of a number between one and a hundred and you tell me what it is."

"We don't have time for that kind of foolishness, not with a rapist in town. I'd better call Arly and have her get the sheriff over to Joyce's before something tragic happens." Ruby Bee dialed the number at the PD, and when there was no answer, the number at the apartment, getting grimmer with each ring. At last, a small voice answered. "Hammet, where's Arly?" Ruby Bee demanded.

She listened for a minute, then told him to stay in the apartment with the door locked. "Hammet says she went out to talk to folks and he doesn't know who or where or when she'll be back," she reported to Estelle. "I guess we ought to call the sheriff ourselves, even if it is long distance."

She was reaching for the telephone when Estelle grabbed her wrist and said, "Wait a minute. I just thought of something."

"I already told you we don't have time for parlor games. That maniac might be breaking into Joyce's house right this second, or cutting across Perkins's pasture and heading this way to attack you and me."

"This ain't a parlor game. You said something that jiggled my memory, and it may be important."

"Then spit it out and let me call the sheriff," Ruby Bee said, bowing to the inevitable, as usual.

"When we were talking about Lamont Petrel the other day, you said you let him stay in number four because he was quiet and real good about paying for his long-distance calls."

"So what? I wouldn't have let him stay if I'd known he was a rapist. I don't cater to that sort of customer, not any more than you'd offer to trim his hair."

Estelle shook her head violently, getting so agitated that a bobby pin went flying across the bar. "He made long-distance calls, and they're on your bill. We have a list of all the numbers he called while he was staying in number four."

"That's not going to help Joyce Lambertino. Calling Sheriff Dorfer and telling him to get his fat butt over there might. Let go of my wrist so I can do it."

"Hold your horses," Estelle said, although she did let

go of Ruby Bee's wrist. "I'm not convinced Petrel is a rapist or that Joyce is watching him out the window. If she's so all fired scared, let her call the sheriff instead of all the folks in town. We've got ourselves a clue as to where Petrel might be hiding or if he's in cahoots with somebody."

"You're saying he called a cab to pick him up during the grand opening? There's gonna be a call to a hotel somewhere because he wanted to make reservations to disappear?" She looked at the telephone, but she had to admit (to herself, of course) Joyce was pretty dadburned chatty for someone in imminent danger of being raped.

"I don't know who he called, but I think we ought to have a look at the last bill," Estelle persisted. "It can't hurt to look at it, for pity's sake."

"I suppose not." Ruby Bee grumbled under her breath all the way out to her unit, grumbled all the time she rummaged through her drawer for the latest bill, which had come that very week, and then grumbled all the way back to the bar and grill. "Here it is, Ms. Magnum P.I."

Despite her tone, she was beginning to get excited, too, and she leaned over Estelle's shoulder. "Some of these are mine," she said, squinting at the numbers. "I called for a doctor's appointment here, and this is to the company that delivers the paper goods. The delivery man showed up without napkins, and I knew for a fact I'd ordered two cases, but he said—"

"Here's one to Texas. You didn't call Texas for napkins, did you? Here's another one to the same number, and another one the day of the grand opening!"

"He said something about it being a supermarket company," Ruby Bee said, trying to recollect. "He stopped by and wrote a check Saturday morning, and apologized for having to make a passel of last-minute business calls from his room. Look here, he called this number in Farberville four times, including the day of the grand opening. It's likely to be a wholesale grocer."

"There's a simple way to find out," Estelle said, nibbling on her lip as she studied the bill. "Call it."

Ruby Bee started to mention that it was her bill they were putting long-distance calls on, but she went ahead and dialed the number as Estelle read it aloud. "Hello," she said briskly. "Who's this?"

"Who's this?" a woman's voice responded.

"It's . . . ah, it's possible I dialed the wrong number," Ruby Bee said, giving Estelle a panicky look. "If it's not too much trouble, just tell me who you are and I'll tell you if it's the wrong number."

"It's the wrong number. Trust me."

Frowning, Ruby Bee put down the receiver and said, "She hung up. I don't think this is going to work, Estelle. Folks don't want to tell you their names in case you're getting ready to sell them storm windows or portraits at a photography place."

"I got an idea." Estelle picked up the receiver, dialed the same number, and when the woman answered, said, "This is Miss Oppers with the telephone company. We're verifying a long-distance call that was charged to this number. I'll have to have your name and address, ma'am." After a moment, she handed the receiver to Ruby Bee. "She hung up, and she was right rude about it, too. You'd think she'd have the decency to answer a polite question from the telephone company. I didn't ask her how much she weighed or if her hair color was natural."

"Let's let her cool off," Ruby Bee said as she picked up the bill and studied it. "Here're more numbers that I don't recognize, and in Farberville, too."

One turned out to be a wholesaler with a secretary who announced as much when she answered. Ruby Bee muttered something about the wrong number, hung up, and drew a line through that one. The Miss-Oppers-from-the-telephone-company routine worked on Muriel Petrel, who obliged with the information, even though she'd been in the shower and was standing in an expanding puddle and was wearing a pink and white towel and nothing else. After a certain amount of debate, Ruby Bee grudgingly called the Texas number and spoke to a sugary voice at Market Investments and Management Inc.

"Is Mr. Lamont Petrel there?" she asked slyly.

The sugary voice sounded a little confused. "Mr. Petrel is not a member of our firm. Would you care to speak to Mr. Dow or Mr. Long?"

Even though the meter was ticking, Ruby Bee said sure and shortly thereafter found herself speaking to a male voice with the expansive drawl of a Houston wheeler-dealer wearing six-hundred-dollar cowboy boots. "I'm afraid your secretary got it cattywampus," she said, now so overcome with slyness that she could have ransacked a henhouse and had fried chicken for a month. "I'm calling on behalf of Lamont Petrel."

"How's the old fart doing?" Long said genially.

"Fine, real fine. He asked me to call and see if you had any messages for him."

"Put the lazy son of a bitch on the line. I got a joke for him that'll steam the wrinkles out of his dick."

"He can't come to the telephone just now," Ruby Bee said, slylessly. "He's in the other room. You know what I mean?"

Long did, if she didn't. "Reading on the john, huh? Tell him I'll save the joke for next time. Have yourself a nice day, and watch out for Lamont."

"Wait a second! What about the messages?"

"What messages?"

"Mr. Petrel just wanted me to ask if there's—if there's been any change in the plans," Ruby Bee said, clutching the receiver so tightly her fingers hurt.

"You mean he's not going to sell that little supermarket? Fer chrissake, I've been putting the paperwork together and working on the figures all goddamn week. Now you're telling me . . ." There was a moment of silence. "Who is this?"

"Oops, Mr. Petrel's hollering at me from the other room. It's been real nice talking to you, Mr. Long. You have yourself a real nice day, you hear?" Ruby Bee replaced the receiver and sat down on the nearest stool. "That man thinks Lamont Petrel's going to sell him the supermarket," she told Estelle.

"You think Jim Bob wants to sell it? From what I've heard, he's puffed up about being the manager and having his name in big plastic letters across the front of the building."

"Maybe he didn't before, but now that it's closed down again and everybody's scared because of being poisoned to death, he may have changed his tune," Ruby Bee said thoughtfully. "We ought to tell all this to Arly so she can ask him."

"We don't have anything to tell her yet, and she's real busy with this poisoning investigation. She doesn't have time to wonder if Jim Bob and Lamont are going to sell the SuperSaver—or to find out who the rude woman is at the other end of this telephone number. We can save her a lot of time if we do a little asking on our own."

"She could find out real quick. All she'd have to do is call over to the sheriff's office and have LaBelle call the telephone company." Ruby Bee blinked at Estelle, who blinked back, and within seconds Ruby Bee was doing further damage to her bill by making yet another long-distance call and telling herself she was only saving Arly the bother.

Martin gave me a startled look as I came into his hospital room. I sat down at the end of the bed, patted his leg, and said, "The nurse said you were about ready to go home. We're going to need you tomorrow at the big game."

"Gran's dead."

"Yes, and I'm sorry, Martin. You pa's going to be okay, but he'll have to remain here for a few more days. Lissie's been staying at the Lambertinos' house. I'll ask if you can stay there, too, until your pa gets home and everybody can be together."

He jerked his leg out of reach, then stared out the window and surreptitiously swiped at the wetness on his cheeks. "Yeah, that'll be swell."

"Would you rather stay with me? Hammet sleeps on the couch, but we can fix up something on the floor for you, and I'm sure Hammet would enjoy the company."

"Okay," he said hoarsely. "Did they find what killed Gran and made Pa and me sick?"

"I wanted to talk to you about it yesterday. You and Lissie had breakfast, then she watched television all morning. What about you?"

"I didn't do nothing, just hung around and didn't do nothing special."

"The two of you had spaghetti and corn bread for lunch, right?" He nodded, watching me closely. "At some point in the afternoon, your pa woke up and told Lissie to go outside and play. That left you, your pa, and Gran in the house. We think someone may have tampered with a package of coconut cakes from the supermarket. Did you eat part of one, Martin?"

"No. Pa and Gran might have, but all I had was a root beer and some crackers. I went into my room to work on an airplane model, but later I started feeling bad and lied down on my bed. The next thing I knew, you was squeezing my hand and then I was in an ambulance and then I was here."

My great theory went up in smoke or down the drain, whichever. "You're sure you didn't eat a cake?" I asked.

He gave me an impatient frown. "All I had was a root beer and a handful of crackers, Miss Arly."

The door opened and a young doctor with shiny black hair and a baby face came into the room, humming to himself and swinging a clipboard. When he saw me, however, he stopped abruptly. "Are you this boy's mother?"

"My ma's dead," Martin said. "This is Miss Arly."

"I'm a police officer," I added. "I'm investigating the poisonings."

"And my patient's bruises?" the doctor said angrily.

"Bruises?" I echoed. I tried to think whether Martin had participated in the brawls we referred to as baseball practice. I didn't think he had, but I'd been in the thick of it most of the time and there'd been arms, legs, knees, and fists flying. "Where'd you get bruises, Martin?"

"I fell out of that walnut tree at the side of the house," he said. "I already told this doctor fellow about it. I was chasing after a gimpy squirrel when my foot slipped and I fell on my rear end."

I told the doctor I'd wait in the hall, said goodbye to Martin, and stood by the door until the doctor came out. "I didn't know about any bruises," I said in a low voice. "Could they have resulted from the fall he described?"

"They could have." The doctor glanced at his watch,

made a note on his clipboard, and gave me a cool look. "I was planning to call the Department of Human Services to request an inquiry, but I'll leave that up to you. I've been on call for thirty-six hours and I need to crash."

"Then you don't think the bruises came from an accident?" I said, unable to assimilate the possibilities. "You think there's been physical abuse?"

"I don't know. The boy says he fell, and that may be the truth. Or he may have been paddled with a flat object hard enough to leave some big bruises. If you'll excuse me, I want to finish my rounds and get to bed."

The doctor went into the next room. I hesitated, then went into Martin's room and said, "I forgot to tell you that I'll be here tomorrow morning to take you back to Farberville. You want to stay with Hammet and me?"

"Yeah," he said from the bed, his voice so faint I could barely hear it.

I stood beside the bed and looked down at his pale face and watery eyes. "Did you get into trouble with your pa yesterday morning? Lissie said you went to the back bedroom to talk with him. Did he spank you?"

"Nobody touched me. Pa was pissed because I hadn't done my chores the day before. I did 'em all, but Pa said the toolshed was still messy and someone had left the hammer and a handful of nails on the floor. He didn't believe me when I said it must've been Lissie."

"Was it Lissie?"

"I don't rightly recall," he muttered. "But all Pa did was yell at me about putting tools away properly and not skipping my chores again. I said okay and went outside, and that's when I saw the gimpy squirrel in the walnut tree. I was trying to catch him so I could take care of him until his back leg healed up, but then my foot slipped and I fell. The squirrel was in the next county by the time I got my breath back."

"So your pa didn't spank you?" I persisted.

"I fell out of the tree. Pa doesn't ever whip me or Lissie. He just yells. Gran was too sickly to do anything except gripe about her heart and her very close veins and her red spots. If you don't believe me, ask Lissie."

"I believe you," I said, then told him I'd be back the

next day and took the elevator to the basement and the intensive-care ward. Through the glass wall of the cubicle, I could see Buzz's gray face under a lot of plastic tubes and wires. The nurse told me he was past the threat of respiratory or cardiac failure, but that they would monitor him for at least another twenty-four hours.

As I drove back to Farberville, I tried to think how Martin had taken a dose of the poison that had killed his grandmother and almost done the same to his father. Root beer and crackers. But Martin had the same symptoms the others had evinced, and he clearly had ingested the poison—not at breakfast, not at lunch, and not for high tea.

I was scowling so hard that I didn't even turn my head as I drove past the Airport Arms Apartments.

12

Mrs. Jim Bob was madder than a coon in a poke. She had a list of grievances as long as her arm, and thus far hadn't had any success with any of them. For starters, Brother Verber had dropped off the face of the earth, and just when she wanted to find out if he'd properly chastised Dahlia O'Neill and Kevin Buchanon for their disgraceful behavior.

She'd been of a mind to discuss it with Eilene, but then Eilene had started making unsettling and distinctly un-Christian remarks about lawyers and Mrs. Jim Bob had allowed herself to be distracted. But that didn't give Brother Verber an excuse not to be in his mobile home or at the Assembly Hall in her hour of need.

Then Jim Bob had allowed Petrel to poison half the missionary society, and although everybody knew who was responsible, they were still acting funny about it and refusing her generous invitations for coffee and cake on the sun porch. What's more, no one had called all morning, and Mrs. Jim Bob was beginning to feel as though her fingers had slipped off the pulse of the town.

Furthermore, Jim Bob still hadn't called the sheriff to tell him about Petrel, and instead, he'd had a conversation with snippety Arly Hanks out in the yard, where you couldn't hear a single word, not even from behind the drape in the living room. He'd been downright odd afterward and wouldn't even explain it to his own wife, who deserved an explanation more than anyone else. Then he'd announced (*announced,* mind you) that he was going to the pool hall and just marched out the door.

To make things worse, Ruby Bee's baseball team was scheduled to play against the upstanding boys of the Jim

Bob's SuperSavers, and for all she knew, there'd be an orgy on the field and somehow it would be her fault and she'd be obliged to resign from the presidency of the missionary society.

Perkins's eldest had skipped the top of the refrigerator, and from the looks of it, for several months. There wasn't any way to make a condolence call at the Milvins' house and find out the details of what had happened, because there wasn't anybody home to offer condolence to. Now that the Kwik-Stoppe-Shoppe had been torn down and the SuperSaver built in its place and then closed, Mrs. Jim Bob was going to have to go all the way into Farberville to buy a simple head of lettuce.

It was enough to drive even the most saintly woman to tears, and she was heading that way when the telephone rang. She jerked up the receiver. "What is it?"

Eula sounded breathless, and she was talking so fast, her dentures clicked like castanets. "Just lock your doors and windows and stay inside. He's in town; Joyce saw him."

Mrs. Jim Bob wasn't in the mood for silliness. "Stop blathering like an orphaned calf and calm yourself down, Eula. I'm in the middle of doing my shopping list, and I don't even know what you're talking about."

"Petrel," Eula said, getting control of herself and her upper plate. "He's already raped a dozen women, and now he's in Joyce Lambertino's backyard under the for-sythia bushes, watching the house. She's scared witless, of course, but who wouldn't be?"

"She was born witless, and I'm beginning to wonder about certain other folks. We all know that Lamont Petrel poisoned everybody, but the last I heard, he disappeared and the state police can't find hide nor hair of him. You're saying he's been raping women and is hiding in Joyce's yard?" Even Mrs. Jim Bob was having trouble with that one, but she waited far Eula to elaborate.

Eula elaborated at length about Petrel's rampage and Joyce's terror.

"Then why doesn't she call the police?" Mrs. Jim Bob asked, still having trouble. She'd met Petrel on a few occasions, and he'd been right gentlemanly; she'd been

surprised herself when she realized he was the poisoner
and she was obliged to pass it along. Men that drove nice
black Cadillacs were hardly the rapist sort. Embezzle-
ment, maybe, or stealing from the country club's bank
account, or even telling lies to widows to get their life
savings—but not rape. Rape was—well, common.

Eula was still dithering. "Arly's off somewhere, and
Joyce's husband's getting ready for school to start and is
over there way back in the auto shop where he can't hear
the telephone. Someone's got to go to Joyce's house and
do something."

"Well, I'm not going over there," Mrs. Jim Bob
snapped. "I've got to get salad for dinner, and since I
have to drive all the way to Farberville, I thought I'd run
by the mall and see if winter coats are on sale. My good
wool coat's starting to look a little frayed at the cuffs; I
thought I'd ask Perkins's eldest if she wanted to buy it
from me cheap."

"But what about Joyce?" Eula wailed.

"Oh, all right." Mrs. Jim Bob punched down the button to cut off the wailing, then dialed the operator and
demanded to be put through to the sheriff's department.
She briskly told LaBelle about the crazed madman in the
act of breaking into the Lambertinos' house with rape on
his perverted mind, then hung up and left the house.

I drove to the Satterings' produce stand and parked in
the shade. Jackie was in the yard, tossing up a ball and
attempting to catch it if it came down in his vicinity.

"Where's your ma?" I asked as I walked into the yard.

"She and Pa are down by the apple trees," he said.
He threw the ball up; it came down hard on his shoulder
and rolled under the side of the house. He was standing
there with a puzzled look as I went around the house,
past several good-sized vegetable beds, and through the
gate to the orchard that sloped away from the house. I
caught sight of a figure toward the back row of gnarly
trees, and as I approached, I heard what sounded like
an argument. I halted, of course, being a professional
and all.

"Then you shouldn't have opened the package," Ivy

said. She was not visible, and after a moment I realized she was on a ladder and hidden by the foliage. "What you don't know can't hurt you."

"But I thought it was my ladybugs," Alex said, his back to me. "For all I knew, they might suffocate. You can't use that stuff, damn it! All our produce is organically grown and guaranteed to be free from pesticides. Just because they haven't proved it doesn't mean that stuff can't cause cancer or even build up in your system and kill you."

"Balderdash," came Ivy's voice from above his head. "Starvation's going to kill us first, if we can't get productivity up. The SuperSaver was selling lettuce for less than a dollar a pound, and if they bring in apples from the West Coast, they'll undercut us with those, too."

He grabbed the ladder and began to shake it fiercely. "You've already used some of that pesticide," he said with sudden venom. "What'd you use it on? The squash? The last of the turnips? Whatever it is, I'm going to pull it up and throw it away."

"I used it on everything, Alex. You'd better get an ax and start chopping down the trees. Get a bulldozer and level all the gardens. And don't think about the vegetable soup we had last night. I thought the organophosphates gave it a nice flavor."

I brushed past him and grabbed the ladder to steady it. Ignoring his gurgle of surprise, I called, "Ivy, it's Arly Hanks. I came by to ask you all a few questions."

She came down the ladder, her expression supremely unruffled, and gave me a smile. "Howdy, Arly. I was inspecting the tree for damage from that late frost last spring. Looks okay to me. Alex, take the ladder back to the barn and then set the sprinkler on the yellow squash. Go on, take the ladder to the barn."

He hesitated, regarding her with a flat expression, then nodded to me, took the ladder, and trudged up the slope. Ivy ran her fingers through her hair, sighed, and said, "He'll leave the ladder in the middle of the yard and set the sprinkler on the tomatoes." She frowned. "But I shouldn't underestimate him. Might be dangerous one of these days."

"I happened to overhear some of the conversation," I said cautiously. "You're using pesticides now?"

"I got tired of catering to the insect world. The stuff's used very commonly, and all you have to do is wash the produce before you eat it. Alex is still having flashbacks to the sixties, I'm afraid. He thinks organic is groovy. He thinks ladybugs are the hottest thing since the Beatles."

"I wanted to ask you about Monday evening," I said. "I guess you heard about the pins and so forth?"

She started far the house, forcing me to trail after her. "I heard about Lillith Smew, too. I don't reckon I ever met her, but it's a damn shame."

"I'm talking to everyone who was in the SuperSaver Monday evening," I said to her back. "Someone said you were there for a time, Ivy. Did you see anyone acting suspiciously—returning items to the display, for instance, or looking worried about being observed?"

She glanced over her shoulder but continued walking briskly up the slope. "Can't say I did. I just went to compare prices, then left when I realized that every last one of them was a damn sight less than what we can sell for."

"When did the pesticide package come?"

"Monday morning. I was way down at the end of the orchard, and Alex happened to have gone to the house for a minute. He was so excited about his box of ladybugs that he didn't stop to look at the return address. His box came the next morning, and he spent the day sprinkling the orange polka-dotted things on what's left of the late-summer crop. He was surprised when they bellied-up, but I wasn't. The pesticide worked real well."

We'd reached the gate, but I was seriously out of breath and my shirt was glued to my back. "Wait a minute," I said. "One more question, Ivy. Do you keep syrup of ipecac in the house?"

I finally had her attention. She turned back, scratching her chin with dirt-caked fingernails, and said, "I have a bottle in the medicine cabinet. I also have pins in the sewing box. I was real perturbed when the SuperSaver opened, and real relieved when it was closed down. I've got no fondness for Mayor Jim Bob Buchanon or his self-righteous wife, and I'd just as soon take a tablespoon of ipecac as give either of them the time of day. The brand of organophosphates I'm using is deadly in small doses, and the container's been opened. Any more questions, Arly?"

"That pretty well covers it," I said, blinking at her. "Anything you'd like to add?"

"I hope you nail the person who sabotaged the supermarket. When you find out who it is, let me know so I can send him a bushel of apples."

She stepped over the ladder in the yard and went through the back door into the house. Alex and Jackie had vanished, so there was nothing for me to do but get in my car and leave. All the exertion had left my mouth dry, so I headed for the Dairee Dee-Lishus for a cherry limeade and a conversation.

"This is out-and-out crazy," Ruby Bee whispered. "What's more, the stink is making me sick to my stomach. It's worse here than it was in the picnic pavilion."

"Stakeouts aren't supposed to be Tupperware parties," Estelle whispered back, not real pleased with the overpowering miasma of rotting garbage and stale whiskey emanating from the rusty green dumpster. "Just because some private eye on television sits in his car for two seconds and along comes the suspect doesn't mean that's what really happens. If you ain't interested in staking out this rude woman, then you can run along home and watch television by yourself."

Ruby Bee turned up her nose at a moldy orange peel covered with flies and a thread of little black ants. "We don't even know if she's in there. What if she goes to work every day and comes home after dark? We're not even going to see her face when she drives up and goes into her apartment."

A yellow jacket zoomed down on a lopsided aluminum soda can. Estelle scooted back as far as she could without risking being visible from the upstairs apartment, then said, "We agreed that her name didn't ring a bell and we were going to have to look at her to figure out how she fits into all this."

"It seems to me we could have found a nicer place to watch from," Ruby Bee said rebelliously. "We could have parked the car across the highway and sat there, you know."

"And not had a decent look at the woman. Unless your eyesight's improved mightily, you wouldn't be able to tell if it was a him or a her, much less what he or she looked like."

"And you don't wear reading glasses when you think I'm not looking?"

"So do you. That doctor's appointment last week wasn't with a baby doctor, was it? You had to get your prescription checked, Miss Twenty-Twenty, My Eye!"

Ruby Bee snorted, but she didn't say anything because Estelle was right and she wasn't about to say so. The yellow jackets were coming down by the dozens, buzzing every which way and threatening to fly in her hair. She flapped at them as she moved back and tried to get comfortable on the gravel.

I was driving toward the Dairee Dee-Lishus when a sheriff's department vehicle came careening up the highway, the blue lights flashing and the siren going full blast. I was still thinking about it when a second car did the same, followed by a third, with the sheriff himself at the wheel.

Never one to pass up a promising social occasion, I put the pedal to the metal, so to speak. They'd turned onto a back road and the dust was blinding as I bounced along behind them. I prudently slowed down, and when I came around the curve, they were already stopped in front of the Lambertino house. The deputies were crouched behind the cars, with .38s and sawed-off shotguns pointed at the house.

Harve pulled out a bullhorn and flipped the switch. His voice boomed as he said, "Testing, one, two, three. Okay, buddy boy, we know you're in there. Come out with your hands up and nobody'll get hurt."

I parked behind the last car and ran to Harve's side. "What the holy hell is going on?"

"We got us a—" He realized he was still broadcasting

to the next county and lowered the bullhorn. "We got us a rapist in there, according to an anonymous report."

"In Joyce's house? A rapist? An anonymous report?" I realized I was on the disjointed side, but I couldn't help it.

"The call could have been from the Lambertino woman. According to the dispatcher, the caller just said there was a rapist breaking in and then slammed down the phone. We're presuming she was interrupted. The line's been busy ever since, so it's probably off the hook."

"Are the children in there?"

"No way of knowing." He raised the bullhorn to his mouth. "Listen up, we've got the house surrounded and there ain't no way you can get away. Let the woman and the children come out and then you and I'll have ourselves a talk. How does that sound?"

Joyce appeared at a window, waved frantically at us, and then ducked out of sight. After a moment, Lissie and Saralee came to the same window and stood there talking to each other as they watched Harve, the deputies, and me all watching them.

"The little girls seem okay," one of the deputies said out of the corner of his mouth. "The woman looked frightened, though. You want me to see if I can sneak up on the porch and take down the perp through a window?"

"Hold on," I said to Harve, pulling down his bullhorn. "Are we very, very sure there's a perp in there?"

He looked at the two girls, then at me. He sucked on his lips for a minute, shook his head, and said, "Nope. Let's not start taking down any perps just yet, Bertie. Let's just sit tight for a few minutes and see what all happens." He put the bullhorn on the hood of his car and took a cigar butt out of his shirt pocket. The deputies looked disappointed as they lowered their weapons and straightened up.

I smiled and waved at the girls, who replied in kind. They exchanged a few words, then Saralee unlocked the window, yanked it open, and yelled, "Hi, Miss Arly. What are you and all those fellows with guns doing? Are they gonna shoot us?"

"Is there anyone in there with you?"

"Yeah," Saralee yelled, nodding. "Do you want us to come out with our hands up like that fat man said to do?"

The deputies were nudging each other and chuckling. Harve got the cigar going, then picked up the bullhorn. "Who all's in there?"

"Lissie and me," Saralee answered. "Aunt Joyce, Cousin Larry Junior, Cousin Traci, and the baby. Uncle Larry Joe went to the high school earlier, but he said he'd be back for lunch. We're not coming out until you swear you ain't gonna shoot us."

Harve ordered the deputies to search the yard and adjoining pasture, and gestured at me to follow him as he walked up the sidewalk and knocked on the door.

"Hi, Miss Arly," Lissie said through the window. "This is better'n television, ain't it?"

"Much better," I said.

Joyce opened the door and threw her arms around Harve. "Thank God you're here," she said brokenly. "You, too, Arly."

Harve disengaged her from his neck and checked his pocket to make sure she hadn't smashed his stash. "Where's the rapist, ma'am?"

"I thought I saw him out back under the forsythia bushes."

"Someone called and said he was in the act of breaking into your house. Was it you?" When she shook her head mutely, he continued. "Is your phone off the hook?"

"I was talking to someone when y'all drove up. It liked to have scared me to death, the sirens and lights and that booming voice and those guns aimed at the house."

The deputies came around to the front yard, none of them dragging a rapist, and reported that the only thing under the forsythia was an ugly yellow dog and a chewed-up plastic truck missing a wheel. Harve brusquely ordered them to wait out by the cars, then gave Joyce a mean look.

"So how'd this rapist story get all the way to my office in Starley City?" he asked.

Joyce twisted her hands and looked at me for help,

but I was fresh out. "My second cousin Barbie Buteo called this morning and said that Lamont Petrel had raped a dozen women in the county, escaped from the police, and was likely to be hiding in Maggody. I guess my imagination got loose from me, huh?"

"And where did this Buteo woman hear that?" he asked, still pissed at having had to drive all the way over and make an ass out of himself with the bullhorn and the display of firepower.

"I don't know."

"Who do ya think called my office?"

"I don't know," she repeated meekly.

"But you were on the phone?" I said, fighting back a grin because I figured Harve wouldn't appreciate it one bit. "Who all did you call, Joyce?"

"I felt obliged to warn some of my friends. I called Ruby Bee, Eula, Elsie, and Millicent McIlhaney—but she wasn't home, so I left a message with Darla Jean. I was talking to Lottie when I heard the sirens. She said she'd let everybody else know what was happening."

"So now," I said to Harve, unable to hold back my grin, "three-quarters of the locals are convinced our missing person is in the act of raping Joyce while making a list of his next dozen potential victims. If you listen real carefully, you can hear those telephone wires humming across the county, and by tomorrow, they'll be barricading the doors in Texarkana."

Harve harrumphed at Joyce, then stalked across the porch and down the sidewalk to his car. I caught up with him before he could drive away, and said, "Somebody'd better find Petrel before a lynch mob of husbands, uncles, and brothers beats us to him. Every last one of them will be a hundred percent convinced Petrel raped some woman someplace."

"Think you can run the rumor back to its source?"

"Sure, Harve, sure. I don't have anything to do for the next year or two. I was going to keep working on the poisoning investigation, but if you want me to start calling the roster of the missionary society, I'll be delighted to oblige."

"You know what? Sometimes you got a real smart mouth."

Harve left me standing in a cloud of dust, but I hardly noticed.

Brother Verber had searched every inch of the mobile home, and he was fairly sure he'd gotten all his study material together—except for the two missing issues, which sure as heck weren't under the mobile home or lying in the grass beside it or anyplace of which he could even begin to think.

Their disappearance into thin air was why he was sweating like a pear-shaped pitcher of iced tea. Droplets of sweat were running down his face, some of them curling around his nostrils and gathering on the corners of his mouth like foam from a rabid dog. His back was wet and his armpits downright soggy. He kept wiping his palms on his trousers, but it didn't last long enough to be worth the effort.

He stared at the gray plastic garbage bag filled with back issues of study material. He couldn't set it in the metal can outside the Voice of the Almighty, because there was obviously a devious burglar in and around the grounds. He wasn't about to put it under his bed or in his closet. He considered putting it in the can behind the Emporium, but as he glanced out the window, he saw the hippie woman stacking crates and decided she looked like the kind of person who knew exactly what was supposed to be in her garbage cans and what wasn't.

It was a vexing problem, and to make it worse, he didn't know where Mrs. Jim Bob was or when she was likely to come banging on his door again.

Brother Verber mopped whatever body surfaces were readily available, squared his shoulders, and picked up the garbage bag. Maggody was too small. He was going to have to take a ride to a place where the garbage cans were anonymous and their contents unlikely to be scrutinized by anyone who would then point the finger of accusation in his direction, even though he had a perfectly legitimate reason for possessing half a dozen issues of *Rubber Maid* and twice that many of *Kittens and Tom-*

cats, less two, of course. The August issue of *Of Human Bondage*. A collection of paperback novels, all selected in order to acquaint him with the steamier sins of his flock and featuring characters named Rod and Dick and Pussy Wantsit. And his most recent addition, Suzie Squeezums, neatly deflated and tucked away in her plastic carrying case.

He went out to his car, tossed the bag in the backseat, and drove out of Maggody, sweating all the more as he fondly thought about his little Suzie.

There was a pickup truck in front of the Dairee Dee-Lishus as I drove up and parked. A group of teenaged boys were jostling each other in front of the counter window, including the mutant Buchanon who'd tangled with Saralee during the grand opening. He glowered at me, muttered to his companions, and slunk away behind the truck as I approached. The others waited, their expressions wary.

"So what you want?" Mandozes barked at them through the window. "You want to admire the scenery, you take a hike. Here is where you order food and drinks."

"Forget it, spic," one of them said. He looked at me. "Is it true about this Petrel guy?"

"Is what true?"

"He raped a bunch of women, escaped from the cops, broke into Mr. Lambertino's house earlier today, and shot a deputy when he escaped again. Is it true?"

"You're worse than the missionary society," I said irritably. "Petrel was last seen at the grand opening of the SuperSaver, and no one's admitted seeing him since then. No rapes have been reported to me or to the sheriff. No one broke into the Lambertinos' house and no one's been shot. Where'd you hear this crazy story?"

One of them said his ma, another his sister. The most cocky of the pack said he'd heard it at the pool hall, and from someone who ought to know.

"And who might that be?" I said.

"I don't remember," he said, snickering.

Before I could insist, they piled in the pickup truck

and drove away. I went to the counter window and said, "Sorry, Mr. Mandozes. I didn't mean to run them off before they ordered."

"The cheap little sons of *puntas* only buy drinks," he said without inflection.

"I need to ask you a few questions. Is there a place in back where we can speak?"

"Go around," he said, jabbing toward the corner with his thumb. "I will allow you in my fine, private office. We can sit at my grand walnut desk and allow my secretary to serve refreshments on a silver tray."

I went around to the back and Mandozes opened a door. His office was no more than eight feet square, and dominated by sacks of cornmeal, a case of hot-dog buns, boxes of paper goods, plastic bottles of cleaning supplies, a collection of mops and brooms in the corner, and a card table littered with bills and invoices.

"This is a fine private office," I said gravely. "I only wish mine were as fine as this."

He pulled a chair out for me. "Then you must sit at my desk while we speak. My secretary is gone at the moment, but when she gets back, she will shine the tray. In the meantime, can I offer you a limeade?"

I nodded. He went to the front, leaving me to contemplate a calendar with a winter scene and a drawing of a cactus done by an immature but sincere hand. I was about to admire the latter when a small furry thing darted from under the mop head and regarded me appraisingly.

I did not shriek, although I did get my feet off the floor pretty damn quick. "You have a visitor," I called.

"*Vaya!*" Mandozes said sharply.

I wasn't sure to whom the command was directed, but the mouse scuttled back to the corner and disappeared. I looked more closely at the shelf of cleaning supplies, and was not surprised to see a box of rat poison next to a bottle of bleach. When Mandozes returned with my drink, I said, "I guess you have a running battle with mice?"

"Yes, but it is the least of my worries. I have also a running battle with the wholesale grocer in Starley City, who wants me to pay his bills with money I do not have."

He sat down across from me and twirled the end of his mustache like a bandito. "You have questions, you said?"

"You were at the SuperSaver Monday evening, right?"

"I was. I asked the checker when the deli would open, but he claimed to have no knowledge of such things. I am curious how many tamales they think they will serve after what happened."

"They didn't look very appetizing on Saturday," I said with a wry smile. "You said you tasted one and spit it out. You're lucky, because they were laced with syrup of ipecac before they were served."

"Is this so?" he said. He pushed the paper cup in front of me and said, "But you are hot and thirsty, so please try the limeade and see if it is good. You are my son's baseball coach. It is the least I can do to offer you this small hospitality."

He was still playing with his mustache and smiling as I picked up the cup and took a drink. "It is very good," I said coolly, "and welcome on a hot day. When did you taste a piece of tamale at the grand opening?"

"A few minutes after they came from the kitchen. The fat girl put the tray down and left, and I pushed through the crowd to the table to try one. They tasted very bad, very sweet and oily."

"Who was in this crowd?"

"Gringos look alike," he said, shrugging. "The woman who has red hair like a fire hydrant and wanted Raimundo to play baseball was there. Ruby Bee, who owns the bar and is your mother—she was there, too. The short woman who sells vegetables. A woman with the mouth of someone who has eaten a green persimmon. Many men in denim pants and caps. Some children, all shoving and shrieking. A crowd is made of many people, is it not?"

That was pretty much what I'd heard from other witnesses. I took another sip of limeade while I considered my next brilliant ploy. "Okay, what about Monday evening when you went to the SuperSaver? Did you buy anything?"

"Bah! I will not give them my business. I will drive to Farberville before I will spend my money there."

"There's a display rack by one of the registers that was filled with cupcakes and sponge cakes," I said. "Did you notice anyone standing in front of it or handling the packages?"

"Or putting ipecac in them?" His laugh was brittle and unconvincing.

I wished there was one person in the whole town who wasn't as knowledgeable as I about the case. Just one who didn't receive hourly news bulletins from the grapevine. "How'd you hear about it?" I asked for form's sake.

"My wife went to the produce stand to buy a few things. While she was waiting for change, two other women came and were discussing the poisoning of another. My wife's English is not so good, but she is quick in the mind. So you have come to ask me if I am responsible, Chief of Police Hanks? Do you want to know if I put ipecac in the tamales and in the cakes so that the SuperSaver would be closed?"

"Basically, yes."

"I did not, but if you find out who did, come by and have another limeade with me and tell me the name. I will send him a nice sack of genuine Mexican tamales."

"Duck," Estelle whispered, grabbing Ruby Bee's shoulder so violently that they both wobbled and sat down hard on the gravel. "Get around on this side of the dumpster, and hurry!"

Ruby Bee rubbed her rump. "What is wrong with you, Estelle Oppers? I'm going to have bruises all over me from being knocked over like a bowling pin. You had no call to—"

"Just get around on this side, and quick." Estelle scrabbled around the edge of the dumpster, and after a sniff, Ruby Bee followed her, even though certain parts of her anatomy were sure to be black and blue before morning.

"Now what?" she asked haughtily. "You want I should get inside and hunt up a nice picnic supper for us?"

"I saw a familiar car, that's what," Estelle retorted.

"Whose?"

"You wouldn't believe me if I swore on a stack of Bibles. Crawl around this way and take a gander for yourself."

Ruby Bee took a gander, and when she sat back down, she was having trouble with her eyeballs and her hands were fluttering like a pair of moths. "What on earth . . . ?"

"Hush!" Estelle hissed, going so far as to clamp her hand over Ruby Bee's mouth because the footsteps were coming closer and closer. The two huddled down on the far side of the dumpster, both wondering how they were going to explain the situation should they be caught, because it wouldn't be easy. Something thudded inside the dumpster. The footsteps receded, and after another moment of pained suspense, a car door slammed and the engine started. They held their breaths until the tires crunched across the gravel lot and the sound of the engine was mingled with the stream of noise from the highway.

"Well, I never," Estelle gasped.

"I never, either," Ruby Bee said as she let out her breath and eased off her knees. She picked a piece of gravel off one kneecap, then looked at Estelle. "He threw something in the dumpster. I heard it."

"And I didn't?" Estelle said, picking at her own kneecap.

"Now what do we do?"

They both thought about the challenge of retrieving whatever it was that was somewhere in the foul confusion of the overflowing dumpster. Where there was rotting garbage, there were apt to be unspeakable things. From the scattered litter in the general vicinity, it was obvious the dumpster contained broken glass, razor-sharp lids, dirty diapers, oil, grease, and filth, all baked in the sunshine and thoroughly ripe.

"You said you needed a tetanus shot, anyway," Ruby Bee suggested with more decisiveness than she felt. "I'll give you a boost inside, and you can grab the evidence real quick."

"I beg your pardon," Estelle said, gazing down her nose like she fancied herself to be the Emily Post of Dumpsterdom. "For one, you're not tall enough to give me a boost. I, on the other hand, am tall enough to give you a leg up and help you when you're ready to climb back out."

The debate raged for a good fifteen minutes, but eventually Estelle won out, interlaced her fingers in a stirrup of sorts, and grunted softly as she hefted Ruby Bee over the edge of the six-foot metal wall. The resultant remarks from the interior were about as graphic as she'd ever heard, but she didn't comment on them because she figured she'd be saying the same things and perhaps even more.

After a minute or two, Ruby Bee said, "I think I see something. It's not as . . . nasty as the other bags, and it's kind of on top of . . . other things. Let me see if I can get over there and—"

The next sound was a harrumph of sorts, but said with great unhappiness and accompanied by an explosive clatter and the tinkle of breaking glass. Estelle clutched her cheeks and said, "Are you all right?"

The door of the upstairs apartment they'd been watching opened and a figure in a white bathrobe and a terrycloth turban yelled, "What the hell's going on down there?"

Estelle threw herself around the corner, praying she hadn't been spotted. From inside the dumpster, a low voice said, "Dandy. This is just dandy."

Another door opened. A wizened man dressed in baggy shorts and a baseball cap came out on the balcony. His chest was covered with matted black hair and his arms resembled rolls of barbed wire. He had a beer in one hand and a half-eaten sandwich in the other. "Damn rats back in the dumpster?" he asked his neighbor. "I saw one the other day big enough to tip the thing over and drag it away."

"I just heard the crash, Arnie," the woman said, still scowling down at the dumpster.

"Tell you what, I'll get my shoes and my shotgun and

go have a look. It's bad enough living in this dump without having rats taking up residence in the parking lot."

"Go for it," the woman said. She went back inside and closed the door. The man stuffed the last of the sandwich in his mouth, finished the beer, and went back into his apartment. The door remained ajar.

"Now what?" said a most unfriendly voice.

"I don't know. Lemme think about it," Estelle whispered, panicked to the point of hyperventilation, which was unfortunate considering the redolence of the moment.

"Good idea . . . thinking, that is. You're the one who got me into this. I'm squatting in garbage, and liable any minute to come nose-to-nose with a rat, and you're going to think about it. Would you like to know what I think?"

It came to Estelle about the time she thought she was going to pass out from the panic. As distasteful as it seemed, she had no choice and had to do her duty. "Just wait there," she told Ruby Bee. "I'm going to distract him so he won't shoot you." She stood up, brushed the dust off her skirt, patted her hair back into shape, lifted her chin, and took off for the stairs that led to the second floor.

The wail of desperation was lost as a plane roared overhead and went in for a landing.

13

▼

Plover's car was parked beside the PD, and I found him inside telling whimsically gory tales to Hammet about bandits and bank robbers. I sat down behind my desk and made a few desultory notes about my interviews with Ivy and Mandozes. They didn't amount to a hill of beans (organic or refried), and I was mostly just sitting when Plover finished his lurid story, sent Hammet to the back room to play with the radar gun, and sat down across from me.

"Have you heard from the lab?" I asked.

He nodded. "Yeah, but you're not going to leap into my lap and smother me with kisses when you hear what they reported."

"I'm not?"

"Only in my fantasies, I fear. The lab analyzed the contents of Lillith Smew's stomach and blood and found traces of a toxic compound. Same for the other two victims. To the pathologists' regret, it's not nice, straightforward arsenic or potassium cyanide, or even something charmingly exotic like curare, but some incredibly complicated mess of polysyllabic chemicals. They think it might take several weeks to pin it down."

"Several weeks? What are we supposed to do while they piddle around with their tests? How am I going to identify a poisoner if I don't have any idea where to look? What kind of a lab is it, anyway?" I rattled desk drawers and slammed around pencils and notebooks until I calmed down. "They have no idea what the toxic compound is?"

"Unofficially, my friend said he suspects it'll turn out to be a common industrial pesticide."

"As in ant powder or rat poison or insecticide?" I told him what I'd learned in the last day. "So Ruby Bee, Mandozes, and Ivy Sattering all have access to lethal substances. But so does everyone else in town. Every kitchen has a box of something or other in the cabinet under the sink where curious toddlers can get to it." I sat back and sighed. "I don't know why I'm bothering to conduct an investigation. All I need to do is wait quietly until Eula and Lottie and all the other tongue-flapping magpies figure it out and pass along the solution. Considering the tempo thus far, I ought to have it by baseball practice this afternoon."

Hammet came to the doorway. "The game's tomorrow, you know. I went over to the field at the high school and watched that other team play. I think we got a shit-load of trouble, Arly. They kin throw and catch and one of 'em liked to knock the darn hide off the ball."

"All we can do is try. Team effort and that sort of thing. Ruby Bee's serving supper afterward, so at least we'll eat well."

"Where is she?" Plover asked. "I was going to suggest a late lunch, but the bar and grill is closed."

I shrugged again. "I am not my mother's keeper, for which I am currently and shall remain eternally grateful. She's off running errands or having her hair colored at Estelle's, I would imagine."

"What color?" Hammet demanded, clearly enchanted with the brightly hued images in his mind.

I shooed him out the door, tilted back in my chair, and propped my feet on the corner of the desk. "This whole thing is a polysyllabic mess. Someone managed to lace the tamale sauce with ipecac, perhaps in front of a dozen people, but nobody saw anything. The store was locked from Saturday at three o'clock until Monday afternoon, and that evening someone left the tampered cake packages on the display rack. All but one had pins or ipecac, which resulted in unpleasantness but not serious injury. One package contained a lethal poison. Why?"

"Beats the hell out of me," Plover said affably. "Why did Lamont Petrel disappear at the grand opening? Why did Jim Bob lie about his whereabouts Monday night? Why did Martin Milvin have the same symptoms as his father and grandmother? Why do fools fall in love?"

"Beats the hell out of me," I said, although not affably. I flipped through my notebook, scowling at the question marks sprinkled here and there as if they'd drifted down from the ceiling, and replaying bits of conversations. I looked up abruptly. "Jim Bob made an odd comment when I went back to tell him what Cherri Lucinda said. He sputtered something about having a hundred witnesses to prove she lied."

"Exhibitionism to an extreme?"

"I don't think so," I said, trying not to visualize Hizzoner and the blonde engaging in sexual antics on the runway. "When's the last time there was a gathering of that many people in Maggody? At the grand opening, of course. And Jim Bob had a really funny expression for a moment—as if he'd spotted a familiar face in the crowd."

"Is this leading somewhere, Chief? What difference does it make if Jim Bob's girlfriend came to the grand opening?"

Plover went into the back room and started the coffeepot, allowing me time to try to come up with an answer to his obnoxiously smug questions. When he returned, I said, "Because she lied. I doubt either of them will admit she was there, but if we're lucky, there is a way to prove it." I told him about the freewheeling cheerleader and the subsequent disaster in the crowd. "The cameraman caught every last squeal and curse. I don't know if it was deemed worthy of the six o'clock news, but he still might have the film. I noticed a blond woman—and I'll bet all three of my bullets it was Cherri Lucinda Crate."

"And?"

"If Jim Bob didn't invite her, maybe someone else did. Lamont's car is parked at the motel, so he didn't drive away. He had a ride."

"So you're theorizing that he left voluntarily with the Crate woman? Any ideas why he'd do that?"

"No," I admitted.

"You could ask her."

"We didn't hit it off real well," I said glumly. I found

the telephone book in a bottom drawer under my beloved travel guide, looked up the number of the television station, and persuaded the gum-snapping receptionist to put me through to the cameraman who'd covered the grand opening. He told me the film had been played several times for the amusement of the staff, who'd particularly enjoyed the expletives and one exceptional flash of thigh. The film had then been taped over at a Cub Scouts awards banquet. I hung up and regarded Plover. "Crate might talk to you, especially if you crinkle your nose and produce the boyish grin while staring in awe at her body."

"You're convinced she knows where Petrel is, then?" Plover said, crinkling his nose and producing the boyish grin but not staring in awe at my body, which was adequate but hardly awesome.

"No, but it's a lead, and we're not exactly swimming in them. We're not even wading in them. All we've got is unsubstantiated gossip and harebrained rumors. Even Hammet is keeping secrets—and from me, his very own coach."

Plover agreed to question Cherri Lucinda Crate and left. I decided to indulge myself with a quick trip to Amsterdam, but not even the flower market and canals could take my mind off the madness in Maggody. I put the book back in the drawer, dealt with a rebellious bobby pin, and went out into the humorless heat of my car.

The Milvin house had the dispirited look of an empty house. The grass looked a little shaggier than I had remembered, and the porch furniture shabbier and less inviting. The seals on both doors were intact, but I had no qualms about ripping one off in order to go inside. The key was under a flowerpot; the only other place it might have been was under the mat. We're not obsessed with security in Maggody. Otherwise, how would your neighbors get in to water your African violets, feed your cats, and snoop through your bedside drawers while you're on vacation?

The house had been bottling up the heat, and the odor was almost enough to send me back outside. I left the door open, yanked open the nearest window, and forced myself to breathe slowly until the odor seemed less oppressive. The recliner was still extended. A magazine lay beside it, offering a glimpse of a football player poised to fling himself at an enemy.

I hurried past Lillith Smew's bedroom and went into the children's room. It was more orderly than many I'd seen (and one I'd inhabited), and I wondered which of the house's inhabitants was responsible for this unchildlike tidiness.

Interesting, but not useful, I told myself as I packed some of Martin's clothes in a bag, then continued to wander through the house, trying to imagine the sounds of a family going about its daily grind.

The children had had breakfast at the kitchen table. Buzz had come home, had a conversation with Lillith, scolded Martin about the mess in the toolshed, and then gone to bed. Martin had climbed a tree to chase a gimpy squirrel, and Lissie had watched television until her father sent her outside. No one had stopped by for a visit.

At some point, Lillith and Buzz had shared the package of coconut cakes laced with a polysyllabic pesticide. Martin had not, but had ended up with the same poison in his system.

"Root beer and crackers," I snapped at a cockroach on the counter. I grabbed a fly swatter off a hook, but the little bugger had vanished by the time I turned around. I slapped the swatter down anyway to hear the crack of plastic on plastic, replaced it, and looked at the artwork taped on the front of the refrigerator, along with coupons and an unpaid electric bill. The last item reminded me of what Buzz had said about needing his mother-in-law, which made me feel even worse. There would be no more Social Security checks.

I let myself out, locked the door, and put the key back under the flowerpot. I then remembered the open window, but decided to leave it so the house would be slightly more bearable when Buzz and his children returned home.

None of this had accomplished anything, and I figured

I wasn't going to get anywhere until I talked to Buzz.
There were a couple of hours until practice, so I decided
to pick up Lissie and drive once again to the hospital.

"Isn't this just amazing?" Estelle gushed. "Here I am to
ask a few questions about your telephone service, and it
turns out you drive one of those monster trucks all the
way to California! That sounds so romantic I can hardly
stand to think about it."

Arnie smiled modestly. "I like to think of myself as a
lone rider, like a cowboy running a herd up the canyon.
And lemme tell ya, it ain't easy making the long haul. I
drive twenty or thirty hours at a time, listening to my
tape player or talking on my CB with the other boys."

"Just amazing," she said, crossing her legs so he could
appreciate her ankles, which she secretly felt were every
bit as good as a lot of Hollywood starlets'. "I do believe
I'll accept your kindly offer of a beer. Being a telephone
company pollster can make you dry as the desert."

As soon as he went into the kitchen, she hurried to
the window and looked down at the dumpster. The lid
covered the half nearest the building and obscured the
view of most of the interior. She thought she caught a
flicker of motion, but at that moment, Arnie came pad-
ding back into the living room.

"Watching the planes come in?" he said as he gallantly
opened her beer and handed it to her.

"Nothing to see at the moment." She moved away
from the window and perched on the edge of the sofa.
"I do wish you'd sit right there across from me and tell
me more about truck driving. Those ol' things are so big,
I don't see how you can steer them."

He flexed his muscles. "It ain't a job for a weakling.
Now the rig's got a hydraulic system, of course, but it
boils down to man against machine."

"Really?"

He went into a long rigmarole about the philosophical
implications of changing gears, but Estelle was having a
hard time trying to look fascinated while fretting about
poor Ruby Bee in the dumpster with the rats. There was
an increasingly loud rumble from outside, as if Arnie's

truck was pulling in, and she finally realized it wasn't an airplane landing.

"Excuse me for interrupting," she said, "but what in tarnation is that racket outside?"

"Sanitation truck. What I was saying was that life's like that black ribbon of asphalt that disappears into the distance. You think you can see where it's going, but then you come—"

"Sanitation truck?" Estelle put down her beer and ran to the window. An enormous white truck was approaching the dumpster. Two metal arms reached out to embrace it on either side, and a rectangular section in the back of the truck slid open.

It was all she could do to keep from shrieking as she dashed out to the balcony. "Stop that!" she shouted sternly. "You in the truck! I said stop that, and I mean it!"

"Are you okay?" Arnie asked from the doorway.

The driver looked up, puzzled, and said, "You talking to me, lady?"

"Who else do you think I'm talking to?"

"I dunno, but I've got to finish my route earlier 'cause of my bowling league having a tournament." He turned back to the controls, and again the metal arms reached for the dumpster.

"Stop!" Estelle screeched as she stumbled down the stairs. Her eyes felt as though they were going to pop right out of their sockets, and the blood pounding in her veins was hotter than chili con carne. "Stop!" she repeated in the same voice. "You're about to commit murder!"

"You're the one who needs to be committed," the driver said. The metal arms slid into their allotted slots. The truck let out a groan as the dumpster began to rise on its trip over the front of the truck to be emptied into its belly.

Estelle was jumping up and down and squawking her head off, but the driver refused to acknowledge her, and Arnie, who was watching from the balcony above, somberly resolved never again to invite women from the telephone company in for a beer. Other residents wandered out of their apartments to gawk at the crazy redheaded lady and offer opinions to each other.

The dumpster had passed its zenith and was beginning to be tilted as a state police car pulled into the lot. Estelle ran to the driver's side and pounded on the window. "Thank God it's you! Make him stop! He's gonna kill her and it's all my fault!"

Plover dutifully ordered the driver to stop. He later admitted, but only in private, that the ensuing scene was the weirdest damn thing that had ever happened to him in his entire career, and if he lived to be as old as Methuselah, he'd just as soon not go through it again.

"Where'd you say you found these?" Kevin demanded, feeling a mite faint as he gaped and gulped at the grainy photographs. He was terrified he would hear footsteps on the stairs outside, but he couldn't stop gaping and gulping.

"On the dirt," Hammet said. "I was hightailin' it past the trailer when they came out the window and liked to flap me in the face and make me fall. I jest grabbed 'em and scuttled under the trailer to have a look-see, 'cause it dint make no sense for someone to be throwing things out the window."

"And that was yesterday," Kevin said slowly. His eyes were slightly crossed as he tried to think things over without getting more confused than usual. "Kinda late in the afternoon, you said."

"You ain't gonna tell Arly, are you? I don't want her to get all riled at me for looking at pictures of . . ." Hammet couldn't find the appropriate words, so he settled for rolling his eyes and twisting up his mouth. He wasn't real sure about Kevin, who didn't appear to be much smarter than a possum heading for certain death on the highway. Hammet had been sitting on the top step outside the apartment and hadn't noticed Kevin until he heard a gasp and realized he'd been caught red-handed with the magazines. Now he figured he was at this dumbshit's mercy. "You ain't gonna tell Arly?" he repeated urgently.

"I ain't gonna tell Arly."

"You ain't gonna tell nobody, right?"

After a moment of silence, Kevin smiled just a tad and said, "I think I'd like to buy those magazines off you, Hammet. How much do you reckon it'll cost me?"

"Why do you want to buy them? They ain't nothing but a lot of . . ." Again, words failed him and he made a face.

"How much?"

"Gosh, I dunno. It ain't like I bought them myself. I jest saw 'em flying out the window. Here, you kin have 'em for free. I don't want 'em anymore."

"Thanks. I'll buy you a tamale and a soda pop one of these days, okay?" Kevin rolled up the magazines and stuck them in his back pocket. "See you later. I got to talk to someone."

Hammet watched Kevin go down the stairs and pedal away, wondering all the while what he wanted nasty magazines for, anyway. He then turned on the television and settled down for thirty minutes of animated mayhem, which was a helluva lot more entertaining than pictures of folks poking their puds in funny places.

Lissie and Saralee were in the Lambertinos' front yard. I told Lissie where we were going, and Saralee promised to relay the information to Joyce, who reportedly was in the den being kinda quiet and not even watching television or anything.

"Martin's coming home tomorrow," I told Lissie as we drove toward Farberville. "He's going to stay with Hammet and me."

"What about Pa?"

"He's going to be fine, but they want to keep him at the hospital for a few more days."

"That's good," she said, brightening. "Is Martin gonna play ball at the game tomorrow?"

We were passing the airport on the right, and therefore the Airport Arms Apartments on the left. Everything looked calm there; I didn't know if Plover had attempted to charm the fingernails off Crate yet, but he'd promised to report back to me when he knew something.

"Yes, we need everyone tomorrow," I said. We dis-

cussed our chances of beating the SuperSavers, which
took no time at all, then rode in silence to the hospital.
"Martin will be excited to see you," I said as I parked in
the flat expanse of concrete. "Let me ask you something,
Lissie. Does your pa ever spank you or Martin?"

She shook her head. "All he does is yell sometimes,
especially if we don't get our chores done or come in late
for supper. Once he made me stay in my room all afternoon 'cause the television was too loud and woke him
up. I didn't know it was too loud."

"What about Gran?"

"She just talked about how hard it was on account
of her heart and all that junk. She said we gave her
headaches."

"But she never spanked either of you?"

"No, she just talked and talked. It was worse. Can we
go see Martin and Pa now?"

"In one second," I said, watching her closely. "Martin
had some bruises on his behind, and he said he fell out
of a tree in the yard. Did he tell you about it?"

"When he was chasing that gimpy squirrel? It sure is
hot in the car, Miss Arly. It's making me dizzy and my
stomach's feeling like it's full of lumpy oatmeal."

We went into the hospital and took the elevator to
Martin's floor. He was watching cartoons, which suited
Lissie, so I left her there and went to the basement floor
and the intensive-care ward. Buzz had fewer wires and
tubes attached, and he was breathing without visible
assistance. The nurse grudgingly allowed me a few
minutes with our patient, as long as I promised not to
tire us out.

"Hi," I said softly.

His eyes fluttered open, and when he saw me, his
mouth curled into a faint smile. "Howdy," he said in a
hoarse voice.

"I brought Lissie to visit Martin. He's to be released
tomorrow and I'll keep him with me until you can come
home."

"Thanks." He coughed in a low wheeze, then gave me
an apologetic look. "Sorry, but they had these damn

tubes down my throat. They told me what happened to Lillith. Did you find the person who did it?"

"Not yet," I admitted. "I'm hoping you can help. The poison seems to have been in the coconut-covered cakes. I had half a dozen reports of tampering that day, although everyone else experienced only mild reactions."

"I bought the cakes on my way out of the store. I just picked 'em up off the rack."

"And there was nothing suspicious about the cellophane wrapper?"

He raised his eyebrows. "I didn't think to examine it. I was going to give them to the kids, but I forgot I had them in my pocket until later in the day. Lillith's got a sweet tooth, and we decided to have ourselves a little treat on the sly. I took it and a beer into the living room, opened a magazine, and the next thing I know some nurse is hovering over me and I've got enough needles in me to be a voodoo doll."

He began to cough in harsh spasms that shook his shoulders and brought tears to his eyes. The nurse came to the door of the cubicle, shot me a dirty look, and said, "How are we doing, Mr. Milvin? Would we like a sip of water?"

"I'm okay," he said, waving her away. "Anything else?"

"One quick question. On Monday night, Jim Bob sent you to Starley City to make the deposit. Do you know why he did that?"

"Some woman called the store and asked to speak to him. He hunkered over the receiver and tried to keep it down, but his ears were redder'n raspberries and he was breathing pretty hard by the time he hung up. He told me to take the bags, that he wanted to stay at the store. When I got back, he was gone."

"But Kevin Buchanon was there the entire time?"

"He was supposed to be," Buzz said with a grimace. "But even when he's there, he's not quite there, if you know what I mean."

I assured him that I did indeed, told him I'd come back to visit, and left before the nurse booted me out. I went back to Martin's room, turned off the television,

and stood beside the bed. "Are you sure you didn't have
a bite of your pa's or your grandmother's coconut cake?"
I pleaded. "One little bite?"

"Is that what poisoned them?"

"And you, too," I said with as much control as I could
rally in my seriously frustrated frame of mind.

He shook his head. "I don't like coconut. It gets stuck
between my teeth."

I told him I'd see him in the morning, and took Lissie
out to the car.

"One short errand on the way back to Maggody," I
told her as we headed down the highway.

She nodded, uninterested in the foolish vagaries of
adults, and was humming to herself as I parked next to
the dumpster at the Airport Arms Apartments. I went
upstairs and along the balcony to the last door. My knock
was as officious as I could make it, and the door opened
within seconds.

This time Cherri Lucinda's curly blond hair was not
hidden, and I was fairly sure she was the woman who'd
been sent sprawling into the van during the ceremonies
outside the SuperSaver. In fact, her scowl was strikingly
similar to the one she'd had that day.

"I'm sick and tired of you people," she said angrily.
"I mean, I've had it up to here with cops and spies and
crazy women. I'm in the middle of packing my bags, and
with luck I'll be in the next state by sunset."

"Wait a minute," I said as she tried to close the door.
"I need to ask you some questions."

"I don't give a damn what you need. I am sick, sick,
sick of this whole stupid nonsense! Screw the gold Le
Baron convertible, screw Jim Bob Buchanon, and screw
you!"

The door slammed in my face.

Lissie didn't glance up as I got back in the car, started
the engine, and drove out of the lot in a cloud of dust.
I dropped her at Joyce's, pulled back onto the highway,
and was considering the idea of driving to France when
I spotted Kevin pedaling along the side of the road in
front of the pool hall. I pulled in front of him and
stopped.

"I want to talk to you," I said as I got out of the car. "And if you so much as sniffle, I'm going to put your head between the spokes of that bicycle and pedal like hell to the East Coast."

"Hi, Arly," he said cheerfully.

"Don't 'hi' me, Kevin Buchanon," I continued. I was aware I wasn't at my coolest, professionally speaking, but I was as sick as Crate of all the gossip and evasions of the last five days, and he was a prime evader. "What happened Monday night at the SuperSaver?"

He swallowed several times, glanced over his shoulder, then rolled his bicycle forward until the front tire went over my foot. "Dahlia came by at ten to talk to me," he said in a whisper, although there was no one in sight except for Roy Stiver sitting in front of his store and therefore a block away. "Buzz told me to git back to work, but we—Dahlia and me, not Buzz and me—had some more talking to do, so she went to the break room and waited there."

"And then?"

His eyes darted like minnows and he began to play with a pimple on his chin. "Well, Jim Bob came in and went to the office. I was shelving boxes of dried potatoes when I heard Jim Bob tell Buzz to go to Starley City. Then Jim Bob ups and leaves, too, so I went back to the break room to talk to my betrothed. You do know Dahlia and I are betrothed, don't you?"

"Yes, Kevin, I do know that. Then what happened?"

"Golly, Arly, that's kind of personal," he stammered, his Adam's apple bouncing.

"I do not—repeat, do not—want to hear what transpired between you and Dahlia. Did the two of you remain in the break room until Buzz returned?"

"It's kind of funny," he said, reattacking the pimple, "but just as Dahlia was gitting ready to slip out the door, we heard Jim Bob come back for a minute. I guess he forgot his notebook or something. We stayed in the break room till he left again, then I hustled Dahlia out and went back to the dried potatoes. There's a new kind with cheddar cheese that—"

"Did you see Jim Bob?" I inserted.

"No, but it wasn't Buzz 'cause he was gone for more than an hour and stayed once he came back. We figured it was Jim Bob."

"And how did you reach that conclusion, Sherlock?"

"He had a key. Otherwise, how would he get back inside the store?"

I stared at him. "I wish you'd mentioned this earlier, Kevin. Did you and your betrothed work out your problems?"

"Oh, yeah, everything's gonna be just swell. I got something to show her that'll make her brighten up like the Christmas lights on the square in Farberville." He stopped abruptly, then finished off the pimple and said, "Mebbe I'll just tell her about it, rather than show it to her. Dahlia's got a real delicate constitution."

And so do Sherman tanks, I thought. I left Kevin sitting on his bicycle and in imminent peril of being run down by a chicken truck (one of the more imminent perils in Maggody). A few of the threads were beginning to come together. As tedious as it sounded, I needed to hear all the gossip floating around town, so I drove briskly to headquarters, aka Ruby Bee's Bar & Grill.

It was still closed.

I turned around in the parking lot and drove back to the PD just as Plover pulled up. He had a peculiar look on his face, so peculiar it was impossible to define or even take a stab at. But thirty minutes later, after hearing his story, I had the same expression on my own face.

14

The next morning I ambled down to Ruby Bee's, found my favorite bar stool, and warned myself to tread very carefully if I ever again wanted to savor a square of lemon icebox pie. "Anybody home?" I called to the kitchen.

Ruby Bee came out to the bar. Her expression reeked of danger, although I'm relieved to report she no longer reeked of more tangible things. "What do you want?"

"I came to talk to you."

"What about? I got to get lunch started. The potatoes need to be peeled and the pies are awaitin' to go in the oven. If you want to talk, why don't you call somebody long distance?"

"I heard you did some of that yourself," I murmured, keeping one foot on the floor just in case.

"Did you?" she said, then wheeled around and started shifting glasses on the back counter. "Where'd you hear that?"

"From Sergeant Plover. He told me the whole story, from the calls to the . . . unpleasant situation in the apartment parking lot yesterday afternoon." My chin started twitching, and I realized I was, as Hammet would say, in a shitload of trouble. I covered the lower part of my face with my hands and feigned a coughing fit, all the while watching her back. It was rigid enough to withstand a bullet.

When she turned around, her stare was enough to stop said bullet in midair. "You getting a summer cold?" she said challengingly. "Is that your problem, missy?"

I nodded helplessly and coughed until I could trust myself as much as I ever would be able to. "But at least we learned where Petrel has been hiding out," I said. "It's unfortunate that he slipped away during the . . . ah, the situation. Plover's confident the state police will be able to run him down today. He couldn't have gone too far on foot."

"The airport's not too far. It's across the street."

"I don't think he'll make a run for Brazil. He didn't commit a crime; he simply chose to hole up in a crummy apartment for the best part of a week."

"With that woman," Ruby Bee said with a growl that would have intimidated a grizzly bear. "I could use another word if I were a mind to, but I won't. She was right uppity when I politely asked to use her bathroom to freshen up. You'd have thought I asked to use her toothbrush or prance around in her black lace underwear."

I was overcome with another fit of coughing. I finally wiped my eyes and said, "According to what I heard, you had a noticeable aroma about you that may have put her off."

"Like a cesspool being dredged after fifty years," Estelle contributed as she came across the room. "Not to mention the coffee grounds in your hair, and that curlicue of apple peel hanging off your ear, and the big ol' brown splotch on your dress, and—"

"Thank you so much for not mentioning any of that," Ruby Bee snapped. "Do you happen to recollect whose brilliant idea it was for me to climb into that nasty thing? Do you?"

Estelle tilted her head and pretended to think. "It seems to me it was a matter of height and who was going to be able to boost the other one over the side and help her out, Miss Five Foot Three On Her Tiptoes."

"Why did you climb in the dumpster?" I asked. "Plover said you claimed that you were going after evidence, but he wasn't clear what it was or why it would be in the dumpster, or even whether or not you found it."

"I was merely investigating. I was hoping to find proof that Petrel was hiding in that awful woman's apartment.

I didn't, but she admitted he had been there, so it doesn't matter, does it?"

"What kind of proof?" I said, not buying a word of it.

"I really couldn't say. You realize the big game's this afternoon, doncha? I got your pink Flamingo shirt in the kitchen; wait and I'll fetch it for you."

I waited, and when she returned, tried my damnedest to badger a straight story out of her and/or Estelle. It paled after a while, so I switched to the less threatening topic of current gossip. What I heard was enough to peel the paint off a '57 Chevy. "Do you believe any of this?" I demanded.

Ruby Bee shook her head. "To tell the truth, I don't rightly know what to believe. I know Petrel wasn't breaking into Joyce's house, and I can't figure out why he'd tamper with the little cakes at his own store, much less put enough poison in one to kill Lillith Smew. But Elsie told Estelle that the Riley girl now claims he raped her— but that doesn't fit in with what Lottie said happened." She frowned at Estelle. "Do you think there were two different cheerleader tryouts?"

Estelle chewed on her lip. "Doesn't make an ounce of sense that there would be. Why would that girl go back after what happened between her and Jim Bob?"

"It's puzzling," Ruby Bee admitted, "but no more so than imagining Kevin and Dahlia carrying on like everybody said they was, and doing it right there on the porch swing, with Eilene and Earl watching television in the living room. I don't think the swing's all that wide."

"Not as wide as Dahlia," Estelle said. "But that's what Johnna Mae Nookim heard when she was buying a broom at the Emporium. She said Perkins's eldest heard all about it while she was cleaning at Mrs. Jim Bob's last week."

"But she told Elsie that she heard it from a woman in the Homemakers' Extension in Hasty not one day ago," Ruby Bee said doubtfully.

"They serve sherry after the meetings."

"During, from what I hear."

I couldn't take any more of it. I left them debating the

relative merits of their sources and drove to the hospital in Farberville to pick up my shortstop. As I passed the Airport Arms, I couldn't keep from staring at the dumpster. I was still chuckling when I reached the hospital. To this day, I get a little smirky when I see one. Ruby Bee, on the other hand, gets very grim.

"The missionary society will be selling canned sodas and cookies," Mrs. Jim Bob said to herself. She made a checkmark by that item and moved on. "Brother Verber will make the opening invocation about playing baseball for Jesus. If he should happen to add a comment or two about the immorality of the other team, I think it might be appropriate, don't you?"

Jim Bob glanced up from the paperwork spread out in front of hiin on the dining room table. "Yeah, what the"—he caught himself—"heck, let him blast into Ruby Bee and Arly. Might be amusing."

"We are speaking of a religious invocation, not a stand-up comedian's routine."

"Right." He looked back down at the papers, wondering how the bankers could generate such quantities of small print without going blind, fer chrissake. He'd managed to appease the wholesale grocer with a partial payment and the promise of the rest of it that afternoon, 'cause now he knew where Lamont was, or figured he had a pretty damn good idea, anyways. He also figured Lamont was going to be a sight more cooperative about putting up his share of the cash. The loan closing wasn't until after the game, and Jim Bob had scraped together his share. Now that Lamont was back (sort of), there'd be enough money to pay the goddamn points, pay off the wholesaler, and maybe pay off the health inspectors and get Jim Bob's SuperSaver Buy 4 Less open again.

He realized, however, he was going to have trouble with Arly Hanks, who'd run whining to the sheriff and her pet trooper. Not being employees of his, they might be less inclined to take orders from him.

"Then Lottie Estes leads the singing of the national anthem," Mrs. Jim Bob said, making yet another checkmark. She was in a much better mood now that she was running the show again, which of course was only fitting since she was the mayor's wife and the president of the missionary society—and was more than prepared to tackle the tricky passage from Corinthians II when the moment arose.

"Is the band playing?" Jim Bob asked, wrinkling his nose.

"I've already explained that we shall use a tape player. I do not trust that group of pimply pubescents to play the sacred strains of the national anthem. I shall hold the flag, and all the players will line up with their caps on their chests as a sign of respect."

"Yeah, I forgot."

"Then I throw out the first ball and we get this game over and done with as quickly as possible. Afterward, there'll be a nice buffet supper at the Assembly Hall for the players and their parents. Perkins's eldest has fixed several quarts of chicken salad and her fair-to-middlin' homemade cinnamon rolls. You will present the trophy, which will then be displayed in the front window of the SuperSaver—if it ever reopens, that is."

"It'll reopen," Jim Bob said in a cold voice. "Just you wait. Lamont'll show up this afternoon and we'll hustle ourselves to the bank to close the loan. Then Arly can arrest him for tampering with the cakes and maybe even for murdering the Smew woman, if he did it on purpose. When he disappears this time, it'll be to a lice-infested cell with a bunch of fags the size of gorillas. They'll learn him a thing or two about trying to pull a quick one on his partner."

Luckily, she'd stopped listening to him. "Does Arly know when she's supposed to arrest him?" she asked as she frowned at her list. There was no reference to Lamont's impending arrest and she wasn't quite sure where it best fit into her schedule. If it took place before the game, it might distract the players, but if it took place afterward, she'd be obliged to make small talk with a criminal for all those dreary innings.

"After the closing. It has to be after the closing, which is set for four o'clock. Arly'd better not so much as look cross-eyed at him until we've closed the loan." Jim Bob realized he sounded a shade frantic, and warned himself to settle down. "We can't accuse him until everything's settled at the bank. I've got my share, but I need his. If the loan folks get spooked, gawd knows what they'll do."

"We do not take the Lord's name in vain in this house," she said mechanically, still wishing she could make a note about the arrest, if only for her own peace of mind. "Perhaps we might plan on having him arrested after you award the trophy," she suggested. "Then we'll have the players clean up the plates and forks and we can all go home knowing justice was served, along with chicken salad and cinnamon rolls."

The telephone rang. Confident that it was for her, Mrs. Jim Bob answered with a curt "Yes?" Fifteen minutes later when she sat back down on the newly re-covered divan, she looked as bumfuzzled as he'd ever seen her. Her eyes were zipping back and forth, and her normally tight mouth was nigh onto invisible. It was rare that she needed to think things over, since she pretty much always had her mind made up in advance.

"What was that about?" he asked.

"That was Millicent. She said she'd just heard an amazing story from Darla Jean, and I must say it takes the cake. Darla Jean and another girl were driving into Farberville to shop for school clothes, and they had the misfortune to have a flat tire right by the airport. They were struggling with the spare when they saw someone they knew across the road at that derelict apartment building. Do you know which one I mean?"

He certainly did, but he prudently hesitated for a moment and scratched his head. "Yeah, the one that should have been torn down a decade ago."

Mrs. Jim Bob went on to relate the rescue of Ruby Bee and the ensuing scene with a blond woman on the balcony. "Darla Jean and her little friend couldn't hear anything, of course, and they were about to walk across the street when a truckload of Maggody boys drove up and fixed the flat for them. The girls went on to the mall. I can't begin to imagine what in tarnation Ruby Bee Hanks was doing in a dumpster. And Darla Jean swears

Estelle Oppers came out of an upstairs apartment—and she wasn't alone. I find this most peculiar."

"Which apartment?" Jim Bob said, doing his level best not to break out in a telltale sweat, despite the fact his bowels had iced over like a sump hole in January.

"I couldn't say, but the point is that she was in a half-naked man's apartment and Ruby Bee was in a dumpster. I would like very much to find out what those two were up to, but my first duty is to report this to Brother Verber. I'm sure he will share my outrage at this immoral behavior."

Brother Verber had the decency to answer the telephone, and she plunged in briskly.

"This is Sister Barbara. Now you'd best sit down and take notes concerning what I'm about to tell you. It has all the makin's of a splendid sermon."

"Why, certainly, Sister Barbara. I'm sure what you have to tell me is very important, very important indeed. Let me get a pencil and a piece of paper."

She could hear his heavy footsteps and a good deal of huffing and puffing as he fetched his supplies, but he sounded fine when he came back on the line to assure her of his readiness.

"Are you familiar with the Airport Arms Apartments?" she began.

"I don't reckon I am, but I devote all my time to saving souls in our little community. I can't remember when I last had call to leave my trailer parked right here in the righteous shade of the Voice of the Almighty Lord Assembly Hall."

"I know where your trailer is parked, Brother Verber. The apartment house is that disreputable place across from the airport in Farberville." She waited for him to say something, but all she heard was his breathing, which suddenly sounded right raspy. He didn't say anything, though, so she went on. "What I have to tell you concerns the dumpster."

His breathing took a turn for the worse. Wanting to get to the gist of her story, Mrs. Jim Bob was beginning to lose her saintly patience. "Are you having a seizure? You haven't even heard the half of it yet."

"I haven't?" he croaked.

"Millicent McIlhaney said her daughter Darla Jean saw one of our citizens in the dumpster and another come out of an upstairs apartment with a half-naked man with a beer can in his hand."

She was quite pleased that he grasped the implications so readily. She could tell from the gurgly noises he made that he was as outraged as she, if not more so. It was most satisfying.

Martin was waiting in the hospital lobby. The pallor of his face was accented by dark smudges beneath his eyes, but he managed a smile for me. He didn't look like an energetic shortstop; then again, it didn't much matter, because we didn't have the proverbial bat's chance.

I stopped at the information desk and learned that Buzz had been moved to a semiprivate room and was now upgraded to good condition. I asked Martin if he wanted to visit his father. He blinked at me for a moment, then said, "Yeah, Miss Arly. That'd be great."

Buzz was sleeping as we entered the room. The tubes were gone except for an IV in his arm, and his color was better than Martin's. He opened his eyes and said, "Martin, good to see you. I've been real worried about you and Lissie, and it's comforting to know Arly's watching out for the both of you. How are you feelin', son?"

"Okay," Martin said quietly. "You don't have to worry about us."

Buzz glanced at me. "You found out anything about who poisoned us?"

"The preliminary lab report is less than detailed, but they've speculated that it was an industrial pesticide. It may take weeks to get more specific information. In the meantime, I'm trying to pick out snippets of truth from all the rumors and gossip."

"So folks are talking?" He let out a low laugh that became a cough. I poured him a glass of water and hovered beside the bed until he regained control. "Sorry, those damn tubes liked to leave scratch marks all the way to my stomach. What's everybody saying?"

"Ninety-nine percent of it is pure malarky," I said,

shaking my head. "The hottest theory is that Lamont Petrel tampered with the packages, then eluded a county-wide dragnet, has been raping women nonstop for the last week, and is numero uno on the FBI's most wanted list."

"He struck me as a nice enough guy. I guess you never can tell, can you?"

"We'll let you rest," I murmured, not in the mood to explain the fine line between hysterically explosive rumors and tedious truth.

Martin and I drove back to Maggody. Hammet was watching television, but as we came into the living room, he switched it off and gave me a worried look. "Is it true what I heard about Miss Ruby Bee being squashed flatter than road kill—and in a big ol' square garbage can?"

"Not exactly," I said. I showed Martin where I'd put his clothes, then sat down across from Hammet and said, "Where'd you hear this latest tidbit?"

"From Saralee, who heard her aunt talking to some lady who was drinking coffee. Lissie said she supposed there was bank robbers' money in the garbage. I dunno, though. I can't figure out why the hell they'd hide money in the garbage."

"Neither can I," I said, amused in spite of myself. Hammet's link to the grapevine was as slippery as any-one's in town. I shuddered to think what the younger side of the population was making of the snatches of conversation they were picking up. Bank robbers and road kill, obviously.

I told the boys to rest up for the big game, then walked across the street to the PD and allowed myself a walking tour of Brussels and a glass of lager at a sidewalk café in the main square.

It calmed me down to the point of idle musing, and after a few minutes, I got out my notebook and reread the notes from all the interviews. It became increasingly interesting, this collection of half-truths, gossip, and out-and-out lies, and shortly thereafter some things began to fall into place. Not everything, mind you, because some witnesses (i.e., Ruby Bee) were about as recalcitrant as diving mules.

Cherri Lucinda Crate had admitted to Plover that Lamont Petrel had been at her apartment since the afternoon of the grand opening. She'd continued to deny that Jim Bob visited her Monday night, but once I decided that was a lie, all sorts of things began to make sense, including Kevin's avowal that Jim Bob had returned to the supermarket and Ruby Bee's screwy story about a serial killer in the motel parking lot. Petrel's motive for disappearing was obvious, and his current whereabouts unknown but within bounds of speculation. I was fairly sure I'd be hearing about it soon, thanks to Hizzoner, but for the moment there wasn't much I could do.

I knew who had laced the tamale sauce and sponge cakes with ipecac, and who had stuck pins in the cupcakes. I knew how and why and when and where, thus qualifying my theory for a journalism class exercise. I moved on to the mysterious poisonings at Buzz Milvin's house. It was possible that the same perp had doctored the coconut cakes, perhaps underestimating the toxicity of the polysyllabic substance. But unless Martin had lied, he hadn't consumed the damn things.

I called Plover and asked him to call back with the lab report on the contents of Martin's stomach. He tried to weasel answers out of me, but I hung up and waited, drumming my fingers on my notebook and staring at the visitor's chair.

It took him only a few minutes to report back to me. "Spaghetti, corn bread, soda pop, crackers, a minute trace of cereal, milk," he said. "Just what the kid's been saying all along. What're you thinking, Arly?"

"That he didn't lie," I said, mostly to myself.

"Lie about what?"

"About what he ate that day, of course." I was hedging, but I wasn't quite ready to explain the fuzzy idea that was struggling to take shape. "I'll get back to you shortly." I hung up, called Ruby Bee, and demanded she repeat the one bit of gossip that nobody had shared with me. She hemmed and hawed, but finally she told me what I'd suspected I would hear. I confirmed it with a second source, then called Plover back to relate my theories.

"I think you're right," he said after a minute of silence. "So what's our schedule?"

"I'm going to call Harve with all this, and then, Sergeant Plover, I'm going to a baseball game. The grande dame of the dumpster is having a party for the team afterward, so I can leave Hammet and Martin in her care. I should be in your office by four-thirty."

After I'd made the final call, I went back to my apartment, put on the pink T-shirt, gathered up the equipment and the two players, and we drove to the baseball field behind the high school.

Most of the town was there for the big shootout, and it took some maneuvering to find a parking place among the pickup trucks and station wagons. Raz was there, as were the Satterings, Perkins and his eldest, Earl Boy Nookim's parents, and the entire force of both the missionary society and the pool hall coterie. Picnic baskets and coolers were everywhere.

The Ruby Bee's Flamingos were milling around near third base, which was not a burlap bag. Georgie McMay, Saralee, and Earl Boy Nookim were exchanging ominous looks, but not blows. Lissie and Jackie were after butterflies, and Enoch was watching reruns in his head. Ray was talking to his father, who went to the bleachers when he spotted us approaching.

I put down the equipment bag, said hello to the team, and shaded my eyes to look across the field at the SuperSavers. If anything, they'd all grown half a foot and a couple had sprouted whiskers. Larry Joe Lambertino was pointing here and there and presumably offering last-minute advice. Hizzoner and Mizzoner stood nearby, both wearing insufferably smug smiles. Petrel was not in sight, but if my theory was correct, he would be before too long.

I turned around to assess the fans in the bleachers. Brother Verber was mopping his face and neck, and looking as composed as a deer caught in the glare of headlights. Dahlia and Kevin were at the far end. Kevin fluttered his fingers at me, but Dahlia didn't even blink, which was fine with me. Joyce was passing out cookies to keep her kids relatively contented. Several high-school girls were sitting together, but a goodly number of their boyfriends were not in sight.

As Ruby Bee walked past the bleachers, there was a low murmur and a few snickers. She held her chin up, however, and I doubted anyone had enough courage to make any remarks within her earshot. Estelle trailed after her, carrying a large plastic bag that bulged oddly but didn't seem heavy.

It looked as if we were all present and accounted for, except for Petrel. I went over to Larry Joe and inquired about procedure. Before he could answer, Mrs. Jim Bob marched over and stuck a piece of paper under my nose.

"I have made all the arrangements," she said with a pinched smile. She consulted her watch. "The pregame ceremonies will begin in three minutes, so I suggest you instruct your team to commence their warm-up."

"Who's the umpire?"

"Why, Jim Bob, of course. I believe he's selected a couple of his employees to umpire out in the field. There are only two minutes remaining."

I thought about protesting, but it wouldn't have done any good and it didn't really matter, since the game was predetermined by relative size (monsters versus dwarfs) and athletic ability (some versus none). There wasn't much reason for our team to warm up, so I told them to sit down and try to remember some of the basic rules.

The SuperSaver cheerleaders tried to rouse the crowd out of its amiable indolence by shrieking and cartwheeling into each other. When they finally gave up (and got up), Mrs. Jim Bob dragged Brother Verber to home plate and clapped her hands until everybody settled down.

"Brother Verber will now lead us in the invocation," she announced.

He wiped his forehead, shot a fearful look at the bleachers, and finally found his voice. "We are gathered here today," he began sonorously, "to test the skills of these two teams of Maggody children—but we are not here with God's blessings. God is wincing as He looks down at this field. He is gnashing His teeth. He is rubbing His hands together and sighing. Why? Do you want to know why God's unhappy today in heaven?"

Nobody admitted to possession of an inquiring mind. After a quick swipe with the handkerchief, Brother Verber sucked in a lungful and told us, anyway. "Because one team is made up of outstanding young boys, each dedicated to the principles of competition and fair play."

"How young are they?" Saralee called.

"Young, little lady. Now this other team"—he made a grandiose sweep in our direction—"this other team has violated the laws of God, not to mention all standards of human decency. This other team has girls and boys playing together! And do you know what that means?" He had to pause to get another lungful, but he had enough sense not to demand any response from the crowd, most of whom were eyeing the Flamingos in case they commenced violating standards right there on the spot. "It means they have wicked thoughts running through their previously innocent little minds. They are seeing each other's bodies, and boys are wondering what all there is under those curvaceous pink T-shirts and the girls are wondering the same about those tight-cut jeans. They are thinking about sex!"

"I'm thinking you're an asshole," Hammet volunteered.

"Me, too," Saralee added loyally.

"That's an example of what I'm talking about," Brother Verber said, his nose pulsating and his face beginning to drip. "There is a passel of wickedness in Maggody, and it comes from boys and girls being thrown together—on baseball teams and on porch swings. It leads to lust and depravity and—"

"Magazine subscriptions?" Kevin Buchanon said loudly. It would have been more impressive if his voice hadn't cracked, but now all heads turned to the far end of the bleachers. "What about magazine subscriptions?"

"I don't know what you're talking about, but I think it's Satan hisself I'm hearing," Brother Verber blustered. "Satan hisself is perched on your shoulder, ain't he? Satan hisself!"

Dahlia had remained motionless thus far. She rose ponderously, inch by inch and with such steeliness that the crowd was holding its collective breath. "What does Satan know about kittens and tomcats except what he reads in your magazine?" she said very slowly and clearly. Her black eyes were burning within the fleshy mounds of her cheeks. Her lips went in and out as she stared at him. She was not anyone to meet in a dark alley.

Brother Verber clutched his bow tie. "They was planted by some sinner to discredit me," he managed to say. "They were put beside my trailer so that I would be made to look like a weak-kneed sinner and unworthy of guiding my flock down the path of righteousness."

Mrs. Jim Bob gave him a quick look, then put one fist on her hip and shook her finger at Kevin and Dahlia. "You're a fine pair to be casting the first stone. Everybody in town knows how you two were fornicating on the porch swing."

Eilene leapt to her feet, although she kept a tight grip on Earl's shoulder to hold him down. "That's a lie!"

"Everybody knows," Mrs. Jim Bob replied complacently.

"I say it's a lie," Eilene said, beginning to snivel. Beside her, Earl was too stunned to do anything, and Kevin and Dahlia had sunk down to their seats and then some.

Estelle and Ruby Bee were whispering. They made a decision, and Estelle stepped into the lion's den. "Satan may have planted those magazines by your trailer, but he didn't plant them in a certain dumpster at the edge of Farberville, did he?" She put the plastic bag down and opened it. A bright pink figure popped up, its painted eyes wide in surprise and its other anatomical projections jiggling so realistically that the crowd let out a collective gasp. "What about your little inflatable friend?" Estelle continued. "Surely you felt bad about leaving Suzie Squeezums, didn't you?"

Brother Verber's face resembled tomato aspic, from the color to the quiver. His jaw opened and closed, and we could see his tongue swelling as if he'd contracted a mild case of bubonic plague. "I don't know what you're talking about," he said hoarsely.

"And you're a fine one to speak," Mrs. Jim Bob

added, although she was sending dark looks at her companion. "Why don't you explain what you were doing in an apartment with a half-naked man, and in the afternoon, too? I think we're entitled to an explanation of this outrageous conduct."

"Sez who?" Ruby Bee snapped.

What was I doing all this time? you ask. Nothing. And why not? you ask. Because every last one of them deserved it, that's why. The entire town had been obsessed with tacky rumors. Life in Puritan Salem had been a damn sight saner, and the only reasons these good citizens hadn't pilloried anyone was because we didn't have a convenient spot for the pillory.

"I've never hidden in a dumpster," Mrs. Jim Bob retorted. It was a non sequitur of monumental proportion, but nobody minded because, in truth, they figured they deserved an explanation of that, too. Several folks nodded and said as much to each other.

Ruby Bee waited until there was dead silence and the tension was as hot as the sun. "I was fetching a bag someone had thrown in there. The bag contained a whole stack of pornographic magazines and books, along with this perverted balloon creature. You want to know who threw it in the dumpster?"

Brother Verber was deteriorating badly, but he nudged Mrs. Jim Bob aside, noisily cleared his throat, and gave it his all. "I did it in the name of the Lord. I was cleansing the town of depravity and filth and perversion by making sure that material was discarded outside the city limits of Maggody, so that not one of our innocent youths might stumble onto it. No, I didn't want a single child to be tainted by that sort of wickedness. No, I didn't want it to creep inside your very homes and destroy your family values. No, I had to fight the devil by my lonesome."

A few of the spectators clapped hesitantly, although most of them were tugging on their lips or scratching their heads as they struggled to follow his logic.

Raz Buchanon expelled an arc of tobacco juice. "But jest exactly where did they come from in the first place?"

Brother Verber clasped his hands over his belly and

rocked back on his feet. "Why, they came from Satan hisself."

"Some of the magazines have subscription labels," Estelle called. "They weren't addressed to Satan, either."

Even Mrs. Jim Bob was growing perturbed. "Where did they come from, Brother Verber?"

He thudded to his knees and put his entwined hands under his chin. His eyes welling with tears, he bleated, "Satan."

This divinely diverting moment was interrupted by the sound of an unmuffled engine coming around the corner of the high school. We all stared at the pickup truck as it drove across the grass and right onto the field, and we stared a damn sight harder as we caught an increasingly better view of the figure crouched in the back.

My first thought was that it was some giant skunk on its hind legs. It was basically black, with a white fluttery streak down its spine.

"Oh my goodness," Mrs. Jim Bob said in a strangled voice. "It's Lamont Petrel. They tarred and feathered him!"

15

The boys in the cab of the truck tumbled out like circus clowns, slapping each other on the back and whooping at the stunned crowd. With all the animation of zombies, those in the bleachers came out to the field and encircled the truck to get a better look at the very unhappy Lamont Petrel.

He was clad only in boxer shorts. The tar had been slathered on by a generous hand, as had the curly white chicken feathers. I presumed the tar had been warmed only to the point of spreadability, in that it was lumpy and Lamont was not only alive but also not screaming about second- and third-degree burns. All in all, it was a rather impressive piece of work.

He spotted me. "I demand to file charges. This is quite intolerable and painful, not to mention humiliating. I want all of these vicious animals arrested at once."

"He's the one oughta be arrested," one of the boys jeered. "Rapist skunks deserve what they get."

"Yeah, that'll teach him to leave our women alone," said another.

I recognized the group from the Dairee Dee-Lishus—short the mutant Buchanon, who was suited up for the game and keeping a wary distance from me. "Glad to see you found Mr. Petrel at the Airport Arms Apartments," I said pleasantly. "I know Hizzoner told you where to find the crazed rapist. I'm curious to know if he suggested the . . . costume, too."

"Hell, no," Jim Bob said, shaking his head in disbelief as he shoved through the crowd. "I didn't tell the shitheads to do this. All of you shitheads are fired! Don't even bother to come by for your paychecks. What'll they say at the closing in an hour? Jesus H. Christ, Lamont, you look about as stupid as a pig in a pinafore."

"Then get me out of here," Lamont said through clenched teeth. He scraped a lump of black goo off his cheek and flipped it off his finger. The stripe of white feathers down his back fluttered each time he moved; it fascinated the crowd, all of whom were rumbling and grumbling at each other.

"Not until we've cleared up a few things," I said. "As chief of police, I have an obligation to find out exactly what happened to our guest—and why." I looked at the boys and said, "The gentleman has been at the apartment since the grand opening almost a week ago. Precisely whom did he rape and when did he do it?"

"Heather Riley," the boys chimed in in unison, although not in the melodious style of the Vienna Boys Choir.

"Did he?" I said smoothly. "Why, look, here's Heather hiding behind Darla Jean McIlhaney. Why don't you come confront your attacker and give me enough information to arrest him? Come on, don't be shy, Heather. There's no point in not repeating what every last person in town already knows."

Lamont watched as the blond girl came forward. "I've never seen her in my life! I sure as hell didn't attack her. How can I have raped her if I've never even seen her?"

Heather approached me with a pleading look. "Maybe I was confused," she whispered. "Maybe I was so traumatized that I didn't remember exactly what all happened."

"But, Heather," Darla Jean said, running up to put her arm around her friend's trembling shoulder, "you did remember his name and face. You told me all about it in your bedroom. You told me how he held you down and ripped your clothes off and hurt you real bad, and then how you ran screaming into the street and barely escaped being run down by a truck. It couldn't have been more than a couple of days ago when you told me how you cried out for Beau to save you from this here monster."

"What the hell is she talking about?" Lamont demanded, the whites of his eyes in sharp contrast with the smeary blackness of his face.

The most verbal of the boys hitched up his jeans and gave the crowd a self-satisfied grin. "When I heard it, I decided to teach this no-good sumbitch not to mess with my woman. Us boys dragged him out of the whore's apartment and kept him busy all night long, dint we? He ain't gonna bother anyone for a long while."

"They're maniacs," the purported sumbitch howled. "Arrest them."

"If'n he raped the girl, he oughta be shot," someone from the crowd muttered. This proved to be a popular sentiment, and I had to shout to make myself heard.

"Shut up! This is a farce. If all of you weren't so ready not only to believe what you hear but also to expand upon it for your own amusement, this sort of thing wouldn't get out of hand. Heather, what happened when you interviewed to be a SuperSaver cheerleader?"

"Jim Bob put his hand on my knee."

"Anything else?" I said, turning on all my wattage.

She looked at her feet. "No, nothing else. It just bothered me, so I told Miss Estes. The next thing I hear is this big story of how I was raped. I . . . I, uh, got confused."

We all turned to Jim Bob, who was as miserable as the girl and kicking up a decent-sized cloud of dust. "I was showing her how long the miniskirt was. I distinctly remember saying that the skirt would come to her knee."

The leader of the pack didn't look much happier, but he managed a cocky voice. "Oh, well, the sumbitch probably raped somebody else. Most likely that whore. That's why the FBI's after him."

"No," I said, "the FBI's not after him, and he and the woman were friends. Cherri Lucinda Crate was nice enough to pick him up outside the supermarket and take him back to unit number twelve of the Airport Arms. Lamont wanted to make Jim Bob sweat, and he was doing a fine job of it until the supermarket reopened Monday afternoon. That was most annoying, because it meant all that wonderful ill will he'd stirred up with the tamale-sauce episode might be assuaged and Jim Bob might be less inclined to sell to an outfit in Texas."

I had everybody's attention except for Mrs. Jim Bob, who looked as if she might attack her husband—but not with amorous intent. She sidled over to Brother Verber and began to hiss at him.

Jim Bob was breathing so loudly we could hear it, and he clenched his fist as he glared at the cartoonish skunk in the bed of the pickup truck. "Then he dumped stuff in the tamale sauce? Is that what I just heard?"

I nodded. "He had a key, so it wasn't much of a challenge to return to the deli Friday night and dump several ounces of ipecac in the quart of sauce. He'd even jotted down the quantity in his notebook so he could calculate how many bottles of ipecac to use. Monday night was more of a challenge, because Buzz Milvin and Kevin were supposed to be there all night and Lamont didn't want to surface quite yet. He was obliged to watch the store from the shadows of the bar and grill until he saw Jim Bob arrive to pick up the receipts. He went into his room at the Flamingo Motel and called Cherri Lucinda, who then called Jim Bob and invited him over for a . . . visit."

Everybody swung around to see how Mrs. Jim Bob was going to field this one, but she was so intent on her conversation with Brother Verber that it was hard to tell if she'd heard any of it. Disappointed, they looked back at me.

I was tempted to get on the bed of the truck so no one would miss a word. However, I opted for decorum, and merely raised my voice in hopes Mrs. Jim Bob would catch on. "The invitation was so vividly couched that Jim Bob told Buzz to take the deposits to the bank, then hopped in his car and drove to her apartment, not the least bit worried about leaving Kevin in charge of the supermarket."

"It was an interview," Jim Bob croaked. This created so much tittering and snickering that I had to wait a full minute before my audience settled down again.

"Whatever you say," I said graciously. "In any case, when Lamont saw Kevin go to the break room, he

slipped into the store, using his key, to place the tampered packages on the display rack in hopes the store
would be closed down again. It worked well."

Dahlia rumbled like the onset of an earthquake. "He
put that stuff in the sponge cakes that made me sick?
Him, the fellow in the tar and feathers? I don't care if
he raped some girl or not—he deserves to be tarred and
feathered and strung up from a tree."

Again, a popular sentiment. Lamont was crouched
down so low that we could barely see him, but we could
hear his sputters of protest and piteous avowals of
innocence.

"You mean," Jim Bob said, rather sputtery himself,
"that Lamont did all this shit to make me sell the Jim
Bob's SuperSaver Buy 4 Less? He put me through a
week of nightmares and cold sweats so I'd belly-up like
a trout in a sewage ditch?"

"And murdered Lillith Smew?" Ruby Bee said from
behind me. "Just to make Jim Bob sell his share? Don't
that seem kinda going overboard?"

"No, he didn't lace the package with a lethal pesticide," I said. "That, indeed, would have been going
overboard. He just wanted to keep the pressure on Jim
Bob right up to the time of the loan closing. Jim Bob
would have been so frantic by then that he'd have been
grateful for whatever offer he received for his share of
the supermarket. I would imagine Lamont anticipated a
fat finder's fee, along with his share, and—"

With a primitive howl born of generations of inbreed-
ing, Jim Bob leapt onto the truck bed and swung wildly
at Lamont. His fist stuck in a glob of tar, and he was
frowning at it as Lamont shoved him over backward,
jumped out of the truck, and ran with surprising agility
through the parked cars and around the corner of the
high school.

Jim Bob got to his feet, rubbed his tarred fist on his
pants, and took off after Lamont. "What about the goddamn loan, you goddamn sumbitch?"

Heather's boyfriend started to follow, but I grabbed
his arm and said, "Let him go. The sheriff's got half a
dozen deputies waiting out front for him. He'll be

charged with felonious assault on various folks' gastrointestinal systems, and we may be able to work out an interstate conspiracy charge that really will attract the attention of the FBI."

The entire scene lapsed into chaotic babbling, which was okay with me. As much as I enjoyed my fifteen minutes of fame, I still had business to attend to, and I dreaded it worse than anything I'd faced before.

"What about the ball game?" Hammet said, tugging on the hem of my gawdy pink Flamingo shirt. "Kin we play now?"

I glanced over his head at Ruby Bee, who hadn't moved and was watching me with an unfathomable expression. "I wish you'd volunteered the gossip when you first heard it," I said to her. "If you had, I could have tried to do something."

"There are some things folk don't like to talk about," she said quietly. "I reckon it was awhile back when I heard something vague, but it was so nasty that I put it out of my mind. No one likes to think that sort of thing goes on next door or down the road. I just figured it wasn't true and that I wasn't going to repeat it, not even to you and Estelle."

"Nobody wanted to talk about it, not even Hammet." I gently shook his shoulder and said, "But sometimes it needs to be talked about, to be brought out like all the other dirty laundry."

"I promised," he said. "I wanted to tell ya, but I promised. Lissie made me swear to keep it a secret. She said she tried to tell her teacher, but the dumb sow didn't believe her and she had to miss recess for lying."

We were on an island in the middle of the noisy crowd. I could hear my heart beating, and I thought I heard Hammet's, too. His eyes filled with tears and he flung his arms around me, his body convulsed with painful sobs. Once he'd calmed down, I told him where I was going and why, then told Ruby Bee that the game was postponed. Indefinitely.

"Guess we showed him," Kevin cackled as he and his honey bun sat on the porch swing, enjoying the breeze.

"Did you see how he fell on his knees? He was so red, he looked like a fire hydrant, didn't he? I'm just sorry a dog didn't wander by and lift a hind leg."

"Don't you go talking like that again, Kevin Fitzgerald Buchanon," Dahlia said. She polished off the last crumbs of chocolate cake, put the plate down in the respectable area between them, and gazed at him until he started to squirm, which didn't take long. "Now if'n I agree to rebetroth with you, you got to swear you ain't gonna act all crazy ever again until we're married and have our own cozy little house."

She may have said *house,* but Kevin would have sworn on his great-granny's urn on the mantel that she said *bed.* It was unfortunate. Not only had he been deprived of his darling dumpling's soft, warm body all these long months, recently he'd been obliged to listen to all sorts of gossip and look at photographs that had left some real vivid images in his head.

He glanced over his shoulder. In the living room, his pa was watching television and his ma was clipping coupons out of a magazine. He gave the swing a little push, then said, "Do you happen to be wearing something other than your best blue blouse, my sweetness?"

He was astonished when she slapped the living daylights out of him. He was so plum astonished that he couldn't for the life of him think of anything to say, which was probably for the best.

Mrs. Jim Bob made one list after another. Groceries; chores Perkins's eldest had best do next week—if she intended to keep her job, that is. Refreshments at the next missionary society meeting. Pieces of furniture to have re-covered. Bible verses that could be used as weapons. The Ten Commandments, all of which Jim Bob had violated in the last week. Well, maybe not failing to honor his father and mother, since they were buried side by side in the old cemetery down by Boone Creek. She scratched that one out and wrote, "Thou shall not humiliate thy wife in front of everybody in town."

She put the other lists aside. This was the one to work on, she decided with a grim smile. When Jim Bob came back, she intended to sit him down on the newly recovered divan for a long while and go over each and every commandment as many times as it took. By the time she finished with him, he was going to wish he'd been tarred and feathered like that disgusting Lamont. It would seem a minor inconvenience compared to what she had in store for him.

Then, she told herself, she would have to do her Christian duty and march right down to the trailer next to the Voice of the Almighty, because she had some questions and was going to get some answers. Her lips tightened as she recalled the bright pink doll, and she grabbed for another piece of paper.

The telephone rang, and she was feeling brightened enough to answer with a brisk "What is it?" She listened for a minute, then said, "No, neither of them's coming in to the bank today. Last seen, my husband was chasing a giant skunk toward Cotter's Ridge."

The man at the other end seemed to want to discuss it further, but she didn't, so she replaced the receiver and went back to Jim Bob's list. She had him on adultery, taking the Lord's name in vain, coveting, and at least partially on some of the others.

Mrs. Jim Bob fixed herself a nice cup of tea and went to work.

When Plover and I returned from Farberville, I admitted I couldn't face the PD or the magpies eagerly awaiting a choice morsel to devour. We drove down to Boone Creek and parked under a clump of oak trees. October was nearly a month away, but the relentless heat had turned some of the leaves brown, and we could hear them rustling above us. The water was low, exposing mud bars and expanses of rough yellowish-green rocks.

Plover called the sheriff's dispatcher for an update. Lamont had last been seen scampering into the brush in the direction of Cotter's Ridge, with Jim Bob hot on his heels and bellowing some highly creative threats. The dispatcher conveyed Harve's apology for letting the two get past his deputies, but none of us was terribly perturbed. Cotter's Ridge was a rocky, brambly wasteland.

The dispatcher assured us that all the roads were being watched, then told us to have a nice day.

I replayed the last two hours in my mind. The scene at home plate had had a certain charm, but what had happened at the hospital had not. "I'm glad he admitted it," I said, sighing. "The last thing I wanted to do was to confront him with his own daughter. Gawd, I wish I'd caught on sooner, but I was listening so hard to the ludicrous gossip that I missed the subtle messages. Both kids afraid of him, defending him, and denying he did more than raise his voice. Lissie saying she had to be a big girl, worrying about being accused of making up stories. Martin lying about being beaten."

"We all missed the messages."

I let my head fall back against the seat and glanced at him out of the corner of my eye. "Nobody did a thing to keep that poor little girl from being sexually abused. Martin tried to tell his grandmother, but she refused to believe him. He did the only thing he could."

Plover took my hand and squeezed it. "It's a good thing he didn't taste too much of the roach powder before he laced the coconut cakes in his pa's coat pocket."

"Guess he wanted to know if it had a weird taste. We can write off his grandmother's death as accidental, since he was trying to . . . stop his father."

"She refused to believe him. He may have suspected she might eat one of the cakes."

"No, he didn't. I'm not about to charge a twelve-year-old with homicide, or even manslaughter. Those kids don't deserve to go through any more ordeals. A caseworker from the Department of Human Services will be here tomorrow to take them into protective custody—and she's not going to hear a single word about coconut cakes and roach powder. God, I hope some therapist can help Lissie understand why he did it. All his pitiful excuses about being so lost and frightened after his wife died, being so lonely, being so desperate for love and physical affection"—I slammed my fist on the dashboard—"those aren't excuses. There is no excuse for what he was doing to that child!"

I shoved open the car door and stalked down the side of the road, grinding my fists into my pockets and kicking the clumps of weeds. When I heard Plover's footstep behind me, I wheeled around and said, "No one listened, damn it. That kind of thing's not entertaining—so we've made it unspeakable." My voice rose an octave. "Let's talk about Kevin and Dahlia in the porch swing, or turn Lamont Petrel into a rapist, or anything worthy of a three-part miniseries on television—anything that has no more than a tiny kernel of truth, because the truth's too damn unpleasant. What the hell—let's bury our heads in a travel book, pretending to be on another continent where everything is romantic and carefree!"

"It's okay," he said, putting his hands on my shoulders. "It's not your fault."

I tried to get my voice down, but I couldn't, and I could barely see him through my watery eyes. "It's everybody's fault. Ruby Bee admitted she'd heard something, but she put it out of her mind. After I talked to you this morning, I called Lissie's fourth-grade teacher from last year. She stammered around, and finally said she'd wondered about the possibility but didn't want to get involved in something like that. *Something like that!*"

I broke free and started down the road again. He let me go for a minute but eventually caught up with me and we sat on a mossy log until long past dusk.

"Georgie McMay, if you don't stop that, I'm going to tan your hide," Estelle said, even though it was an empty threat because he probably outweighed her. "You, too, Ray. We are not going to hit each other with catsup and mustard bottles. Fix your hamburgers and sit down nicely."

When Georgie hesitated, Earl Boy Nookim took the opportunity to curl his foot around Georgie's ankle and bring him facedown on the floor. Enoch leapt on Earl Boy's back and, with the enraged roar of the Hulk (Enoch was a great fan of the green machine), did his best to throttle his victim. Georgie rolled over and grabbed Earl Boy's foot. He regretted it almost immediately when the wrestlers crashed down on him, and he expressed his displeasure both verbally and with an attack on Earl Boy's hair.

Ruby Bee put her hands on her hips and tried the voice that usually broke up barroom brawls. "I am not about to have this sort of thing going on in this bar and grill. Y'all either settle down or I'll settle you down myself."

"Who wants more chips?" Estelle trilled.

Lissie, Jackie, and Martin raised their hands. There wasn't any point in saying anything, because the din from the barroom floor would have drowned out a bulldozer.

In the back booth, Saralee gazed pensively across the tabletop at Hammet. "You are mighty mysterious," she said, twirling a yellow braid around her finger.

"I ain't neither."

"Yes, you are."

"Ain't."

"Are too!"

By the time Ruby Bee brought the wedges of pie to the back booth, the occupants were on their feet, pushing, shoving, and yelling at each other. She noted there was no serious damage being done, and returned to the bar at the very moment a man in a khaki jumpsuit and a baseball cap came in.

"Private party," she said wearily.

"I just came by to give you the tournament schedule," he said. He handed her a piece of paper, noticed the brawl still in progress, winced, and said, "The other team was disqualified, naturally. We can't have seventeen-year-olds in the intermediate league, not even ones repeating sixth grade for the fifth time, or fifth for the sixth. Your team has its first game Saturday morning. I . . . ah, I look forward to seeing you and your players at the ballpark." He left, quickly.

"Lookee here," Ruby Bee said loudly, "the Ruby Bee's Flamingos are the champions of Maggody! Ain't that something? We're gonna play in a real tournament this week."

"And won't Arly be excited when she hears this," Estelle murmured.

Ruby Bee hesitated as a whole lot of things went

through her mind. However, she told herself coolly, she could handle Arly. "Let's celebrate with ice cream!"

Lamont finally gave up and stopped, mostly because he was panting so hard that he was afraid he'd have a heart attack in the middle of the woods. Some of the tar had been left on tree trunks and logs submerged in dry leaves. Most of the white feathers on his back were gone, although he was unaware of it and therefore equally unaware of the Hanselish trail he'd left all the way up the side of the ridge.

He sat down on a stump and listened for the sound of someone crashing through the leaves in pursuit. It was hard to think, what with the roar in his head and the black blotches rotating before his eyes, and he finally conceded as much. He attempted to run his fingers through his silver hair, but the result was not good. The sudden crackle of leaves behind a dense clump of scrub firs was not good, either. He wiped his hand on the side of the stump, cursed the barbarians who'd done this to him, and struggled to his feet.

Jim Bob charged into the clearing. "I'm going to cut off your balls and feed them to the squirrels," he said in way of greeting. "One at a time. Then I'm going to cut off your—"

"Hey, Jim Bob, I thought we were partners," Lamont said. He held out his hand but shrewdly began to edge around the stump. "We can work this out. I'll call the loan officer, at home if I have to, and tell him we'll be there bright and early Monday morning to finish the paperwork."

He had the stump between them now. He would have preferred a chain-link fence topped with barbed wire, but he figured the stump was better than nothing, since Jim Bob had the look of a pissed-off pit bull. "What's more," he said magnanimously, "we can work out a deal for you to buy me out. You'll be the sole owner of Jim Bob's SuperSaver Buy 4 Less."

Jim Bob advanced. "You're some fine sumbitch, ain't you?"

"Now listen here, you don't have any reason to carry on like a school-yard bully," Lamont said. Each time Jim Bob sidled around the stump, he followed suit. "We can work it out."

"Some fine sumbitch, using me and sweet Cherri Lucinda like you did. We're gonna work it out right here and right now."

What neither of them noticed was the entrance to the burrow beneath the stump. It was small but cozy and had been excavated for the sole intent of protection. The *Mephitis mephitis* (Mustelidae), being a nocturnal creature, was frightened by the loud voices and commotion outside its burrow. It twitched its nose and warily turned its tapered snout toward the opening.

"You keep away from me!" Lamont said shrilly.

A foot kicked the stump, sending its occupant into deep-seated panic. In order to protect itself, it scurried out and took a hard look at the two combatants, who were staggering around the stump, swinging wildly at each other, grunting and cursing, and sending up explosions of dusty leaves.

The *Mephitis mephitis* (also called polecat or zorrino, or sometimes wood pussy) felt no kinship with this distorted version of itself. It turned around, lifted its tail, and spewed out a fine yellow mist that enveloped the two in a noxious haze. It then stalked away to find a few grubs for an early supper.

Jim Bob pushed Lamont away, but it was too late to escape. His eyes burned and his throat felt like someone had poured boiling water down it. His lungs threatened to shut down then and there. His words were barely audible, even in the sudden silence. "Aw, shit."

ABOUT THE AUTHOR

JOAN HESS is the author of the now four books in the Maggody series, as well as the popular Claire Malloy series. She is the winner of the American Mystery Award and lives in Fayetteville, Arkansas.

SPELLBINDING THRILLERS ...
TAUT SUSPENSE

There's an epidemic with 27 million victims. And no visible symptoms.

It's an epidemic of people who can't read.

Believe it or not, 27 million Americans are functionally illiterate, about one adult in five.

The solution to this problem is you... when you join the fight against illiteracy. So call the Coalition for Literacy at toll-free **1-800-228-8813** and volunteer.

Volunteer Against Illiteracy. The only degree you need is a degree of caring.